D0482322

THE THREE MUSKETEERS

ALEXANDRE DUMAS

THE THREE MUSKETEERS

PICTURES BY

BRETT HELQUIST

ADAPTED BY

CLARISSA HUTTON

WITHDRAWN

HARPER

An Imprint of HarperCollins*Publishers*

For Henry

—B.H.

The Three Musketeers
Adapted text copyright © 2011 by HarperCollins Publishers
Illustrations copyright © 2011 by Callister-Helquist Creative LLC
All rights reserved. Printed in the United States of America.
No part of this book may be used or reproduced in any manner whatsoever without written permission except in the case of brief quotations embodied in critical articles and reviews.
For information address HarperCollins Children's Books, a division of HarperCollins Publishers, 10 East 53rd Street, New York, NY 10022.
www.harpercollinschildrens.com

Library of Congress Cataloging-in-Publication Data
Hutton, Clarissa.
The three musketeers / Alexandre Dumas ; illustrated by Brett Helquist ; adapted by Clarissa Hutton.—1st ed.
p. cm.
Summary: An adaptation of Alexandre Dumas' classic tale of seventeenth-century France, when young D'Artagnan initially quarrels with, then befriends, three musketeers and joins them in trying to outwit the enemies of the king and queen.
ISBN 978-0-06-208230-5
1. France—History—Louis XIII, 1610–1643—Juvenile fiction. [1. France—History—Louis XIII, 1610–1643—Fiction. 2. Adventure and adventurers—Fiction.] I. Helquist, Brett, ill. II. Dumas, Alexandre, 1802–1870. Trois mousquetaires. English. III. Title.
PZ7.H966Thr 2011 2010045635
[Fic]—dc22 CIP
AC

Typography by Ray Shappell
11 12 13 14 15 CG/RRDB 10 9 8 7 6 5 4 3 2 1

❖

Adapted by Clarissa Hutton from the original *The Three Musketeers* by Alexandre Dumas, first serialized in 1844.

CONTENTS

THE THREE MUSKETEERS

ONE

In 1625, a young man of eighteen arrived in the town of Meung. Too big for a youth, too small for a grown man, an experienced eye might have taken him for a farmer's son had it not been for the long sword.

His steed was an elderly pony, yellow in hide, without a hair in its tail. Unfortunately, young d'Artagnan—for such was his name—could not conceal from himself the ridiculous appearance the steed gave him. He had sighed when accepting the pony from his father. The words that had accompanied the present were above all price.

"My son," said the old Gascon gentleman, "sustain worthily your name of gentleman. Endure nothing from anyone except Monsieur le Cardinal and the king. It is by courage alone that a gentleman can make his way. You ought to be brave for two reasons: first that you are a Gascon, second that you are my son. I have taught you how to handle a sword; you have a wrist of steel. Fight on all occasions. Fight the more for duels being forbidden.

Young d'Artagnan could not conceal from himself the ridiculous appearance the steed gave him.

I have nothing to give you, my son, but fifteen crowns, my horse, and the counsels you have just heard. Your mother will add a recipe for a balsam which cures all wounds that do not reach the heart. Live happily and long.

"I propose an example to you: Monsieur de Treville, captain of the Musketeers. Go to him with this letter, and make him your model."

Upon which M. d'Artagnan the elder girded his own sword round his son.

With such advice, d'Artagnan took every smile for an insult—his fist was constantly doubled, his hand on the hilt of his sword; and yet the fist did not descend, nor did the sword issue from its scabbard. The sight of the pony excited smiles from passersby; but as against the side of this pony rattled a sword, they repressed their hilarity. D'Artagnan remained majestic till he came to Meung.

There, alighting from his horse at the gate of the Jolly Miller, d'Artagnan spied, through an open window, a gentleman talking with two persons. The gentleman was enumerating d'Artagnan's horse's qualities to his listeners, who every moment burst into fits of laughter. As a half-smile was sufficient to awaken the irascibility of the young man, the effect of this mirth may be easily imagined.

D'Artagnan perceived a man of some forty years, with black eyes, a strongly marked nose, and a black and well-shaped mustache. At the moment in which d'Artagnan saw him, the gentleman made one of his remarks, his listeners laughed louder, and he himself smiled. There could be no doubt; d'Artagnan was insulted. Endeavoring to copy the court airs he had picked up among young traveling nobles, he advanced with one hand on the hilt of his sword and the other on his hip. As he advanced, his anger increased; and instead of lofty speech, he found nothing at the tip of his tongue but a gross personality.

"I say, you, hiding behind that shutter—yes, you, tell me what you are laughing at, and we will laugh together!"

The gentleman raised his eyes as if to determine whether it could be to him that such strange reproaches were addressed, then replied, "I was not speaking to you, sir."

"But I am speaking to you!" replied the young man.

The stranger came out of the hostelry and placed himself by d'Artagnan. The ironical expression of his countenance redoubled the mirth of the persons with whom he had been talking.

D'Artagnan drew his sword out of the scabbard.

"This horse is decidedly a buttercup," resumed the stranger, "a color well known in botany, but rare among horses."

"There are people who laugh at the horse that would not dare to laugh at the master," cried d'Artagnan.

"I do not often laugh, sir," replied the stranger, "but I retain the privilege of laughing when I please."

"And I," cried d'Artagnan, "will allow no man to laugh when it displeases me!"

"Indeed, sir," continued the stranger, calmer than ever, and turning on his heel, was about to reenter the hostelry.

D'Artagnan followed him, crying, "Turn, Master Joker, lest I strike you behind!"

"Strike me!" said the other, turning and surveying him with astonishment. "Why, you must be mad!" D'Artagnan made such a furious lunge at him that if he had not sprung nimbly backward, it is probable he would have jested for the last time. The stranger drew his sword, saluted his adversary, and placed himself en garde. At the same moment, his two auditors, accompanied by the host, fell upon d'Artagnan with sticks. This caused such a diversion from the attack that d'Artagnan's adversary sheathed his sword and became a spectator, muttering, "A plague upon him! Replace him on his orange horse, and let him begone!"

"Not before I have killed you, poltroon!" cried d'Artagnan.

"By my honor," the other said, "these Gascons are incorrigible! When he is tired, he will tell us that he has had enough."

But d'Artagnan was not the man ever to cry for quarter. The fight was prolonged; but at length d'Artagnan dropped his sword, which was broken in two pieces by the blow of a stick. Another blow full upon his forehead brought him to the ground, covered with blood. The host carried the wounded man into the kitchen.

As to the gentleman, he resumed his place at the window.

"How is it with this madman?" he exclaimed, turning as the noise of the door announced the entrance of the host.

"He is better," said the host, "he fainted quite away. First, he collected all his strength to challenge you."

"Why, this fellow must be the devil!" cried the stranger.

"No, not the devil," replied the host, with a grin of contempt. "We rummaged his bag and found nothing but a clean shirt and eleven crowns—which did not prevent his saying that if such a thing had happened in Paris, you should have cause to repent of it. He struck his pocket and said, 'We shall see what Monsieur de Treville will think of this insult offered to his protégé.'"

"Monsieur de Treville?" said the stranger. "He put his hand upon his pocket while pronouncing the name Monsieur de Treville? You did not fail, I am sure, to ascertain what that pocket contained?"

"A letter addressed to Monsieur de Treville, captain of the Musketeers."

The host did not observe the expression that his words had given to the stranger. The latter knitted his brow.

"Can Treville have set this Gascon upon me?" murmured he. "A sword thrust is a sword thrust, whatever the age of him who gives it. Host, where is he?"

"In my wife's chamber, they are dressing his wounds."

"His things are with him?"

"Everything is in the kitchen. If he annoys you—"

"To be sure he does. Go; make out my bill and notify my servant."

"What the devil!" said the host to himself. "Can he be afraid of this boy?" He bowed and retired.

"It is not necessary for Milady to be seen by this fellow," continued the stranger. "I should like, however, to know what this letter contains."

And the stranger directed his steps toward the kitchen.

In the meantime, the host, who entertained no doubt that it was the presence of the young man that drove the stranger from his hostelry, reascended to his wife's chamber and found d'Artagnan recovering his senses. Giving him to understand that the police would deal with him severely for having sought a quarrel with a great lord—for in the opinion of the host the stranger could be nothing less—he insisted d'Artagnan depart.

D'Artagnan, half stupefied, began to descend the stairs; the first thing he saw was his antagonist talking calmly at the step of a carriage to a woman.

This woman's beauty struck d'Artagnan more forcibly from its being totally different from that of the southern countries in which he had resided. She was pale and fair, with long curls falling over her shoulders, had large, blue, languishing eyes, rosy lips, and hands of alabaster. She was talking with great animation with the stranger.

"His Eminence, then, orders me—" said the lady.

"To return instantly to England. Inform him as soon as the duke leaves London."

"My other instructions?" asked the fair traveler.

"Are contained in this box, which you will open on the other side of the Channel."

"Very well; what will you do?"

"I return to Paris."

"Without chastising this insolent boy?" asked the lady.

D'Artagnan precipitated himself over the threshold of the door.

"This insolent boy chastises others," cried he, "and this time he whom he ought to chastise will not escape him. Before a woman you would dare not fly, I presume?"

"Remember," said Milady, "the least delay may ruin everything."

"You are right," cried the gentleman. "Begone, and I will depart." He sprang into his saddle, while the lady's coachman applied his whip vigorously to his horses. They took opposite directions.

"Base coward!" cried d'Artagnan, springing forward. Scarcely had he gone ten steps when a cloud of blood passed over his eyes, and he fell, crying, "Coward!"

"He is a coward, indeed," grumbled the host, endeavoring to make up matters with the young man.

"Yes," murmured d'Artagnan, "but she was very beautiful."

"What she?" demanded the host.

"Milady," faltered d'Artagnan, and fainted a second time.

"I have lost two customers, but one remains," said the host. "There will be eleven crowns gained."

It is to be remembered that eleven crowns was just the sum in d'Artagnan's purse.

The host had reckoned upon eleven days of confinement at a crown a day, but had reckoned without his guest. The next morning d'Artagnan asked, among other ingredients, for oil, wine, and rosemary, and with his mother's recipe composed a balsam, with which he anointed his wounds, and was almost cured by the morrow.

When the time came to pay for his rosemary, oil, and wine, d'Artagnan found nothing in his pocket but his purse; the letter for M. de Treville had disappeared. The young man flew into such a rage as was near costing him a fresh consumption of wine, oil, and rosemary—for upon seeing this hotheaded youth threaten to destroy everything in the establishment, the host seized a spit, his wife a broom handle, and the servants the sticks they had used the day before.

"My letter of recommendation!" cried d'Artagnan. "I will spit you like ortolans!"

There was an obstacle to the accomplishment of this threat;

his sword had been in his first conflict broken in two. When d'Artagnan drew, he found himself armed with a stump about eight inches long.

This would not have stopped our fiery young man if the host had not reflected that the reclamation his guest made was perfectly just.

"But, after all," said he, lowering his spit, "where is this letter?"

"Yes, where is this letter?" cried d'Artagnan. "It is for Monsieur de Treville, and he will know how to find it."

His threat completed the intimidation of the host. After the king and the cardinal, M. de Treville was perhaps the most respected man in France. Throwing down his spit, he commenced a search for the lost letter.

"Does the letter contain anything valuable?" demanded the host.

"It does indeed!" cried the Gascon, who reckoned upon this letter for making his way at court. "But the money is nothing; that letter was everything."

A ray of light broke upon the mind of the host.

"That letter is not lost!" cried he. "It has been stolen. The gentleman who was here yesterday came down into the kitchen, where your doublet was. He remained there some time alone. I would lay a wager he has stolen it."

"Do you think so?" answered d'Artagnan, little convinced, as he knew how entirely personal the value of this letter was.

"I am sure of it," continued the host. "When I informed him that your lordship was the protégé of Monsieur de Treville, and had a letter for that gentleman, he asked where that letter was, and immediately came down into the kitchen."

"That's my thief," replied d'Artagnan. "I will complain to Monsieur de Treville, and Monsieur de Treville will complain to the king." He drew two crowns majestically from his purse and gave them to the host, then remounted his yellow horse, which bore him to Paris, where his owner sold him for three crowns. The dealer to whom d'Artagnan sold him did not conceal that he only gave that sum on the account of the originality of his color.

Thus d'Artagnan entered Paris and walked about till he found an apartment to be let on terms suited to the scantiness of his means.

As soon as the money was paid, d'Artagnan took possession of his lodging, and passed the remainder of the day sewing onto his doublet some ornamental braiding and having a new blade put to his sword.

After this, full of hope for the future, he retired to bed and slept the sleep of the brave. This sleep brought him to nine o'clock in the morning, at which hour he rose, in order to repair to the residence of M. de Treville.

TWO

M. de Treville had commenced life as d'Artagnan did: without a sou in his pocket, but with a fund of audacity and intelligence.

Treville was endowed with an obedient intelligence like a dog, with a blind valor, a quick eye, and a prompt hand; to him sight appeared to be given to see if the king were dissatisfied with anyone, and the hand to strike this displeasing person. At last Louis XIII made Treville the captain of his devoted Musketeers.

The cardinal had his Musketeers as Louis XIII had his, and these powerful rivals vied in procuring the most celebrated swordsmen. It was not uncommon for Richelieu and Louis XIII to dispute over their evening game of chess the merits of their servants.

Treville paraded his Musketeers before the cardinal with an insolent air that made the mustache of His Eminence curl with ire. Loose, half-drunk, imposing, the king's Musketeers spread themselves about in the cabarets, in the public walks, and the public sports, shouting, twisting their mustaches, clanking their swords, taking pleasure in annoying the Guards of the cardinal, drawing in the open streets, sometimes killed, often killing others, but certain of not rotting in prison, M. de Treville being there to claim them.

The court of his house resembled a military camp. In the antechamber, upon long circular benches, reposed the elect, while M. de Treville in his office, like the king in his balcony at the Louvre, had only to place himself at the window to review his men.

On the day on which d'Artagnan presented himself, the assemblage was imposing. When he had passed the massive door, he fell into the midst of a troop of swordsmen playing tricks one with another. Our young man advanced with that half-smile of the embarrassed provincial who wishes to put on a good face. For the first time in his life, d'Artagnan felt ridiculous.

At the staircase, it was worse. There were four Musketeers on the steps, amusing themselves. One, upon the top stair, naked sword in hand, endeavored to prevent the three others from ascending. These others fenced against him with their agile swords. D'Artagnan at first took these weapons for foils, but soon perceived that every weapon was pointed and sharpened. D'Artagnan had seen a few of the preliminaries of duels; but the daring of these four fencers appeared to him the strongest he had ever heard of.

On the landing they were no longer fighting, but amused themselves with stories about women, and in the antechamber, with stories about the court. On the landing d'Artagnan blushed; in the antechamber he trembled. His imagination had never dreamed of half the amorous wonders or a quarter of the feats of gallantry set forth. His morals were shocked on the landing, his respect for the cardinal was scandalized in the antechamber. That great man served as an object of ridicule to the Musketeers, who cracked jokes upon his bandy legs and crooked back. Some sang ballads about his mistress; while others formed parties to annoy the Guards of the cardinal duke—all things that appeared to d'Artagnan monstrous impossibilities.

"These fellows will be imprisoned or hanged," thought the terrified d'Artagnan, "and I with them." He dared not join in the conversation, only looked and listened; and felt himself led by his instincts to praise rather than blame the unheard-of things taking place.

At length somebody came and asked him what he wanted. D'Artagnan begged the servant to request a moment's audience of M. de Treville.

D'Artagnan, a little recovered from his first surprise, had now leisure to study costumes and physiognomy.

The center of the most animated group was a Musketeer of great height and haughty countenance, dressed in a costume so peculiar as to attract general attention. He did not wear the uniform cloak, but a cerulean-blue doublet, and over this a magnificent baldric, worked in gold, which shone like water in the sun. A long cloak of crimson velvet fell in graceful folds from his shoulders, disclosing in front the splendid baldric, from which was suspended a gigantic rapier. This Musketeer complained of having a cold, and coughed from time to time. It was for this reason, he said, that he wore his cloak; and while he twisted his mustache disdainfully, all admired his baldric.

"What would you have?" said the Musketeer. "One must lay out one's inheritance somehow."

"Ah, Porthos!" cried one of his companions. "Don't try to make us believe you obtained that baldric by paternal generosity. It was given to you by that veiled lady I met you with the other Sunday."

"No, I bought it with the contents of my own purse," answered he whom they designated Porthos.

"Yes, in the same manner," said another Musketeer, "that I bought this purse with what my mistress put into the old one."

"Is it not true, Aramis?" said Porthos, turning toward another Musketeer.

This other Musketeer formed a perfect contrast to his interrogator. He was a stout man, of about three-and-twenty, with an open countenance and cheeks rosy and downy as an autumn peach. He answered his friend by an affirmative nod.

This affirmation appeared to dispel all doubts. They continued to admire the baldric, but said no more about it.

"Monsieur de Treville awaits Monsieur d'Artagnan," cried a servant, throwing open the door of the cabinet.

At this announcement, during which the door remained open, everyone became mute. The young man entered the apartment of the captain of the Musketeers.

THREE

M. de Treville saluted the young man, but making a sign as if to ask his permission to finish with others before he began with him, called:

"Athos! Porthos! Aramis!"

The two Musketeers with whom we have already made acquaintance advanced. Their appearance, although not quite at ease, excited by its carelessness the admiration of d'Artagnan.

When the door was closed behind them, when M. de Treville had three or four times paced in silence the whole length of his cabinet, he stopped in front of them, and, with an angry look, "Do you know what the king said to me," cried he, "yesterday evening?"

"No," replied the two Musketeers, "sir, we do not."

"But I hope that you will tell us," added Aramis, in his politest tone.

"He told me that he should henceforth recruit his Musketeers from among the Guards of Monsieur le Cardinal."

The two Musketeers reddened. D'Artagnan wished himself

a hundred feet underground.

"His Majesty was right," continued M. de Treville. "The Musketeers make a miserable figure at court. The cardinal related yesterday that those *damned Musketeers*, those *braggarts* had made a riot in a cabaret, and that a party of his Guards had been forced to arrest them! Arrest Musketeers! You were among them! You, Aramis, why did you ask me for a uniform when you would have been better in a cassock? And you, Porthos, do you only wear such a fine golden baldric to suspend a sword of straw from it? And Athos—where is he?"

"Ill—"

"Of what malady?"

"It may be smallpox, sir," replied Porthos, "and will certainly spoil his face."

"Sick of smallpox at his age! No; wounded, killed, perhaps. Messieurs Musketeers, I will not have this quarreling in the streets. Above all, I will not have occasion given for the cardinal's Guards to laugh at you! They would prefer dying on the spot to being arrested."

Porthos and Aramis trembled with rage. They could have strangled M. de Treville, if they had not felt it was the great love he bore them that made him speak thus. They stamped upon the carpet with their feet, bit their lips till the blood came, and grasped the hilts of their swords.

"The king's Musketeers arrested by the Guards of the cardinal?" continued M. de Treville, as furious as his soldiers. "Six of His Eminence's Guards arrest six of His Majesty's Musketeers! I will give in my resignation as captain of the king's Musketeers to take a lieutenancy in the cardinal's Guards."

D'Artagnan looked for some tapestry behind which he might hide.

"My Captain," said Porthos, "we were six against six. But we were not captured by fair means; before we had time to draw our swords, two of our party were dead, and Athos grievously wounded. And we did not surrender! They dragged us away by force. On the way we escaped. As for Athos, they believed him dead, and left him on the field of battle. What the devil, Captain, one cannot win all one's battles!"

"And I have the honor of assuring you that I killed one with his own sword," said Aramis, "for mine was broken at the first parry."

"I did not know that," replied M. de Treville, in a softened tone. "The cardinal exaggerated, I perceive."

"Pray, sir," continued Aramis, "do not say that Athos is wounded. As the wound penetrates into the chest, it is to be feared—"

At this instant the tapestry was raised and a noble head, frightfully pale, appeared.

"Athos!" cried the two Musketeers.

"You have sent for me, sir," said Athos to M. de Treville, in a feeble yet calm voice. "I am here."

At these words, the Musketeer, in irreproachable costume, entered the cabinet. M. de Treville, moved to the bottom of his heart by this proof of courage, sprang toward him.

"I was about to say," said he, "that I forbid my Musketeers to expose their lives needlessly; brave men are dear to the king, and his Musketeers are the bravest on earth. Your hand, Athos!"

Then Athos fell upon the floor as if he were dead.

"A surgeon!" cried M. de Treville. "Or my brave Athos will die!"

This eager attention might have been useless if the doctor had not chanced to be in the hotel. He pushed through the crowd and required that the Musketeer should be carried into an adjoining chamber.

At length, M. de Treville returned. The injured man had recovered his senses. The surgeon declared that the situation of the Musketeer had nothing in it to render his friends uneasy, his weakness having been caused by loss of blood.

Then M. de Treville made a sign, and all retired except d'Artagnan, who did not forget that he had an audience. M. de Treville found himself alone with the young man. In an instant, he grasped the situation.

"Pardon me," said he, smiling, "but I had forgotten you. A captain is nothing but a father of a family, charged with even a greater responsibility than the father of an ordinary family. I respected your father very much," said he. "What can I do for the son?"

"Monsieur," said d'Artagnan, "it was my intention to request of you the uniform of a Musketeer; but I comprehend that such a favor is enormous."

"It is indeed a favor, young man," replied M. de Treville, "but it may not be beyond your hopes. But no one becomes a Musketeer without the preliminary ordeal of several campaigns, certain brilliant actions, or a service of two years in some other regiment."

D'Artagnan bowed, feeling his desire to don the Musketeer's uniform vastly increased by the difficulties preceding the attainment of it.

"But," continued M. de Treville, fixing upon his compatriot a look so piercing that it might be said he wished to read his heart, "I will do something for you. I dare say you have not brought too large a stock of money with you?"

D'Artagnan drew himself up with a proud air that plainly said, "I ask alms of no man."

"Oh, that's very well, young man," continued M. de Treville, "I myself came to Paris with four crowns in my purse, and would have fought anyone who dared to tell me I was not in a condition to purchase the Louvre."

D'Artagnan's bearing became still more imposing. Thanks to the sale of his horse, he commenced his career with four more crowns than M. de Treville had possessed.

"You ought to husband the means you have; but you ought also to perfect yourself in the exercises becoming a gentleman. I will write a letter to the director of the Royal Academy, and he will admit you without expense. You will learn horsemanship, swordsmanship, and dancing. From time to time call upon me, to tell how you are getting on."

D'Artagnan perceived a little coldness in this reception.

"Alas, sir," said he, "I cannot but perceive how sadly I miss the letter of introduction which my father gave me to present to you."

"I certainly am surprised," replied M. de Treville, "that you should undertake so long a journey without that passport."

"I had one, sir," cried d'Artagnan, "but it was stolen from me."

He then related the adventure of Meung, and described the unknown gentleman.

"This is very strange," said M. de Treville. "Tell me, had this gentlemen a slight scar on his cheek?"

"Yes, such as would be made by the grazing of a ball."

"A fine-looking man of lofty stature?"

"Yes, that is he; you are acquainted with this man?"

"He was waiting for a woman," continued Treville.

"He departed after having conversed for a minute with her. He gave her a box, told her not to open it except in London."

"Was this woman English?"

"He called her Milady."

"It is he!" murmured Treville.

"Sir, if you know who this man is," cried d'Artagnan, "tell me. I wish to avenge myself."

"Beware, young man!" cried Treville. "Do not cast yourself against such a rock; he would break you like glass."

All at once the captain stopped. This hatred which the young traveler manifested for this man, who—a rather improbable thing—had stolen his father's letter—was there some treachery concealed here? This pretended d'Artagnan—was he an emissary of the cardinal? He fixed his eyes upon d'Artagnan, and was moderately reassured. "I know he is a Gascon," reflected he, "but he may be one for the cardinal. Let us try him."

"My friend," said he, slowly, "I wish to discover to you the secrets of our policy. The king and the cardinal are the best of friends; their bickerings only feints to deceive fools. I am devoted to both these masters, and my endeavors have no other aim than the service of the king, and also the cardinal. If you entertain enmities against the cardinal, let us separate. I will aid you without attaching you to my person."

Treville said to himself: "If the cardinal has set this young fox upon me, he will certainly have told his spy that the best means of making court to me is to rail at him. If it be as I suspect, my cunning gossip will assure me that he holds His Eminence in horror."

D'Artagnan answered, with the greatest simplicity: "I came to Paris with exactly such intentions. My father advised me to stoop to nobody but the king, the cardinal, and yourself—whom he considered the first three personages in France."

D'Artagnan added M. de Treville to the others, but thought this addition would do no harm.

"I have the greatest veneration for the cardinal," continued he. "So much the better for me, sir, if you speak to me with frankness; but if you have entertained any doubt, I trust you will not esteem me the less for it."

M. de Treville was surprised. So much frankness created admiration, but did not entirely remove his suspicions. "You are an honest youth; but at the moment I can only do for you that which I offered."

"That is to say," replied d'Artagnan, "that you will wait until I have proved myself worthy. Well, be assured," added he, "you shall not wait long." And he bowed.

"Wait a minute," said M. de Treville. "I promised you a letter for the director of the Royal Academy. Are you too proud to accept it?"

"No, sir," said d'Artagnan. "I will guard it so carefully that it shall arrive at its address!"

M. de Treville smiled and seated himself in order to write. While he was doing this, d'Artagnan amused himself at the window, watching the Musketeers who went away.

M. de Treville approached the young man in order to give him the letter, but was astonished to see his protégé become crimson with passion and rush from the cabinet, crying, "He shall not escape me!"

"Who?" asked Treville.

"He, my thief!" replied d'Artagnan and disappeared.

"The devil take the madman!" murmured M. de Treville. "Unless," added he, "this is a cunning escape, seeing that he had failed in his purpose!"

FOUR

D'Artagnan was darting toward the stairs when he ran against a Musketeer coming out of M. de Treville's rooms, and striking his shoulder violently, made him utter a cry.

"Excuse me," said d'Artagnan, "but I am in a hurry."

Scarcely had he descended the first stair, when a hand of iron seized him by the belt.

"In a hurry?" said the Musketeer, as pale as a sheet. "You say, 'Excuse me,' and believe that is sufficient? Do you fancy because you heard Monsieur de Treville speak to us a little cavalierly today that other people are to treat us as he speaks to us? Undeceive yourself, comrade, you are not Monsieur de Treville."

"My faith!" replied d'Artagnan, recognizing Athos. "I did not do it intentionally, and I said, 'Excuse me.' Let me go where my business calls me."

"Monsieur," said Athos, letting him go, "it is easy to perceive that you come from a distance."

D'Artagnan had already strode down three or four stairs, but at Athos's remark he stopped.

"Monsieur!" said he. "However far I come, it is not you who can give me a lesson in good manners. If I were not in such haste . . ."

"Monsieur-in-a-hurry, you can find me without running."

"Where, I pray?"

"Near the Carmes-Deschaux."

"At what hour?"

"Noon. Endeavor not to make me wait; at quarter past twelve I will cut off your ears as you run."

"Good!" cried d'Artagnan. "I will be there ten minutes before twelve." And he set off running, hoping that he might yet find the stranger.

At the street gate, Porthos was talking with the soldier on guard. There was just enough room for a man to pass. D'Artagnan sprang forward. As he was about to pass, the wind blew out Porthos's cloak, and d'Artagnan rushed straight into the middle of it. He was particularly anxious to avoid marring the magnificent baldric, but found himself with his nose between Porthos's shoulders, exactly upon the baldric.

Alas, the baldric, glittering with gold in front, was nothing but simple buff behind. Vainglorious as he was, Porthos could not afford to have a baldric wholly of gold.

"Bless me!" cried Porthos. "You must be mad to run against people in this manner."

"Excuse me," said d'Artagnan, reappearing, "I was running after someone—"

"Do you always forget your eyes when you run?" asked Porthos.

"No," replied d'Artagnan, piqued, "and thanks to my eyes, I can see what other people cannot."

"Monsieur," said Porthos, "you stand a chance of getting chastised if you rub Musketeers in this fashion."

"Chastised, monsieur!" said d'Artagnan. "The expression is strong."

"It is one that becomes a man accustomed to look his enemies in the face."

"I know full well that you don't turn your back to yours."

And the young man, delighted with his joke, went away laughing loudly.

Porthos foamed with rage, and made a movement to rush after d'Artagnan.

"Presently," cried the latter, "when you haven't your cloak on."

"At one o'clock, behind the Luxembourg."

"Very well," replied d'Artagnan, turning the angle of the street.

But neither in the street he had passed through, nor in the one that his eager glance pervaded, could he see anyone; the stranger was gone. D'Artagnan inquired of everyone he met, but nothing! As the perspiration broke from his forehead, his heart began to cool.

It was scarcely eleven o'clock, and yet this morning had already brought him into disgrace with M. de Treville, who could not fail to think the manner in which d'Artagnan had left him a little cavalier. Besides this, he had drawn upon himself duels with two men, each capable of killing three d'Artagnans. He finished by hoping that he might survive, with terrible wounds, both these duels; and made the following reprehensions upon his own conduct:

"What a stupid fellow I am! Brave Athos was wounded on that shoulder against which I ran headlong. The only thing that astonishes me is that he did not strike me dead at once. The pain must have been atrocious. As to Porthos—faith, that's droll!"

In spite of himself, the young man began to laugh.

"As to Porthos, that is certainly droll; but I am a fool. Have I any right to go peep under people's cloaks? He would have pardoned me if I had not said anything about that cursed baldric. Friend d'Artagnan," he continued, speaking to himself, "if you escape, I would advise you to practice perfect politeness for the future. Look at Aramis, mildness and grace personified. From this moment I will model myself after him. Ah! Here he is!"

D'Artagnan perceived Aramis, chatting with three Guards, and approached the young men with a smile. All four immediately broke off their conversation.

D'Artagnan perceived that he was one too many, but did not know how to extricate himself gallantly. He was seeking for the least awkward means of retreat, when he remarked that Aramis had let his handkerchief fall, and placed his foot upon it. D'Artagnan stooped, drew the handkerchief from under the foot of the Musketeer, and holding it out, said, "I believe, monsieur, this is a handkerchief you would be sorry to lose?"

The handkerchief was richly embroidered, and had a coronet and arms at one of its corners. Aramis blushed, and snatched it.

"Ah!" cried one of the Guards. "Will you persist in saying, Aramis, that you are not on good terms with Madame de Bois-Tracy, when that lady has the kindness to lend you her handkerchief?"

Aramis darted d'Artagnan one of those looks which inform a man that he has acquired a mortal enemy. Then, resuming his mild air, "You are deceived, gentlemen," said he. "This handkerchief is not mine."

D'Artagnan perceived his mistake. "The fact is," he hazarded, timidly, "I did not see the handkerchief fall from the pocket of Monsieur Aramis. I thought from his having his foot upon it the handkerchief was his."

"And you were deceived, sir," replied Aramis, coldly.

In a moment or two the conversation ceased, and the three Guardsmen and the Musketeer separated, the Guardsmen going one way and Aramis another.

"Now is my time to make peace," said d'Artagnan to himself. "Monsieur," said he, "you will excuse me, I hope."

"Ah, monsieur," interrupted Aramis, "permit me to observe that you have not acted as a gallant man ought."

"What, monsieur!" cried d'Artagnan. "Do you suppose—"

"I suppose, monsieur, that you are not a fool, and that you knew that people do not tread upon handkerchiefs without a reason."

"Monsieur, you act wrongly in endeavoring to mortify me," said d'Artagnan.

"Monsieur, what I say to you," said Aramis, "is not for the sake of seeking a quarrel. Being a Musketeer but for a time, I only fight with repugnance; but a lady is compromised by you. Why did you so maladroitly restore me the handkerchief?"

"Why did you so awkwardly let it fall?"

"I have said, monsieur, that the handkerchief did not fall from my pocket."

"And you have lied, monsieur; I saw it fall."

"You take that tone, do you? I will teach you how to behave."

"Draw, if you please—"

"Not here. I wish to kill you quietly where you will not be able to boast of your death to anybody."

"Take your handkerchief; you may stand in need of it."

"At two o'clock I shall have the honor of expecting you at the hotel of Monsieur de Treville."

The two men bowed and separated, d'Artagnan taking the road to the Carmes-Deschaux, saying to himself, "At least, if I am killed, I shall be killed by a Musketeer."

FIVE

D'Artagnan, acquainted with nobody in Paris, went to his appointment with Athos without a second. He hoped, by means of loyal excuses, to make a friend of Athos. He flattered himself he should be able to frighten Porthos with the adventure of the baldric, which he might, if not killed, relate to everybody. As to Aramis, he did not entertain much dread of him, and determined to dispatch him in good style.

He flew toward the convent of the Carmes-Dechausses, which was generally employed as the place for the duels of men who had no time to lose. When d'Artagnan arrived, Athos was waiting, and twelve o'clock was striking.

"Monsieur," said Athos, "I have engaged two of my friends as seconds; they are not yet come."

"I have no seconds, monsieur," said d'Artagnan. "Having only arrived yesterday in Paris, I know no one but Monsieur de Treville."

Athos reflected, speaking half to himself, "If I kill you, I shall have the air of a boy-slayer."

"Not too much so," replied d'Artagnan, with a bow, "since you do me the honor to draw a sword with me while suffering from a wound which is very inconvenient."

"Very inconvenient; and you hurt me devilishly. I will take the left hand—my custom in such circumstances. Do not fancy that I do you a favor; I use either hand easily. It will be a disadvantage to you; a left-handed man is troublesome to people who are not prepared for it. I regret I did not inform you sooner of this circumstance."

"You have truly, monsieur," said d'Artagnan, bowing again, "courtesy, for which I am very grateful."

"You confuse me," replied Athos, with his gentlemanly air. "Let us talk of something else. Ah, my shoulder quite burns."

"If you would permit me—" said d'Artagnan, with timidity.

"What, monsieur?"

"I have a miraculous balsam for wounds. I am sure that in less than three days it would cure you, and when you would be cured—well, it would do me great honor to be your man."

D'Artagnan spoke these words with a simplicity that did honor to his courtesy.

"*Pardieu,* monsieur!" said Athos. "That's a proposition that pleases me; I cannot accept, but it savors of the gentleman. If we don't kill each other, I foresee I shall have much pleasure in your conversation. Ah, here is one of my friends."

At the end of the rue Vaugirard, Porthos appeared.

"What!" cried d'Artagnan. "Is your first witness Monsieur Porthos?"

"And here is the second."

D'Artagnan perceived Aramis.

"What!" cried he, in an accent of astonishment. "Your second witness is Monsieur Aramis?"

"Are you not aware that we are called the Three Inseparables?"

"My faith!" replied d'Artagnan. "You are well named; my adventure will prove that your union is not founded upon contrasts."

In the meantime, Porthos had come up, waved his hand to Athos, and turning toward d'Artagnan, stood quite astonished. He had changed his baldric.

"This is the gentleman I am going to fight with," said Athos, pointing to d'Artagnan.

"Why, it is with him I am also going to fight," said Porthos.

"But not before one o'clock," replied d'Artagnan.

"And I also am to fight with this gentleman," said Aramis, coming onto the place.

"But not until two o'clock," said d'Artagnan.

"What are you going to fight about, Athos?" asked Aramis.

"I don't very well know. He hurt my shoulder. And you, Porthos?"

"I am going to fight—because I am going to fight," answered Porthos, reddening.

A faintly sly smile passed over the lips of the young Gascon as he replied, "We had a short discussion upon dress."

"And you, Aramis?" asked Athos.

"Oh, ours is a theological quarrel," replied Aramis, making a sign to d'Artagnan to keep secret the cause of their duel.

"And now you are assembled, gentlemen," said d'Artagnan,

"permit me to offer you my apologies."

At this word, a cloud passed over the brow of Athos, a haughty smile curled the lip of Porthos, and a negative sign was the reply of Aramis.

"You do not understand me, gentlemen," said d'Artagnan, throwing up his head. "I asked to be excused in case I should not be able to discharge my debt to all three; Monsieur Athos has the right to kill me first, which must diminish the face value of your bill, Monsieur Porthos, and render yours almost null, Monsieur Aramis. And now—en garde!" With the most gallant air, d'Artagnan drew his sword.

"It is very hot," said Athos, drawing his sword in turn, "yet I cannot take off my doublet; I just felt my wound begin to bleed again, and should not like to annoy monsieur with the sight of blood which he has not drawn himself."

"Monsieur," replied d'Artagnan, "I shall always view with regret the blood of so brave a gentleman. I will also fight in my doublet."

"Enough of such compliments!" cried Porthos. "Remember, we are waiting our turns."

"Speak for yourself," interrupted Aramis. "I think what they say is quite worthy of two gentlemen."

Scarcely had the rapiers clashed, when a company of the Guards of His Eminence, commanded by M. de Jussac, turned the corner of the convent.

"The cardinal's Guards!" cried Aramis and Porthos. "Sheathe your swords!"

But it was too late. The combatants had been seen in a position that left no doubt of their intentions.

"Halloo, Musketeers!" cried Jussac, advancing toward them. "Fighting, are you? And the edicts?"

"You are generous, gentlemen of the Guards," said Athos. "If we were to see you fighting, we would make no effort to prevent you."

"Gentlemen," said Jussac, "it is with great regret that I pronounce the thing impossible. Sheathe, and follow us."

"Monsieur," said Aramis, parodying Jussac, "it would afford us great pleasure to obey your invitation; but unfortunately the thing is impossible—Monsieur de Treville has forbidden it. Pass on."

This chatter exasperated Jussac. "We will charge upon you," said he, "if you disobey."

"There are five of them," said Athos, half aloud, "we are but three; we must die on the spot, for I will never appear again before the captain as a conquered man."

Athos, Porthos, and Aramis drew near one another, while Jussac drew up his soldiers.

This short interval was sufficient to determine d'Artagnan on the part he was to take. It was one of those events that decide the life of a man—a choice between the king and the cardinal. To fight was to disobey the law, to make an enemy of a minister more powerful than the king himself.

Turning toward Athos and his friends, "Gentlemen," said he, "allow me to correct your words. You said you were three, but we are four."

"But you are not one of us," said Porthos.

"That's true," replied d'Artagnan, "but my heart is that of a Musketeer."

"Withdraw, young man," cried Jussac. "Save your skin; begone quickly."

D'Artagnan did not budge.

"Decidedly, you are a brave fellow," said Athos, pressing the young man's hand.

But all three reflected upon the youth of d'Artagnan, and dreaded his inexperience.

"We should only be three, one wounded, with the addition of a boy," resumed Athos, "yet it will be said we were four men."

"Try me, gentlemen," said d'Artagnan. "I swear that I will not go hence if we are conquered."

"What is your name, my brave fellow?" said Athos.

"D'Artagnan, monsieur."

"Well, then, Athos, Porthos, Aramis, and d'Artagnan, forward!" cried Athos.

The nine combatants rushed upon each other. Athos fixed upon Cahusac, a favorite of the cardinal's. Porthos had Bicarat, and Aramis found himself opposed to two adversaries. As to d'Artagnan, he sprang toward Jussac himself. Jussac was a fine blade; nevertheless it required all his skill to defend himself against an adversary who departed every instant from received rules, attacking him on all sides at once.

This contest at length exhausted Jussac's patience. Furious at being held in check by one whom he considered a boy, he began to make mistakes. D'Artagnan redoubled his agility. Jussac, springing forward, aimed a thrust at his adversary, but the latter glided like a serpent beneath his blade and passed his sword through Jussac's body. Jussac fell like a dead mass.

D'Artagnan then cast an anxious glance over the field of battle.

Aramis had killed one of his adversaries. The other pressed him warmly. Nevertheless, Aramis was in a good situation, and able to defend himself.

Bicarat and Porthos had just made counter hits. Porthos had received a thrust through his arm, and Bicarat one through his thigh. Neither wound was serious, and they fought more earnestly.

Athos, wounded anew by Cahusac, became paler, changed his sword, and fought with his left hand.

According to the laws of dueling, d'Artagnan was at liberty to assist whom he pleased. He caught a glance from Athos. Athos would have died rather than appeal for help; but he could look. With a terrible bound, d'Artagnan sprang to the side of Cahusac, crying, "To me, Monsieur Guardsman; I will slay you!"

Cahusac turned. Athos, whose great courage alone supported him, sank upon his knee.

"Do not kill him," cried he to d'Artagnan. "I have an affair to settle with him. Disarm him only. Very well done!"

The exclamation was drawn by seeing the sword of Cahusac fly twenty paces. D'Artagnan and Cahusac sprang forward, one to recover, the other to obtain, the sword; d'Artagnan placed his foot upon it.

Cahusac immediately ran to the Guardsman whom Aramis had killed, seized his rapier, and returned; on his way he met Athos, who had recovered his breath and wished to resume the fight.

D'Artagnan perceived that it would be disobliging Athos not

to leave him alone; and in a few minutes Cahusac fell, with a sword thrust through his throat.

At the same instant, Aramis placed his sword point on the breast of his fallen enemy and forced him to ask for mercy.

There only remained Porthos and Bicarat. Porthos made a thousand flourishes, but gained nothing. Bicarat was one of those iron men who never fell dead.

Nevertheless, it was necessary to finish. The watch might come up and take all the combatants, royalists or cardinalists.

Athos, Aramis, and d'Artagnan surrounded Bicarat and required him to surrender. Though alone against all, Bicarat wished to hold out; but Jussac, who had risen upon his elbow, cried out to him to yield. Bicarat pointed to a spot of earth with his sword. "Here," cried he, "will Bicarat die; for I only am left, and they seek my life."

"There are four against you; leave off, I command you."

"Ah, if you command me, that's another thing," said Bicarat. "As you are my commander, it is my duty to obey." And he broke

his sword across his knee to avoid surrendering it, whistling a cardinalist air.

Bravery is respected even in an enemy. The Musketeers saluted Bicarat with their swords and returned them to their sheaths. D'Artagnan did the same. Then, assisted by Bicarat, the only one left standing, he bore Jussac, Cahusac, and one of Aramis's adversaries under the porch of the convent. The fourth, as we have said, was dead. Then, carrying away four swords out of five, they took their road toward the house of M. de Treville.

They walked arm in arm, taking in every Musketeer they met, so that it became a triumphal march. The heart of d'Artagnan swam in delirium.

"If I am not yet a Musketeer," said he to his new friends, "at least I have entered upon my apprenticeship!"

SIX

M. de Treville scolded his Musketeers in public, and congratulated them in private. In the evening he attended the king's gaming table. The king was winning, and in an excellent humor.

"Come here, Monsieur Captain," said he, "that I may growl at you. Do you know His Eminence has been making complaints? These Musketeers of yours are devils."

"No, sire," replied Treville, "they are good creatures and desire that their swords may never leave their scabbards but in Your Majesty's service. But the Guards of Monsieur le Cardinal are forever seeking quarrels with them, and the poor young men must defend themselves."

"Listen to Monsieur de Treville!" said the king. "Would not one say he was speaking of a religious community? Don't fancy that I am going to take you on your bare word. I am called Louis the Just, Monsieur de Treville, and we will see."

"I shall wait patiently the good pleasure of Your Majesty."

"Wait, then, monsieur," said the king. "I will not detain you long."

Fortune changed; and as the king began to lose what he had won, he arose, and putting the money which lay before him into his pocket, "La Vieuville," said he, "take my place; I must speak to Monsieur de Treville."

Then turning toward M. de Treville, "Well, monsieur," continued he, "you say His Eminence's Guards sought a quarrel with your Musketeers?"

"Three of my best soldiers, Athos, Porthos, and Aramis, had made a party of pleasure with a young fellow from Gascony. They had appointed to meet at the Carmes-Deschaux, when they were disturbed by Jussac and four other Guardsmen, who certainly did not go there in such numerous company without some ill intention."

"Ah!" said the king. "They went thither to fight themselves."

"I do not accuse them, sire; but I leave Your Majesty to judge what five armed men could possibly be going to do in such a deserted place. Upon seeing my Musketeers, they forgot their private hatred; Your Majesty cannot be ignorant that the Musketeers, who belong to the king, are the natural enemies of the Guardsmen, who belong to the cardinal."

"Yes, Treville," said the king, in a melancholy tone, "it is very sad to see thus two parties in France. You say the Guardsmen sought a quarrel with the Musketeers?"

"I say that it is probable, sire. You know how difficult it is to discover the truth; unless a man be endowed with that admirable instinct which causes Louis XIII to be named the Just—"

"You are right, Treville; but they were not alone, your

Musketeers. They had a youth with them?"

"Yes, sire; three of the king's Musketeers—one of whom was wounded—and a youth not only maintained their ground against five of the most terrible of the cardinal's Guardsmen, but brought four of them to earth."

"Why, this is a victory!" cried the king, all radiant.

"Yes, sire."

"Three men, one wounded, and a youth, say you?"

"Who behaved himself so admirably that I will take the liberty of recommending him to Your Majesty."

"How does he call himself?"

"D'Artagnan, sire; he is the son of one of my oldest friends—a man who served under the king your father."

"And you say this young man behaved himself well?"

"Sire," resumed Treville, "as I told you, Monsieur d'Artagnan is little more than a boy; and as he has not the honor of being a Musketeer, was dressed as a citizen. The Guards of the cardinal, perceiving his youth, invited him to retire before they attacked."

"So you may plainly see, Treville," interrupted the king, "it was they who attacked?"

"True, sire; there can be no more doubt on that head. He answered that he was a Musketeer at heart, entirely devoted to Your Majesty, and that he would remain with the Musketeers."

"Brave young man!" murmured the king.

"He did remain; Your Majesty has in him so firm a champion that it was he who gave Jussac the terrible sword thrust which has made the cardinal angry."

"He who wounded Jussac!" cried the king. "Jussac, one of the first swordsmen in the kingdom? I will see this young man,

Treville. Tomorrow, at midday. Bring me all four. I wish to thank them. By the back staircase—it is useless to let the cardinal know."

"Yes, sire."

"You understand, Treville—it is forbidden to fight, after all."

That evening the three Musketeers were informed of the honor accorded them. As they had long been acquainted with the king, they were not much excited; but d'Artagnan saw in it his future fortune, and passed the night in golden dreams.

The next day, at the king's antechamber, they found Louis XIII in high good humor.

"Come in, my braves," said the king, "I am going to scold you."

The Musketeers advanced, bowing, d'Artagnan close behind them.

"What the devil!" continued the king. "Five of His Eminence's Guards placed *hors de combat* by you four! If you go on so, His Eminence will be forced to renew his company."

"Therefore, sire, Your Majesty sees that they are come, quite repentant, to offer you their excuses."

"Quite repentant!" said the king. "I place no confidence in their hypocritical faces. In particular, there is one yonder of a Gascon look. Come hither, monsieur."

D'Artagnan approached, assuming a most deprecating air.

"Why, you told me he was a young man? This is a boy, Treville! Do you mean to say that it was he who bestowed that severe thrust at Jussac?"

"Without reckoning," said Athos, "that if he had not rescued me from the hands of Cahusac, I should not have the honor of making my reverence to Your Majesty."

"Poor cardinal! Five men, and those of his very best! Thanks for your devotedness, gentlemen. I may continue to rely upon it, may I not?"

"Oh, sire!" cried the four companions, with one voice. "We would allow ourselves to be cut to pieces in Your Majesty's service."

"Well, well, but keep whole; that will be better. Treville," added the king, in a low voice, as the others were retiring, "as you have no room in the Musketeers, place this young man in the company of the Guards of Monsieur Dessessart, your brother-in-law."

The king waved his hand to Treville, who left him and rejoined the Musketeers.

The cardinal was so furious that during eight days he absented himself from the king's gaming table. This did not prevent the king, whenever he met him, asking in the kindest tone, "Well, Monsieur le Cardinal, how fares it with that poor Jussac of yours?"

SEVEN

D'Artagnan did all he could to make out who Athos, Porthos, and Aramis really were (for under these pseudonyms each of these young men concealed his name). He addressed himself to Porthos to gain information respecting Athos and Aramis, and to Aramis to learn something of Porthos.

Unfortunately, Porthos knew little of his silent companion. It was said Athos had met with great crosses in love, and that a frightful treachery had forever poisoned the life of this gallant man. What could this treachery be? All the world was ignorant.

As to Porthos, except his real name, his life was very easily known. Porthos was vain and indiscreet, and the only thing to mislead the investigator would have been belief in all the good things he said of himself.

Aramis was a young fellow made up of mysteries. Having learned from him of the success of Porthos with a princess, d'Artagan wished to gain a little insight into the amorous adventures of his interlocutor.

"It seems to me," said d'Artagan, "that you are tolerably familiar with coats of arms—a certain embroidered handkerchief, for instance, to which I owe the honor of your acquaintance?"

Aramis assumed the most modest air and replied, "My dear friend, I wish to belong to the Church. The handkerchief you saw had been left at my house by one of my friends. I neither have, nor desire to have, a mistress."

"But what the devil! You are not a priest, you are a Musketeer!"

"A Musketeer for a time, my friend, but a churchman at heart. But I am taking up your valuable time."

"Not at all; it interests me very much," cried d'Artagnan.

"Yes, but I have my breviary to repeat," answered Aramis, "then some verses to compose. Then I must go to the rue St. Honoré in order to purchase some rouge for Madame de Chevreuse. So you see, my dear friend, I am in a hurry."

Aramis held out his hand to his young companion and took leave of him.

D'Artagnan was unable to learn any more concerning his three friends. He formed the resolution of believing for the present all that was said of their past, hoping for revelations in the future.

As to the rest, the life of the four young friends was joyous enough. Athos played cards, as a rule unfortunately. Nevertheless, he never borrowed of his companions and always awakened his creditor by six o'clock the next morning to pay the debt of the preceding evening.

On the days when Porthos won he was insolent and

ostentatious; if he lost, he disappeared completely for several days, after which he reappeared with a pale face and thinner person, but with money in his purse.

As to Aramis, he never played. He had always something or other to do. Sometimes in the warmth of conversation, Aramis looked at his watch and took leave of the company. At this, Athos would smile his melancholy smile, and Porthos would drink, swearing that Aramis would never be anything but a village curé.

D'Artagnan fell easily into the habits of his friends. He went on guard because he kept company with whoever of his friends was on duty. He was well known at the House of the Musketeers, where everyone considered him a good comrade.

On their side, the three Musketeers were much attached to him. The friendship that united these four men caused them to be continually running after one another like shadows.

In the meanwhile, M. de Chevalier Dessessart admitted d'Artagnan as a cadet in his company of Guards. D'Artagnan donned his uniform, which he would have exchanged for that of a Musketeer at the expense of ten years of his existence. But M. de Treville promised this favor after two years—which might be abridged if d'Artagnan should distinguish himself. Upon this promise, d'Artagnan began service.

Then it became the turn of Athos, Porthos, and Aramis to mount guard with d'Artagnan. The company of M. le Chevalier Dessessart thus received four instead of one when it admitted d'Artagnan.

EIGHT

D'Artagnan reflected that four young, brave, enterprising, and active men ought to have some other object than swaggering walks, fencing lessons, and practical jokes. He was racking his brain to find a direction for this force, when someone tapped gently at his door. A man with the appearance of a tradesman entered.

"I have heard Monsieur d'Artagnan spoken of as a very brave young man," said the citizen, "and this reputation decided me to confide a secret to him."

"Speak, monsieur," said d'Artagnan.

The citizen continued, "I have a wife who is seamstress to the queen, monsieur. Monsieur Laporte, the queen's cloak bearer, is her godfather. My wife was abducted yesterday morning as she was coming out of her workroom. Monsieur, I am convinced that there is less love than politics in all this."

"Less love than politics," replied d'Artagnan, "what do you suspect?"

"I will have confidence in you. It is not on account of any intrigues of her own that my wife has been arrested, but because of those of a lady much greater than herself."

"Of the—" D'Artagnan checked himself.

"Yes, monsieur," replied the terrified citizen.

"With whom?"

"With whom can it be, if not the Duke of—"

"How do you know?"

"Did I not tell you that my wife was the goddaughter of Monsieur Laporte, the confidential man of the queen? Monsieur Laporte placed my wife near Her Majesty in order that our poor queen might have someone in whom she could place confidence, betrayed as she is by everybody. My wife came home four days ago, monsieur. She confided that the queen believes someone has written to the Duke of Buckingham in her name, to make him come to Paris and draw him into some snare."

"But what has your wife to do with all this?"

"Her devotion to the queen is known; they wish either to remove her from her mistress or to seduce her and make use of her as a spy."

"That is likely," said d'Artagnan, "but the man who has abducted her—do you know his name?"

"He is a creature of the cardinal. My wife pointed him out to me one day. He is a noble of very lofty carriage, black hair, and has a scar on his temple."

"A scar on his temple!" cried d'Artagnan. "Why, that's my man of Meung. That simplifies the matter greatly. If your man is mine, I shall obtain two revenges; but where to find this man?"

"I know not. One day, as I was conveying my wife back to the

Louvre, he was coming out, and she showed him to me."

"The devil!" murmured d'Artagnan. "All this is vague enough. From whom have you learned of the abduction of your wife?"

"From Monsieur Laporte."

"And you have learned nothing from any other quarter?"

"By the word of Bonacieux, I have not!" cried the citizen.

"You call yourself Bonacieux?" interrupted d'Artagnan. "Pardon me for interrupting you, but that name is familiar to me."

"Possibly, monsieur. I am your landlord."

"Ah!" said d'Artagnan, half rising and bowing. "You are my landlord?"

"Yes, monsieur. As you have forgotten to pay me my rent and I have not tormented you, I thought you would appreciate my delicacy."

"How can it be otherwise, my dear Bonacieux?" replied d'Artagnan. "If I can be of any service—"

"As I was about to say, by the word of Bonacieux, I have confidence in you."

The citizen took a paper from his pocket and presented it to d'Artagnan.

"A letter?" said the young man.

"'Do not seek your wife,'" he read. "'She will be restored to you when there is no longer occasion for her. If you make a step to find her, you are lost.'

"That's pretty positive," continued d'Artagnan, "but it is but a menace."

"I am not a fighting man, monsieur, and I am afraid of the Bastille."

"Hum!" said d'Artagnan. "I have no greater regard for the Bastille than you. If it were nothing but a sword thrust, why—"

"Seeing you surrounded by Musketeers, and knowing that these Musketeers belong to Monsieur de Treville, and were consequently enemies of the cardinal, I thought that you and your friends, while rendering justice to your poor queen, would be pleased to play His Eminence an ill turn. And I offer you fifty pistoles."

"Admirable! You are rich then, my dear Monsieur Bonacieux?"

"I am comfortably off, monsieur, but—" cried the citizen.

"What!" demanded d'Artagnan.

"Whom do I see yonder?"

"It is he!" cried d'Artagnan and the citizen at the same time.

"He will not escape me!" cried d'Artagnan.

Drawing his sword, he rushed out of the apartment. On the staircase he met Athos and Porthos, and rushed between them like a dart.

"Where are you going?" cried the two Musketeers.

"The man of Meung!" replied d'Artagnan, and disappeared.

D'Artagnan had related to his friends his adventure with the stranger. The opinion of Athos was that d'Artagnan had lost his letter in the skirmish. A gentleman—and according to d'Artagnan's portrait of him, the stranger must be a gentleman—would be incapable of stealing a letter.

Porthos saw nothing in all this but a love meeting, which had been disturbed by the presence of d'Artagnan and his yellow horse.

Aramis said that these sorts of affairs were mysterious, it was better not to fathom them.

They understood, then, what was in hand, and as they thought that overtaking his man, or losing sight of him, d'Artagnan would return to his rooms, kept on their way. When they entered d'Artagnan's chamber, it was empty; the landlord had judged it prudent to decamp.

NINE

As Athos and Porthos had foreseen, d'Artagnan returned. He had run, sword in hand, through the streets, but found nobody resembling the man he sought. While d'Artagnan was running through the streets, Aramis had joined his companions.

"Well!" cried the three Musketeers, seeing d'Artagnan enter.

"Well!" cried he, throwing his sword upon the bed. "This man has disappeared. His flight has caused us to miss a glorious affair, gentlemen."

"Impart it to us, my dear friend," said Aramis, "unless the honor of any lady be hazarded by this confidence."

"Be satisfied," replied d'Artagnan. "The honor of no one will have cause to complain of what I have to tell."

He then related to his friends all that had passed between him and his host, and how the man who had abducted the wife of his worthy landlord was the same with whom he had had the difference at the hostelry of the Jolly Miller.

"Your affair is not bad," said Athos. "One may draw fifty or sixty pistoles from this good man. There only remains to ascertain whether fifty or sixty pistoles are worth the risk of four heads."

"It is not Madame Bonacieux about whom I am anxious," cried d'Artagnan, "but the queen, whom the king abandons, whom the cardinal persecutes, and who sees the heads of her friends fall, one after the other."

"Why does she love what we hate most, the Spaniards and the English?"

"Spain is her country," replied d'Artagnan, "and it is natural that she should love the Spanish. As to the second reproach, I have heard it said that she does not love the English, but an Englishman."

"Well," said Athos, "it must be acknowledged that this Englishman is worthy of being loved. I never saw a man with a nobler air."

"If I knew where the Duke of Buckingham was," said d'Artagnan, "I would conduct him to the queen, if only to enrage the cardinal."

"And Bonacieux," rejoined Athos, "told you that the queen thought that Buckingham had been brought over by a forged letter?"

"She is afraid so. I am convinced," said d'Artagnan, "that this abduction of the queen's woman is connected with the presence of Buckingham in Paris."

"Gentlemen," cried Aramis, "listen to this. Yesterday I was at the house of a doctor of theology, whom I sometimes consult about my studies."

Athos smiled.

"He resides in a quiet quarter," continued Aramis. "When I left his house—"

Here Aramis paused and appeared to make a strong effort, like a man who finds himself stopped by some unforeseen obstacle.

"This doctor has a niece," continued Aramis.

"Ah, a niece!" interrupted Porthos.

"A very respectable lady," said Aramis. The three friends burst into laughter. "If you laugh," replied Aramis, "you shall know nothing."

"We are as mute as tombstones," said Athos.

"This niece comes sometimes to see her uncle," resumed Aramis, "and was there yesterday, and I conducted her to her carriage."

"She has a carriage, then, this niece of the doctor?" interrupted Porthos. "A nice acquaintance, my friend!"

"Gentlemen," cried d'Artagnan, "the thing is serious. Go on, Aramis."

"All at once, a tall, dark gentleman—like yours, d'Artagnan—came toward me, accompanied by six men; and in the politest tone, 'Monsieur Duke,' said he to me, 'and you, madame,' continued he, addressing the lady on my arm—"

"The doctor's niece?"

"Hold your tongue, Porthos," said Athos.

"'—will you enter this carriage, without offering the least resistance?'"

"He took you for Buckingham!" cried d'Artagnan.

"I believe so," replied Aramis.

"But the lady?" asked Porthos.

"He took her for the queen!" said d'Artagnan.

"The fact is," said Porthos, "Aramis is something of the shape of the duke; but it nevertheless appears to me that the dress of a Musketeer—"

"I wore an enormous cloak," said Aramis.

"In the month of July?" said Porthos.

"I can comprehend that the spy may have been deceived by the person; but the face—"

"I had a large hat," said Aramis.

"Oh, good lord," cried Porthos, "what precautions for the study of theology!"

"Gentlemen," said d'Artagnan, "do not let us lose time in jesting. Let us seek Bonacieux's wife—the key of the intrigue."

"A woman of such inferior condition!" said Porthos, protruding his lips with contempt.

"She is goddaughter to Laporte, the confidential valet of the queen. Besides, it has perhaps been Her Majesty's calculation to seek for support so lowly. High heads expose themselves from afar."

At this moment the door was thrown open, and Bonacieux rushed into the chamber.

"Save me, gentlemen!" cried he. "There are men come to arrest me!"

Porthos and Aramis arose.

"A moment," cried d'Artagnan. "It is not courage that is needed; it is prudence."

"And yet," cried Porthos, "we will not leave—"

"You will leave d'Artagnan to act as he thinks proper," said

Athos. "He has the longest head of the four, and I will obey him."

At this moment four Guards appeared at the door, but seeing Musketeers, hesitated.

"Come in, gentlemen," called d'Artagnan. "We are faithful servants of the king and cardinal."

"Then you will not oppose our executing the orders we have received?" asked the leader of the party.

"On the contrary, gentlemen, we would assist you if it were necessary."

"What does he say?" grumbled Porthos.

"You are a simpleton," said Athos. "Silence!"

"But you promised me—" whispered Bonacieux.

"We can only save you by being free ourselves," replied d'Artagnan, in a low tone. "If we defend you, they will arrest us with you. Come, gentlemen!" said d'Artagnan, aloud. "I have no motive for defending monsieur. I saw him today for the first time. Is that not true, Monsieur Bonacieux?"

"That is the truth," cried the mercer, "but monsieur does not tell you—"

"Silence; silence about the queen, above all, or you will ruin everybody without saving yourself! Come, gentlemen, remove the fellow." And d'Artagnan pushed the mercer among the Guards.

The officers were full of thanks, and took away their prey.

"What villainy you have performed," said Porthos, when the four friends found themselves alone. "Shame, shame, for Musketeers to allow a fellow who cried for help to be arrested in their midst!"

"Porthos," said Aramis, "Athos told you that you are a simpleton, and I am quite of his opinion. D'Artagnan, when you occupy Monsieur de Treville's place, I will ask your influence to secure me an abbey."

"And now, gentlemen," said d'Artagnan, "all for one, one for all—that is our motto, is it not?"

"And yet—" said Porthos.

"Swear!" cried Athos and Aramis.

Overcome by example, Porthos stretched out his hand, and the four friends repeated with one voice:

"All for one, one for all."

"Now let us retire," said d'Artagnan, as if he had done nothing but command all his life. "From this moment we are at feud with the cardinal."

TEN

A Mousetrap

As soon as society invented police, police invented mousetraps. When an individual is arrested, the arrest is held secret. The door of the house is opened to all who knock. It is closed after them, and they are arrested; at the end of two or three days the police have all the *habitués* of the establishment. That is a mousetrap.

The apartment of M. Bonacieux became a mousetrap; whoever appeared there was interrogated by the cardinal's people. As a separate passage led to the upper floor, where d'Artagnan lodged, those who called on him were exempted from this detention.

Besides, nobody came but the three Musketeers; they had discovered nothing. Athos had even questioned M. de Treville. But M. de Treville knew nothing, except that the cardinal looked thoughtful, the king uneasy, and the redness of the queen's eyes denoted that she had been sleepless or tearful. But this was not striking; since her marriage the queen had slept badly and wept much.

As to d'Artagnan, he converted his chamber into an observatory. From his windows he saw all the visitors who were caught. Having removed a plank from his floor, nothing remaining but a simple ceiling between him and the room beneath, he heard all that passed.

The interrogatories were always framed thus: "Has Madame Bonacieux sent anything to you? Has Monsieur Bonacieux sent anything to you? Has either of them confided anything to you?"

"If they knew anything, they would not question people in this manner," said d'Artagnan to himself.

On the evening of the day after the arrest of Bonacieux, a knocking was heard at the street door. The door was opened and shut; someone was taken in the mousetrap.

D'Artagnan flew to his hole and listened.

Stifled cries were soon heard. There were no questions.

"The devil!" said d'Artagnan. "It seems like a woman! The scoundrels!"

"But I tell you I am the mistress of the house! I am Madame Bonacieux; I belong to the queen!" cried the unfortunate woman.

"Madame Bonacieux!" murmured d'Artagnan.

The voice could now only be heard in inarticulate sounds.

"They are binding her; they are going to drag her away," cried d'Artagnan to himself. "My sword!"

He let himself gently down through the window, then went to the door and knocked, murmuring, "I will be caught in the mousetrap; woe to the cats that pounce upon such a mouse!"

The knocker had scarcely sounded before the door was

opened, and d'Artagnan, sword in hand, rushed into the rooms of M. Bonacieux.

Then the neighbors heard loud cries, clashing of swords, and breaking of furniture. A moment after, those who had gone to their windows to learn the cause saw four men clothed in black *fly*, like frightened crows. D'Artagnan was conqueror.

On being left alone with Mme Bonacieux, d'Artagnan turned toward her; the poor woman reclined fainting upon an armchair. She was a charming woman, with dark hair, blue eyes, admirable teeth, and a complexion of rose and opal. While d'Artagnan was examining her, he saw on the ground a fine cambric handkerchief, at the corner of which he recognized the same cipher he had seen on the handkerchief that had nearly caused him and Aramis to cut each other's throat.

From that time, d'Artagnan had been cautious with respect to handkerchiefs, and therefore placed this one in the pocket of Mme Bonacieux.

At that moment Mme Bonacieux opened her eyes, looked around with terror, and saw that she was alone with her liberator. She extended her hands to him with a smile.

"Ah, monsieur!" said she. "You have saved me."

"Madame," said d'Artagnan, "I have only done what every gentleman would have done in my place."

"But what could these men want with me, and why is Monsieur Bonacieux not here?"

"Madame, those men are the agents of the cardinal and your husband was yesterday evening conducted to the Bastille."

"My husband in the Bastille!" cried Mme Bonacieux. "What has he done?"

D'Artagnan, sword in hand, rushed into the rooms of M. Bonacieux.

"What has he done?" said d'Artagnan. "His only crime is to have the good fortune to be your husband. I know that you have been abducted, madame, by a man with black hair and a scar on his left temple."

"And did my husband know I had been carried off?"

"He was informed of it by a letter, written by the abductor himself."

"And does he suspect," said Mme Bonacieux, "the cause of this event?"

"He attributed it to a political cause."

"I think as he does. Then Monsieur Bonacieux has not suspected me a single instant?"

"He was too proud of your prudence, and of your love. But," continued d'Artagnan, "how did you escape?"

"I took advantage of a moment when they left me alone; with the help of the sheets I let myself down from the window. Then I hastened hither."

"I believe the men I have put to flight will return reinforced; if they find us here, we are lost."

"You are right," cried the frightened Mme Bonacieux. "Let us save ourselves."

At these words she passed her arm under that of d'Artagnan, and urged him forward. Without taking the trouble to shut the door after them, they descended the rue des Fossoyeurs rapidly.

"Where do you wish me to conduct you?" asked d'Artagnan.

"I am at a loss," said Mme Bonacieux. "My intention was to inform Monsieur Laporte, through my husband, so that Monsieur Laporte might tell us what had taken place at the Louvre, and whether there is danger in presenting myself there."

"I," said d'Artagnan, "can inform Monsieur Laporte."

"No doubt you could, only Monsieur Bonacieux is known at the Louvre, and would be allowed to pass, whereas the gate would be closed against you."

"Ah, bah!" said d'Artagnan. "You have at some wicket of the Louvre a concierge who, thanks to a password, would—"

Mme Bonacieux looked earnestly at the young man.

"If I give you this password," said she, "would you forget it as soon as you used it?"

"By my honor!" said d'Artagnan, with an accent so truthful that no one could mistake it.

"But where shall I go?"

"Is there nobody from whose house Monsieur Laporte can come and fetch you?"

"I can trust nobody."

"Stop," said d'Artagnan. "We are near Athos's door."

"Who is this Athos?"

"One of my friends."

"But if he should be at home and see me?"

"He is not at home, and I will carry away the key, after having placed you in his apartment."

"But if he should return?"

"Oh, he will be told that I have brought a woman with me, and that woman is in his apartment."

"But that will compromise me sadly, you know."

"Nobody knows you. Besides, we are in a situation to overlook ceremony."

As d'Artagnan had foreseen, Athos was not within. He introduced Mme Bonacieux into the little apartment.

"You are at home," said he. "Fasten the door, open to nobody unless you hear three taps like this—" And he tapped thrice—two taps close together, the other after an interval.

"That is well," said Mme Bonacieux. "Present yourself at the wicket of the Louvre and ask for Germain. He will ask what you want, and you will answer by these two words, 'Tours' and 'Bruxelles.' He will put himself at your orders."

"And what shall I command him?"

"To go and fetch Monsieur Laporte, the queen's valet."

"And when Monsieur Laporte is come?"

"You will send him to me."

"But where shall I see you again?"

"Let that care be mine, and be at ease."

D'Artagnan bowed to Mme Bonacieux, darting the most loving glance that he could upon her charming little person; and while he descended the stairs, he heard the door double-locked. In two bounds he was at the Louvre; ten o'clock struck.

In a few minutes, Laporte was at the lodge; d'Artagnan informed him where Mme Bonacieux was. Laporte set off at a run. Hardly, however, had he taken ten steps before he returned.

"Young man," said he to d'Artagnan, "a suggestion. Have you any friend whose clock is too slow? Go and call upon him, in order that he may give evidence of your having been with him at half past nine."

D'Artagnan found his advice prudent. Five minutes after, M. de Treville was asking d'Artagnan what caused his visit at so late an hour.

"Pardon me, monsieur," said d'Artagnan, who had profited by the moment he had been left alone to put back M. de Treville's clock three-quarters of an hour. "I thought, as it was only twenty-five minutes past nine, it was not too late to wait upon you."

"Twenty-five minutes past nine!" cried M. de Treville. "Why, that's impossible!"

"Look, monsieur," said d'Artagnan, "the clock shows it."

"That's true," said M. de Treville. "I believed it later. What can I do for you?"

Then d'Artagnan told M. de Treville a long history about the queen. He expressed the fears he entertained with respect to Her Majesty; he related what he had heard of the projects of the cardinal, and all with a candor of which M. de Treville was the more the dupe, from having himself observed something fresh between the cardinal, the king, and the queen.

As ten o'clock was striking, d'Artagnan left M. de Treville, who thanked him for his information and returned to the saloon; at the foot of the stairs, d'Artagnan remembered he had forgotten his cane. He sprang up again, reentered the office, set the clock right again, that it might not be perceived that it had been put wrong, and certain that he had a witness to prove his alibi, soon found himself in the street.

ELEVEN

In Which the Plot Thickens

For an apprentice Musketeer, Mme Bonacieux was almost an ideal of love. Pretty, mysterious, initiated in the secrets of the court. Moreover, d'Artagnan had delivered her from the hands of demons who wished to harm her, and established one of those feelings of gratitude that easily assume a more tender character.

And M. Bonacieux, whom d'Artagnan had pushed into the hands of the officers, promising in a whisper to save him? D'Artagnan thought nothing about him. Love is the most selfish passion.

D'Artagnan, smiling at the stars, found himself in the quarter in which Aramis lived and took it into his head to pay his friend a visit. This was an opportunity for talking about pretty little Mme Bonacieux, of whom his head, if not his heart, was already full.

D'Artagnan already perceived the door of his friend's house, when a shadow issued from the rue des Fossoyeurs. D'Artagnan soon discovered that it was a woman. This woman, not certain of the house she was seeking, lifted up her eyes to look around her, stopped, went backward, and returned again. D'Artagnan was perplexed.

"Shall I offer my services?" thought he. "By her step she must be young; perhaps she is pretty. But a woman at this hour only ventures out to meet her lover."

There were but three private houses in this part of the street, and only two windows looking toward the road, one belonging to Aramis.

"It would be droll if this dove should be in search of our friend's house," said d'Artagnan to himself. "My dear Aramis, I shall find you out." And d'Artagnan concealed himself in the darkest side of the street.

The young woman continued to advance. She resolutely drew near to Aramis's shutter, and tapped with her bent finger.

"Dear Aramis," murmured d'Artagnan. "Monsieur Hypocrite, I understand how you study theology."

The inside blind was opened and a light appeared through the shutter.

"Ah!" said the listener. "Not through doors, but through windows! We shall see the windows open, and the lady enter. Very pretty!"

But to the great astonishment of d'Artagnan, the shutter remained closed. Still more, the light disappeared, and all was again in obscurity. At the end of some seconds two sharp taps were heard inside. The young woman in the street replied by a single tap, and the shutter opened a little way.

The young woman took from her pocket a white object,

which she unfolded quickly: a handkerchief. She made her interlocutor observe the corner of this unfolded object.

This immediately recalled to d'Artagnan's mind the handkerchief he had found at the feet of Mme Bonacieux, which had reminded him of that which he had dragged from under the feet of Aramis.

"What the devil could that handkerchief signify?"

Placed where he was, d'Artagnan could not perceive the face of Aramis, but entertained no doubt that it was his friend who held this dialogue. Curiosity prevailed, and he stole from his hiding place, positioning himself close to the angle of the wall, from which his eye could pierce the interior of Aramis's room.

Upon gaining this advantage, d'Artagnan was near uttering a cry of surprise; it was not Aramis, it was a woman! D'Artagnan could not distinguish her features.

The woman drew a second handkerchief from her pocket, and exchanged it for that which had just been shown. The shutter closed. The woman outside the window turned round, and passed d'Artagnan, pulling down the hood of her mantle; but d'Artagnan had recognized Mme Bonacieux.

Mme Bonacieux! The suspicion had crossed his mind when she drew the handkerchief from her pocket; but what probability was there that Mme Bonacieux should be running about Paris, at the risk of being abducted a second time?

This must be an affair of importance; and what is the most important affair to a woman? Love. Was it on her own account that she exposed herself to such hazards?

There was a simple means of satisfying himself whither Mme Bonacieux was going: to follow her.

At the sight of the young man, who detached himself from the wall like a statue walking from its niche, and at the noise of the steps behind her, Mme Bonacieux uttered a cry and fled. D'Artagnan ran after her. The unfortunate woman was exhausted by terror. When d'Artagnan placed his hand upon her shoulder, she sank upon one knee, crying, "Kill me, but you shall know nothing!"

D'Artagnan made haste to reassure her. Mme Bonacieux uttered a cry of joy. "Oh, it is you! Thank God!"

"Yes, it is I," said d'Artagnan, "whom God has sent to watch over you."

"Was it with that intention you followed me?" asked the young woman.

"No," said d'Artagnan. "It was chance that threw me your way; I saw a woman knocking at the window of one of my friends."

"One of your friends?" interrupted Mme Bonacieux.

"Without doubt; Aramis is one of my best friends."

"Aramis! Who is he?"

"Come, you won't tell me you don't know Aramis?"

"This is the first time I ever heard his name."

"It was not he you came to seek?"

"Not the least in the world. You must have seen that the person to whom I spoke was a woman."

"That is true; but this woman is a friend of Aramis—"

"I know nothing of that."

"—since she lodges with him."

"That does not concern me."

"But who is she?"

"Oh, that is not my secret."

"My dear Madame Bonacieux, you are charming; but at the same time you are one of the most mysterious women."

"Do I lose by that?"

"No; you are adorable."

"Give me your arm, then. Now escort me."

"Where?"

"You will see, because you will leave me at the door."

"Shall I wait for you?"

"That will be useless."

"You will return alone, then?"

"Perhaps yes, perhaps no."

"I will wait until you come out."

"In that case, *adieu.*"

"But you have claimed—"

"The aid of a gentleman, not the watchfulness of a spy."

"Well, madame, I must do as you wish."

D'Artagnan offered his arm to Mme Bonacieux, who took it, half laughing, and they reached the top of rue de la Harpe. Arriving there, the young woman approached a door. "Now, monsieur," said she, "it is here I have business; a thousand thanks for your honorable company."

"You will have nothing to fear on your return?"

"I shall have nothing to fear from robbers. What could they take from me? I have not a penny about me."

"You forget that beautiful handkerchief with the coat of arms, which I found at your feet, and replaced in your pocket."

"Hold your tongue! Do you wish to destroy me?"

"You see that there is danger, since a single word makes you tremble; you confess that if that word were heard you would be ruined. Come, madame!" cried d'Artagnan, seizing her hands. "Confide in me."

"Ask my own secrets, and I will reveal them to you," replied Mme Bonacieux, "but those of others—that is another thing."

"Very well," said d'Artagnan, "I shall discover them."

"Beware of what you do!" cried the young woman, in a manner so serious as to make d'Artagnan start. "I exist no longer for you, any more than if you had never seen me."

"Must Aramis do as much as I, madame?" said d'Artagnan, deeply piqued.

"I have told you that I do not know him."

"You do not know the man at whose shutter you have just knocked? You believe me too credulous!"

"You say that one of your friends lives in that house?"

"I say so for the third time; that house is inhabited by my friend Aramis. If you could see my heart," said d'Artagnan, "you would there read so much curiosity that you would pity me and so much love that you would instantly satisfy my curiosity."

"You speak very suddenly of love, monsieur," said the young woman, shaking her head.

"That is because love has come suddenly upon me."

The young woman looked at him.

"I am already upon the scent," resumed d'Artagnan. "About three months ago I was near having a duel with Aramis concerning a handkerchief resembling the one you showed to the woman in his house."

"Silence, monsieur! Since the dangers I incur cannot stop you, think of those you yourself run! There is peril of imprisonment, risk of life in knowing me. Monsieur," said the young woman, clasping her hands together, "by the honor of a soldier, by the courtesy of a gentleman, depart! Midnight strikes, the hour when I am expected."

"Madame," said the young man, bowing, "I can refuse nothing asked of me thus. I will depart."

"Ah, I was sure you were a good and brave young man," said Mme Bonacieux, holding out her hand to him. D'Artagnan seized it, and kissed it ardently.

"Well!" resumed Mme Bonacieux, in a voice almost caressing. "What is lost today may not be lost forever. Who knows, when I shall be at liberty, that I may not satisfy your curiosity?"

"Will you make the same promise to my love?" cried d'Artagnan, beside himself with joy.

"Oh, as to that, I do not engage myself. Today, I am no further than gratitude. Be satisfied. Now go, in the name of heaven! I am late."

"By five minutes."

"Yes; in certain circumstances five minutes are five ages."

"When one loves."

"The discussion is going to begin again!" said Mme Bonacieux, with a half smile that was not exempt from a tinge of impatience.

"No, I would have all the merit of my devotion, even if that devotion were stupidity. *Adieu*, madame!"

As if he only felt strength to detach himself by a violent effort from the hand he held, he sprang away, running, while Mme Bonacieux knocked. When he had gained the angle of the street, he turned. The door had been opened, and shut again; the mercer's pretty wife had disappeared.

D'Artagnan pursued his way. Five minutes later he was in the rue des Fossoyeurs.

"Poor Athos!" said he. "He will have returned home, where he will have learned that a woman had been there. A woman with Athos! After all," continued d'Artagnan, "there was certainly one with Aramis. I am curious to know how it will end."

"Badly, monsieur!" replied a voice, which the young man recognized as that of his valet; for, soliloquizing aloud, he had entered the alley, at the end of which were the stairs that led to his chamber.

"Badly?" asked d'Artagnan. "What has happened?"

"Monsieur Athos is arrested. He was found in your lodging; they took him for you."

"By whom was he arrested?"

"By Guards brought by the men in black whom you put to flight."

"Why did he not tell them he knew nothing about this affair?"

"On the contrary, he said to me, 'It is your master that needs his liberty, since he knows everything and I know nothing. In three days I will tell them who I am, and they cannot fail to let me go.'"

"Bravo, Athos! Noble heart!" murmured d'Artagnan. "And what did the officers do?"

"Four conveyed him away. Two remained with the men in black, who rummaged and took all the papers. Then, when all was over, they went away, leaving the house empty."

"If Porthos and Aramis come, tell them what has happened. I will run to Monsieur de Treville, and meet them there."

And with all the swiftness of his legs, d'Artagnan directed his course toward M. de Treville's.

M. de Treville was not at his house. His company was on guard at the Louvre.

It was necessary to reach M. de Treville, so that he should be informed of what was passing. D'Artagnan resolved to try and enter the Louvre. His costume of Guardsman in the company of M. Dessessart ought to be his passport.

He therefore came up to the dock and saw two persons whose appearance very much struck him. One was a man and the other a woman. The woman had the outline of Mme Bonacieux; the man resembled Aramis.

The woman's hood was pulled down, the man held a handkerchief to his face. Both, as these precautions indicated, had an interest in not being recognized.

They took the bridge. D'Artagnan followed them. He had not gone twenty steps before he became convinced that the woman was really Mme Bonacieux and the man Aramis.

He felt at that instant all the suspicions of jealousy agitating his heart. Mme Bonacieux had declared that she did not know Aramis and yet he found her on the arm of Aramis. D'Artagnan did not reflect that he had only known the mercer's pretty wife three hours; that she owed him nothing but a little gratitude; and that she had promised him nothing. He considered himself an outraged lover.

The two perceived they were watched, and redoubled their speed. D'Artagnan passed them, then returned so as to meet them before a lamp that threw its light over all that part of the bridge.

"What do you want, monsieur?" demanded the Musketeer, with a foreign accent, which proved to d'Artagnan that he was deceived in one of his conjectures.

"It is not Aramis!" cried he.

"No, monsieur, it is not Aramis; I perceive you have mistaken me for another, and pardon you. Allow me to pass."

"You are right, monsieur, it is not with you that I have anything to do; it is with madame."

"Ah," said Mme Bonacieux, in a tone of reproach, "monsieur, I had your promise as a soldier and your word as a gentleman. I hoped to be able to rely upon that."

"And I, madame!" said d'Artagnan, embarrassed. "You promised me—"

"Take my arm, madame," said the stranger, "and let us continue our way."

D'Artagnan, however, stood, with crossed arms, before the Musketeer and Mme Bonacieux.

The Musketeer pushed d'Artagnan aside with his hand. D'Artagnan drew his sword. With the rapidity of lightning, the stranger drew his.

"In the name of heaven, my lord!" cried Mme Bonacieux, throwing herself between the combatants.

"My lord!" cried d'Artagnan, enlightened by a sudden idea. "Pardon me, monsieur, but you are not—"

"My lord the Duke of Buckingham," said Mme Bonacieux, in an undertone. "Now you may ruin us all."

"My lord, a hundred pardons! I love her and was jealous. You know what it is to love, my lord. Tell me how I can serve Your Grace?"

"You are a brave young man," said Buckingham, holding out his hand to d'Artagnan, who pressed it respectfully. "Follow us as far as the Louvre, and if anyone watches, slay him!"

D'Artagnan placed his naked sword under his arm and followed, ready to execute the instructions of the noble and elegant minister.

The young woman and the handsome Musketeer entered the Louvre without interference. As for d'Artagnan, he repaired to the cabaret, where he found Porthos and Aramis. Meanwhile, we must leave our three friends, and follow the Duke of Buckingham and his guide through the labyrinths of the Louvre.

TWELVE

THE DUKE OF BUCKINGHAM

Mme Bonacieux and the duke entered the Louvre without difficulty. Mme Bonacieux was known to belong to the queen; the duke wore the uniform of the Musketeers, who were that evening on guard.

Once within the court, Mme Bonacieux pushed a little door. Both entered, and found themselves in darkness; Mme Bonacieux took the duke by the hand, and began to ascend the staircase. The duke counted two stories. She turned to the right, followed a long corridor, descended a flight, opened a door, and pushed the duke into an apartment lighted by a lamp, saying, "Remain here, my lord duke; someone will come." She went out by the same door, which she locked, so that the duke found himself literally a prisoner.

The Duke of Buckingham did not experience an instant of fear. Brave, rash, and enterprising, this was not the first time he had risked his life in such attempts. He had learned that the message, upon the faith of which he had come to Paris, was a snare; but instead of returning to England, had declared to the queen that he would not depart without seeing her. The queen at length became afraid that the duke would commit some folly. She had already decided upon seeing him when Mme Bonacieux, charged with conducting him to the Louvre, was abducted. Once free, she accomplished the perilous enterprise that, but for her arrest, would have been executed three days earlier.

Buckingham, left alone, walked toward a mirror. His Musketeer's uniform became him marvelously.

At thirty-five, he was the handsomest gentleman and the most elegant cavalier of France or England. Convinced of his own power, he went straight to the object he aimed at, even an object so elevated that it would have been madness for any other to have contemplated.

Buckingham placed himself before the glass, twisted his mustache, and smiled upon himself with pride.

At this moment a door opened, and a woman appeared. Buckingham saw this apparition in the glass; he uttered a cry. It was the queen!

Anne of Austria was then twenty-six years of age, in the full splendor of her beauty. Her carriage was that of a goddess; her eyes, which cast the brilliancy of emeralds, were full of sweetness and majesty. Her mouth was small and rosy, lovely in its smile. Her skin was admired for its velvety softness; her arms were of surpassing beauty. Her hair, which she wore curled very plainly, and with much powder, admirably set off her face. Buckingham threw himself at her feet, and before the queen could prevent him, kissed the hem of her robe.

"Duke, you know that it is not I who wrote to you."

"Yes, Your Majesty!" cried the duke. "I know that I must have been mad to believe that snow would become animated or marble warm; they who love believe in love. I have lost nothing by this journey because I see you."

"Yes," replied Anne, "because you persist in remaining in a city where you run the risk of your life, and make me run the risk of my honor. I see you to tell you that everything separates us—the depths of the sea, the enmity of kingdoms, the sanctity of vows. I see you to tell you that we must never see each other again."

"Speak on, madame," said Buckingham. "The sweetness of your voice covers the harshness of your words."

"My lord," cried the queen, "I have never said that I love you."

"But you have never told me that you did not; truly, to speak such words would be an ingratitude. Where can you find love like mine—love which neither time, nor absence, nor despair can extinguish? It is now three years, madame, since I saw you first, and during those three years I have loved you."

"What folly," murmured Anne of Austria.

"Every time I see you is a fresh diamond which I enclose in the casket of my heart. In three years, madame, I have only seen you four times—the third, in the garden of Amiens."

"Duke," said the queen, blushing, "never speak of that evening."

"You remember what a beautiful night it was? I was able for one instant to be alone with you. I felt, bending my head toward you, your beautiful hair touch my cheek, and I trembled from head to foot. For that night, madame, you loved me."

"My lord, you saw the queen come to the aid of the woman.

At the first word you uttered, I called for help."

"You believed that you would fly from me by returning to Paris. Eight days after, I was back, madame. I risked my life and favor to see you but for a second. I did not even touch your hand."

"Calumny seized upon all those follies in which I took no part, as you well know, my lord. The king, excited by the cardinal, made a terrible clamor. Madame de Chevreuse fell into disgrace, and when you wished to come as ambassador to France, the king himself opposed it."

"Yes, and France is about to pay for her king's refusal with a war. I am not allowed to see you, madame, but you shall hear of me. Tell me what woman has a lover more truly in love?"

"My lord, all these proofs of love are almost crimes."

"Because you do not love me, madame! Ah, Madame de Chevreuse was less cruel than you. Holland loved her, and she responded to his love."

"Madame de Chevreuse was not queen," murmured Anne of Austria.

"You would love me, then, if you were not queen! Thanks for those sweet words!"

"I did not mean to say—"

"Silence!" cried the duke. "If I am happy in error, do not lift me from it. For I have had a presentiment that I should shortly die." And the duke smiled, with a smile at once sad and charming.

"Oh, my God!" cried Anne of Austria, with an accent of terror.

"I do not tell you this to terrify you. The words you have just spoken will have richly paid all."

"Oh, but," said Anne, "I dreamed that I saw you lying wounded."

"In the left side, with a knife?" interrupted Buckingham.

"Yes. Who can have told you I had had that dream?"

"I ask for no more. Would God send the same dreams to you as to me if you did not love me?"

"Oh!" cried Anne of Austria. "This is more than I can bear. If your love for me was the cause of your death, I should run mad. Depart! Come back as ambassador, surrounded with guards, and then I shall no longer fear for your days."

"Some pledge of your indulgence; something you have worn that I may wear—a ring, a necklace, a chain."

"Will you depart, if I give you that—return to England?"

"I swear."

Anne of Austria reentered her apartment, and came out holding a small rosewood box in her hand.

"Here, my lord," said she, "keep this in memory of me."

Buckingham took the small box and fell again on his knees.

"You have promised to go," said the queen.

"And I keep my word. Your hand, madame, and I depart!"

Anne of Austria stretched forth her hand, closing her eyes.

Buckingham pressed his lips to that beautiful hand, and rising, said, "Within six months, if I am not dead, I shall see you again, madame—even if I have to overturn the world." And he rushed out of the apartment.

In the corridor he met Mme Bonacieux, who conducted him out of the Louvre.

THIRTEEN

The officers who arrested M. Bonacieux conducted him to the Bastille. At the end of half an hour or thereabouts, a clerk came to give the order to conduct M. Bonacieux to the Chamber of Examination.

Two guards pushed him into a low room, where the only furniture was a table, a chair, and a commissary. The commissary was seated in the chair and was writing at the table. He began by asking M. Bonacieux his name, age, condition, and abode.

The accused replied that his name was Jacques Michel Bonacieux, that he was fifty-one years old, a retired mercer, and lived at rue des Fossoyeurs, no. 14.

The commissary made him a speech upon the danger of meddling with public matters, complicated by an exposition in which he painted the power and the deeds of the cardinal. He bade poor Bonacieux reflect upon the gravity of his situation.

The reflections of the mercer were already made; he cursed

the instant when M. Laporte had formed the idea of marrying him to his goddaughter, and the moment when that goddaughter had been received as lady of the linen to Her Majesty. At bottom the character of M. Bonacieux was one of selfishness mixed with cowardice.

"Monsieur Commissary," said he, "I know, more than anybody, the merit of the incomparable eminence by whom we have the honor to be governed."

"Indeed?" asked the commissary, with an air of doubt. "If that is so, how came you in the Bastille?"

"How I came," replied Bonacieux, "is impossible for me to tell you; it is not for having disobliged Monsieur le Cardinal."

"You must have committed a crime, since you are accused of high treason."

"High treason!" cried Bonacieux, terrified. "How is it possible for a poor mercer to be accused of high treason?"

"Monsieur Bonacieux," said the commissary, "you have a wife?"

"Yes, monsieur," replied the mercer, in a tremble, "I *had* one. They have abducted her, monsieur."

"They have abducted her," said the commissary. "Do you know the man who has committed this deed?"

M. Bonacieux was in the greatest perplexity possible. Had he better tell everything?

"I suspect," said he, "a tall, dark man, who has the air of a great lord. He has followed us several times when I waited for my wife at the wicket of the Louvre. As to his name, I know nothing; if I were to meet him, I should recognize him."

The face of the commissary grew darker.

"You should recognize him?" continued he. "That is enough; someone must be informed that you know the ravisher of your wife."

"But I have not told you that I know him!" cried Bonacieux, in despair.

"Take away the prisoner," said the commissary to the guards.

"Alas!" said M. Bonacieux to himself. "My wife must have committed some frightful crime. They believe me her accomplice."

The guards led the prisoner away. Bonacieux sat all night on his stool; when the first rays of the sun penetrated into his chamber, the dawn itself appeared to him to have taken funereal tints.

All at once he heard his bolts drawn, and believed they were come to conduct him to the scaffold; so that when he saw, instead of the executioner, only his commissary of the preceding evening, he was ready to embrace him.

"Your affair has become more complicated. I advise you to tell the whole truth."

"Why, I am ready to tell everything," cried Bonacieux.

"Where is your wife?"

"Did not I tell you she had been stolen from me?"

"Yes, but yesterday, thanks to you, she escaped."

"My wife escaped!" cried Bonacieux. "Monsieur, it is not my fault."

"What business had you to go into the chamber of Monsieur d'Artagnan?"

"To beg him to assist me in finding my wife. I believed I had a right to endeavor to find her. Monsieur d'Artagnan promised me his assistance; but he was betraying me."

"Monsieur d'Artagnan made a compact with you, put to flight the police who had arrested your wife, and placed her beyond reach. Bring in Monsieur d'Artagnan," said the commissary. The guards led in Athos.

"But," cried Bonacieux, "this is not Monsieur d'Artagnan."

"Not Monsieur d'Artagnan?" exclaimed the commissary. "What is this gentleman's name?"

"I cannot tell you."

"Your name?" asked the commissary.

"Athos," replied the Musketeer.

"You said that your name was d'Artagnan."

"Somebody said to me, 'You are Monsieur d'Artagnan?' I did not wish to contradict."

At this moment the door was opened, and a messenger gave a letter to the commissary.

"Oh, unhappy woman!" cried the commissary.

"Of whom do you speak? Not my wife!"

"Yours is a pretty business."

"But," said the agitated mercer, "how can my own affair become worse by anything my wife does while I am in prison? I am a stranger to what she has done!"

The commissary designated by the same gesture Athos and Bonacieux. "Let them be guarded more closely."

"And yet," said Athos, "if Monsieur d'Artagnan is concerned in this matter, I do not perceive how I can take his place."

"Do as I bade you," cried the commissary.

Athos shrugged his shoulders, while M. Bonacieux uttered lamentations enough to break the heart of a tiger.

They locked the mercer in the same dungeon where he had passed the night. In the evening, the guards appeared.

"Follow me," said an officer, who came up behind the guards.

"Follow you!" cried Bonacieux. "At this hour! Where, my God?"

"Where we have orders to lead you."

"My God!" murmured the mercer. "I am lost!" At the gate he found a carriage surrounded by men of the Cardinal's Guards on horseback. They made him enter this carriage, the door was locked, and they were left in a rolling prison. Through the closely fastened windows the prisoner could perceive the houses and pavement; true Parisian as he was, Bonacieux recognized every street. He soon realized they were taking the road to Traitor's Cross.

It was at Traitor's Cross that lesser criminals were executed. He could not yet see that dreadful cross, but he felt as if it were coming to meet him. When within twenty paces of it, the carriage stopped. Bonacieux uttered a feeble groan and fainted.

FOURTEEN

Guards received Bonacieux in their arms from the officer, carried him up a flight of stairs, and deposited him in an antechamber.

All these movements had been effected mechanically, as far as he was concerned. He had walked as one walks in a dream. He might have been executed at that moment without making a gesture in his own defense.

He remained exactly where the Guards placed him.

On looking around him, he perceived that his fear was exaggerated, and began to turn his head to the right and the left. Then he ventured to draw up one leg, then the other. At length, he lifted himself. At this moment an officer opened the door. "Bonacieux?" said he.

"Yes, Monsieur Officer," stammered the mercer.

"Come in," said the officer.

It was a large cabinet. A square table, covered with books and papers, upon which was unrolled an immense plan of the city of la Rochelle, occupied the center of the room.

Standing before the chimney was a man with a proud expression on a thin face. This man had the appearance of a soldier; and his buff boots still slightly covered with dust indicated that he had been on horseback in the course of the day. He was Armand Jean Duplessis, Cardinal de Richelieu, an active and gallant cavalier. At first sight, nothing denoted the cardinal; it was impossible for those who did not know his face to guess in whose presence they were.

"Is this that Bonacieux?" asked he.

"Yes, monseigneur," replied the officer.

"Give me those papers, and leave us."

The officer took the papers pointed out, gave them to him, bowed, and retired. Bonacieux recognized the questions he was asked at the Bastille. At the end of ten minutes of reading, the cardinal was satisfied.

"That head has never conspired," murmured he, "but it matters not.

"You are accused of high treason," said the cardinal.

"So I have been told, monseigneur," cried Bonacieux, giving his interrogator the title he had heard the officer give, "but I know nothing about it."

"You have conspired with your wife, with Madame de Chevreuse, and with my lord Duke of Buckingham."

"No, monseigneur," responded the mercer, "I have heard her pronounce those names. She said that the Cardinal de Richelieu had drawn the Duke of Buckingham to Paris to ruin him and the queen."

"She said that?" cried the cardinal, with violence. "Your wife has escaped. Did you know that?"

"I learned it from Monsieur the Commissary."

"Then you are ignorant of what has become of your wife since her flight."

"She has likely returned to the Louvre."

"At one o'clock this morning she had not returned."

"What can have become of her?"

"We shall know, be assured. Nothing is concealed from the cardinal."

"In that case, monseigneur, do you believe the cardinal will tell me what has become of my wife?"

"Perhaps; you must first reveal all you know of your wife's relations with Madame de Chevreuse."

"But, monseigneur, I know nothing."

"When you went to fetch your wife from the Louvre, did you return directly home?"

"Scarcely ever; she had business to transact with linen drapers, to whose houses I conducted her."

"How many were there of these linen drapers?"

"Two, monseigneur."

"Did you go into these houses with her?"

"Never, monseigneur; I waited at the door."

"You are a very complacent husband, dear Monsieur Bonacieux," said the cardinal.

"He calls me dear monsieur," said the mercer to himself. "Matters are going all right."

"Where are those doors?"

"No. 25 in the rue de Vaugirard; 75 in the rue de la Harpe."

"That's well," said the cardinal. He took up a silver bell and rang it; the officer entered.

"Go," said he, "and find Rochefort. Tell him to come to me immediately."

The officer sprang out of the apartment with alacrity. Five seconds had scarcely elapsed when a new personage entered.

"It is he!" cried Bonacieux. "The man who abducted my wife."

The cardinal rang a second time. The officer reappeared.

"Place this man in the care of his guards; let him wait till I send for him."

"It is not he!" cried Bonacieux. "This is another man, and does not resemble him at all."

The officer took Bonacieux by the arm, and led him into the antechamber.

The moment the door closed, "They have seen each other," said the newly arrived personage, approaching the cardinal eagerly.

"The queen and the duke?" cried Richelieu. "How did it come about?"

"At half past twelve the queen was with her women, when someone brought her a handkerchief. The queen turned pale—'Ladies,' said she, 'I shall soon return.'"

"Did she return?"

"Yes; but only to take a little rosewood box."

"When she finally returned, did she bring that little box with her?"

"No."

"Does your spy, Madame de Lannoy, know what was in that casket?"

"The diamond studs which His Majesty gave the queen."

"Madame de Lannoy is of the opinion that she gave them to Buckingham?"

"She is sure of it."

"Meanwhile, do you know where the Duchesse de Chevreuse and the Duke of Buckingham are concealed?"

"No, monseigneur."

"But I know. They were: one in the rue de Vaugirard, no. 25, the other in the rue de la Harpe, no. 75."

"Does Your Eminence command that they be arrested?"

"Take ten Guardsmen, and search the two houses thoroughly."

"Instantly, monseigneur." And Rochefort went out of the apartment.

The cardinal reflected and rang the bell a third time. The same officer appeared.

"Bring the prisoner in again," said the cardinal.

M. Bonacieux was introduced afresh.

"You have deceived me!" said the cardinal, sternly.

"I," cried Bonacieux, "I deceive Your Eminence?"

"Your wife, in going to rue de Vaugirard and rue de la Harpe, did not go to find linen drapers. She went to meet the Duchesse de Chevreuse and the Duke of Buckingham."

"Yes," cried Bonacieux, recalling the circumstances, "I told my wife that it was surprising that linen drapers should live in houses that had no signs; but she laughed at me."

A smile played upon the cardinal's lips, and he said, offering his hand, "Rise, my friend, you are a worthy man."

"The cardinal has touched me with his hand!" cried

Bonacieux. "The great man has called me his friend!"

"Yes, my friend," said the cardinal, with that paternal tone that deceived none who knew him. "You have been unjustly suspected, take this purse and pardon me."

"I pardon you, monseigneur!" said Bonacieux. "You can have me arrested, you can have me tortured, you can have me hanged; I could not have the least word to say."

"My dear Monsieur Bonacieux, you are generous. Take this bag, and go away without being too malcontent."

"I go away enchanted."

Bonacieux bowed to the ground. He went out, and the cardinal heard him crying aloud, "Long life to the great cardinal!" The cardinal listened with a smile. "Good!" said he. "That man would henceforward lay down his life for me." And the cardinal began to examine the map of la Rochelle. As he was in his meditations, the door opened, and Rochefort returned.

"Well?" said the cardinal.

"Well," said the latter, "a young woman and a man have indeed lodged at the houses; the woman left last night, and the man this morning."

"It was they!" cried the cardinal. "And it is too late to have them pursued. Not a word. Let the queen be ignorant that we know her secret."

"And Bonacieux, what has Your Eminence done with him?"

"I have made him a spy upon his wife."

The Comte de Rochefort bowed like a man who acknowledges the superiority of the master, and retired.

Left alone, the cardinal wrote a letter. Then he rang. The officer entered for the fourth time.

"Tell Vitray to come to me," said he, "and to get ready for a journey."

An instant after, the man he asked for was before him.

"Vitray," said he, "go to London and deliver this letter to Milady. Be back within six days."

The messenger bowed and retired.

Here is what the letter contained:

MILADY,

Be at the first ball at which the Duke of Buckingham shall be present. He will wear on his doublet twelve diamond studs; get near him and cut off two.

As soon as these studs are in your possession, inform me.

FIFTEEN

The next day, Athos not having reappeared, M. de Treville repaired to the office of the *lieutenant-criminel* and learned that Athos was lodged in the Fort l'Eveque.

M. de Treville, on leaving the residence of the *lieutenant-criminel,* arrived at the palace, where the cardinal was with the king. As captain of the Musketeers, M. de Treville had the right of entry at all times.

It is well known how violent the king's prejudices were against the queen, and how carefully kept up by the cardinal. One of the grand causes of this prejudice was the friendship of Anne of Austria for Mme de Chevreuse, who in his eyes not only served the queen in her political intrigues, but in her amorous intrigues.

At the first word the cardinal spoke of Mme de Chevreuse—who, though exiled to Tours, had come to Paris—the king flew into a furious passion. When the cardinal added that at the moment of arresting the queen's emissary to the exiled duchess, a Musketeer had interrupted the course of justice, Louis XIII could not contain himself. Yet the cardinal had not said a word about the Duke of Buckingham.

At this instant M. de Treville entered, cool, polite, and in irreproachable costume.

"You arrive in good time, monsieur," said the king. "I have learned some fine things concerning your Musketeers."

"And I," said Treville, coldly, "have some pretty things to tell Your Majesty concerning a party of commissaries who have taken upon themselves to throw into the Fort l'Eveque one of your Musketeers, sire, Monsieur Athos. Let Your Majesty remember, Athos is the Musketeer who had the misfortune to wound Monsieur de Cahusac so seriously." Addressing the cardinal, "Monsieur de Cahusac is quite recovered?"

"Thank you," said the cardinal, biting his lips with anger.

"Athos went to pay a visit to one of his friends," continued Treville. "Scarcely had he arrived, when a crowd of bailiffs laid siege to the house—"

The cardinal made the king a sign, signifying, "That was the affair about which I spoke to you."

"Monsieur de Treville," said the cardinal, "does not tell Your Majesty that this innocent Musketeer had an hour before attacked four commissaries delegated to examine into an affair of importance."

"I defy Your Eminence to prove it," cried Treville. "One hour before, Monsieur Athos was conversing in my house."

The king looked at the cardinal.

"In the house in which the arrest was made," continued the impassive cardinal, "there lodges, I believe, a friend of the Musketeer."

"Your Eminence means Monsieur d'Artagnan. D'Artagnan passed the evening with me."

"Well," said the cardinal, "everybody seems to have passed the evening with you."

"Does Your Eminence doubt my word?" said Treville, flushed with anger.

"God forbid," said the cardinal. "Only, at what hour was he with you?"

"As to that I can speak positively, Your Eminence; as he came in I remarked that it was half past nine."

"At what hour did he leave your hotel?"

"At half past ten—an hour after the event."

"Well," replied the cardinal, who felt that victory was escaping him, "Athos *was* taken in the house in the rue des Fossoyeurs."

"That house is suspected, Treville," said the king.

"The house may be suspected; but not the part inhabited by Monsieur d'Artagnan; there does not exist a more devoted servant of Your Majesty."

"Was it not this d'Artagnan who wounded Jussac?" asked the king, looking at the cardinal, who colored with vexation.

"Yes, sire; Your Majesty has a good memory."

"Come, how shall we decide?" said the king. "Send the case before the judges."

"Only," replied Treville, "the army will be little pleased at being exposed to rigorous treatment on account of police affairs."

"Police affairs!" cried the king, taking up Treville's words. "According to your account, if a Musketeer is arrested, France is in danger."

"From the moment they are suspected by Your Majesty," said Treville, "the Musketeers are guilty; therefore, you see me prepared to surrender my sword."

"Come," said the king, "will you swear that Athos was at your residence during the event?"

"By yourself, whom I venerate above all the world."

"Be so kind as to reflect, sire," said the cardinal. "If we release the prisoner, we shall never know the truth."

"Athos may always be found," replied Treville. "He will not desert, Monsieur le Cardinal."

"Order it as you please, sire; you possess the right of pardon."

"The right of pardoning only applies to the guilty," said Treville. "My Musketeer is innocent."

"The devil!" murmured the king. "What must be done?"

"Sign an order for his release," replied the cardinal. "I believe with Your Majesty that Monsieur de Treville's guarantee is sufficient."

Treville bowed respectfully, his joy mixed with fear; he would have preferred an obstinate resistance to this sudden yielding.

The king signed the order for release. As Treville was about to leave the presence, the cardinal gave him a friendly smile and said, "A perfect harmony reigns, sire, between the leaders and the soldiers of your Musketeers."

"He will play me some dog's trick or other," said Treville.

M. de Treville then made his entrance triumphantly into the Fort l'Eveque, whence he delivered the Musketeer.

Scarcely had the captain of the Musketeers closed the door after him, than His Eminence said to the king, "Sire, Buckingham has been in Paris five days, and only left this morning."

SIXTEEN

The king grew pale; the cardinal saw that he had recovered by a single blow all the ground he had lost.

"Buckingham in Paris!" cried he. "Why does he come?"

"To conspire with your enemies."

"To conspire against my honor."

"Oh, sire, what an idea! The queen loves Your Majesty."

"Woman is weak, Monsieur le Cardinal," said the king. "As to loving me, I have my own opinion."

"I maintain," said the cardinal, "that the Duke of Buckingham came to Paris for a project wholly political."

"And I am sure he came for quite another purpose, Monsieur le Cardinal."

"Indeed," said the cardinal, "Madame de Lannoy told me that the night before last Her Majesty sat up very late, that this morning she wept much, and that she was writing all day."

"That's it!" cried the king. "Cardinal, I must have the queen's papers."

"Neither Your Majesty nor myself can charge himself with such a mission. The august spouse of Your Majesty is one of the greatest princesses in the world."

"The more she has forgotten the high position in which she was placed, the more degrading is her fall."

"I believe that the queen conspires against the power of the king, but not against his honor."

"I tell you against both. The queen does not love me; she loves that infamous Buckingham! Why did you not have him arrested?"

"Arrest the prime minister of King Charles I!"

"All the time he was in Paris, you did not lose sight of him?"

"No, sire."

"You are certain that the queen and he did not see each other?"

"I believe the queen to have too high a sense of her duty, sire."

"But they have corresponded. I must have those letters!"

"There is but one way, to charge the keeper of the seals with this mission. The matter enters completely into the duties of the post."

"Let him be sent for instantly."

"The queen will refuse to obey, if she is ignorant that these orders come from the king."

"I will inform her myself. Cardinal, send for Monsieur the Keeper of the Seals. I will go to the queen."

The queen was in the midst of her women. Her thoughts, gilded as they were by a last reflection of love, were nevertheless sad. Anne of Austria, deprived of the confidence of her husband, pursued by the hatred of the cardinal, had seen her most devoted servants fall around her. Mme de Chevreuse was exiled, Laporte did not conceal that he expected to be arrested.

She was plunged in the darkest of these reflections when the king entered.

The ladies rose. The king made no demonstration of politeness, only stopping before the queen. "Madame," said he, "you are about to receive a visit from the chancellor, who will communicate certain matters with which I have charged him."

The unfortunate queen, constantly threatened with divorce and exile, could not refrain from saying, "But what can the chancellor have to say that Your Majesty could not say yourself?"

The king turned upon his heel without reply. When the chancellor appeared, the king had already gone out.

The queen was standing; scarcely had the chancellor entered then she reseated herself, and with supreme hauteur said, "What do you desire, monsieur?"

"To make, madame, in the name of the king, an examination into all your papers."

"An investigation of my papers! Truly, this is an indignity!"

"Pardon me, madame; I am but the instrument which the king employs."

"Search, then, monsieur! Estafania, give up the keys of my drawers and my desks."

For form's sake the chancellor paid a visit to the pieces of furniture named; but he knew that it was not in a piece of furniture that the queen would place an important letter. When the chancellor had opened and shut the drawers, it became necessary to search the queen herself. The chancellor advanced and said with an embarrassed air, "And now the principal examination."

"What is that?" asked the queen, unwilling to understand.

"His Majesty is certain that a letter has been written; he knows that it has not yet been sent to its address."

"Would you dare lift your hand to your queen?" said Anne of Austria, drawing herself up to her full height.

"I am a faithful subject of the king, madame; all that His Majesty commands I shall do."

"It is true!" said Anne of Austria. "The spies of the cardinal have served him faithfully. I have written a letter today. The letter is here." And the queen laid her beautiful hand on her bosom.

"Give me that letter, madame," said the chancellor.

"I will give it to none but the king," said Anne.

"If the king had desired that the letter should be given to him, madame, he would have demanded it. If you do not give it up, he has charged me to take it. I am authorized to seek even on the person of Your Majesty."

"I would rather die!" cried the queen, in whom the imperious blood of Spain and Austria began to rise.

The chancellor bowed. Then, with the intention quite patent of not drawing back, he approached Anne of Austria, whose eyes sprang tears of rage. He stretched forth his hands toward the place where the paper was to be found.

Anne of Austria became pale, drew the paper from her bosom, and held it out to the keeper of the seals.

"There, monsieur, is that letter!" cried the queen, with a trembling voice. "Take it, and deliver me from your odious presence."

"There, monsieur, is that letter!" cried the queen.

The chancellor took the letter, bowed to the ground, and retired. The queen sank, half fainting, into the arms of her women. The chancellor carried the letter to the king, who took it with a trembling hand, opened it slowly, then seeing that it was addressed to the king of Spain, read it rapidly.

It was a plan of attack against the cardinal. The queen pressed her brother and the emperor of Austria to declare war against France, and as a condition of peace, to insist upon the dismissal of the cardinal; as to love, there was not a word.

"The queen is my enemy, but not yours, sire," said the cardinal. "She is an irreproachable wife. Allow me to intercede for her with Your Majesty."

"Let her come to me first."

"On the contrary, sire, set the example. Give a ball; you know how much the queen loves dancing. It will be an opportunity for her to wear those beautiful diamonds you gave her on her birthday, with which she had no occasion to adorn herself."

"We shall see, Monsieur le Cardinal," said the king, who, in his joy at finding the queen guilty of a crime that he cared little about, and innocent of a fault of which he had great dread, was ready to make up all differences with her.

Anne of Austria was astonished the next day to see the king make some attempts at reconciliation. She could not come round at the first advance; but at last had the appearance of beginning to forget. The king took advantage of this moment to tell her that he had the intention of giving a fete.

A fete was so rare a thing for poor Anne of Austria that the last trace of resentment disappeared, if not from her heart, at least from her countenance. She asked upon what day this fete would take place, but the king replied that he must consult the cardinal upon that head.

Every day the king asked the cardinal when this fete should take place; every day the cardinal deferred fixing it.

On the eighth day after the scene we have described, the cardinal received a letter that contained these lines: "I have them; but am unable to leave London for want of money. Send me five hundred pistoles, and four or five days after I shall be in Paris."

On the same day the cardinal received this letter, the king put his customary question to him.

Richelieu said to himself, "She will arrive four or five days after having received the money. Four or five days for the transmission of the money, four or five days for her to return; that makes ten days. Allowing for contrary winds, twelve days."

"Well, Monsieur le Cardinal," said the king, "have you made your calculations?"

"Yes, sire. Today is the twentieth of September. The aldermen of the city give a fete on the third of October. That will fall in wonderfully well."

Then the cardinal added, "Sire, do not forget to tell Her Majesty the evening before the fete that you should like to see how her diamond studs become her."

SEVENTEEN

It was the second time the cardinal had mentioned these diamond studs. Louis XIII began to fancy that this recommendation concealed some mystery. He went to the queen and accosted her with fresh menaces. Anne of Austria lowered her head; but Louis XIII wanted a discussion from which some light might break, convinced as he was that the cardinal was preparing for him some terrible surprise.

"Sire," cried Anne of Austria, "it is impossible that Your Majesty can make all this ado about a letter to my brother."

The king did not know what to answer, and thought that this was the moment for expressing the desire which he was not going to have made until the evening before the fete.

"Madame," said he, with dignity, "there will shortly be a ball. I wish you should appear ornamented with the diamond studs I gave you on your birthday."

Anne of Austria believed that Louis XIII knew all. She was unable to reply.

"You hear, madame?" said the king.

"Yes, sire, I hear," stammered the queen.

"You will appear at this ball?"

"Yes."

"With those studs?"

"Yes."

The queen's paleness increased; the king enjoyed it with that cold cruelty which was the worst side of his character.

"On what day will this ball take place?" asked Anne of Austria.

"Oh, shortly, madame," said he. "I will ask the cardinal."

"It was he who told you to invite me to appear with these studs?"

"What does it signify? You will appear?"

The queen made a curtsy as the king departed. "I am lost," she murmured, "the cardinal knows all, and the king soon will."

Her position was terrible. Buckingham had returned to London; Mme Chevreuse was at Tours. The queen felt certain that one of her women had betrayed her. Laporte could not leave the Louvre; she had not a soul in whom she could confide.

"Can I be of service to Your Majesty?" said a voice full of sweetness and pity.

The queen turned round. At one of the doors appeared Mme Bonacieux. She had been arranging the dresses in a closet when the king entered; she had heard all.

"Fear nothing, madame!" said the young woman. "I have discovered a means of extricating you from your trouble."

"You!" cried the queen. "Can I trust in you?"

"Oh, madame!" cried the young woman, falling on her knees.

"I am ready to die for Your Majesty!" This expression sprang from the very bottom of the heart; there was no mistaking it.

"No one is more devoted to Your Majesty," continued Mme Bonacieux. "Those studs, you gave them to the Duke of Buckingham?"

"Oh, my God!" murmured the queen, teeth chattering with fright.

"We must have them back," continued Mme Bonacieux. "I will find a messenger."

"But I must write."

"Oh, yes; two words from the hand of Your Majesty and your private seal."

"These two words would bring about my condemnation, divorce, exile!"

"Yes, if they fell into infamous hands. But I will answer for these words being delivered to their address."

"I must then place my life, my honor, my reputation, in your hands?"

"Yes, madame; I will save them all. My husband will set out, without knowing what he carries, and carry Your Majesty's letter."

The queen took the hands of the young woman, and seeing nothing but sincerity in her eyes, embraced her tenderly.

"Do that," cried she, "and you will have saved my honor!"

"I have nothing to save; you are the victim of perfidious plots."

The queen ran to a little table, wrote two lines, sealed the letter with her private seal, and gave it to Mme Bonacieux.

"You see the address," said the queen, speaking low. "To my

lord Duke of Buckingham, London."

Mme Bonacieux kissed the hands of the queen and disappeared with the lightness of a bird.

Ten minutes afterward she was at home. She had not seen her husband since his liberation; she was ignorant of the change in him with respect to the cardinal. The mercer fancied himself on the road to honors and fortune.

On her side, in spite of herself, her thoughts reverted to that handsome young man who appeared to be so much in love.

The couple, then, accosted each other with a degree of preoccupation.

"I have something to tell you," said she.

"The complexion of our fortune has changed since I saw you, Madame Bonacieux," said he.

"Yes, particularly if you follow the instructions I am about to give you."

Mme Bonacieux knew that in talking of money to her husband, she took him on his weak side. But a man, when he has talked with Cardinal Richelieu, is no longer the same man.

"You must go away immediately," she said. "I will give you a paper which you will deliver into the proper hands."

"Whither am I to go?"

"To London. An illustrious person sends you; an illustrious person awaits you. The recompense will exceed your expectations."

"Nothing but intrigues! Monsieur le Cardinal has enlightened me on that head."

"The cardinal?" cried Mme Bonacieux. "Have you seen the cardinal?"

"He sent for me," answered the mercer, proudly. "He gave me his hand, and called me his friend. I am the friend of the great cardinal!"

"The great cardinal!"

"As his servant, I will not allow you to serve the intrigues of a woman who has a Spanish heart."

The poor wife, who had answered for him to the queen, trembled at the danger into which she had cast herself. Nevertheless, she did not despair of bringing him round.

"Ah, you are a cardinalist, monsieur?" cried she. "You serve the party of those who maltreat your wife and insult your queen?"

"I am for those who save the state," said Bonacieux, emphatically.

"And what do you know about the state?" said Mme Bonacieux, shrugging her shoulders. "Be satisfied with being a plain citizen, and turn to that side which offers the most advantages."

"Eh!" said Bonacieux, slapping a plump bag, which returned a sound of money. "What do you think of this?"

"From the cardinal?"

"From him, and from my friend the Comte de Rochefort."

"The Comte de Rochefort! Why, it was he who carried me off! You receive silver from that man?"

"Have you not said that that abduction was entirely political?"

"Yes; but had for its object to draw from me by torture confessions that might compromise the honor, and perhaps the life, of my august mistress."

"Madame," replied Bonacieux, "your august mistress is a perfidious Spaniard, and what the cardinal does is well done."

"Monsieur," said the young woman, "I know you to be cowardly, avaricious, and foolish, but I never till now believed you infamous!"

"Hold your tongue, madame! You may be overheard."

"Yes, you are right; I should be ashamed for anyone to know your baseness."

"What do you require of me?"

"I have told you. You must depart instantly, monsieur. You must accomplish loyally the commission with which I charge you. On that condition I pardon everything, and"—she held out her hand to him—"I restore my love."

Bonacieux was cowardly and avaricious, but he loved his wife. Mme Bonacieux saw that he hesitated.

"Come! Have you decided?" said she.

"Reflect a little upon what you require of me. London is far from Paris, and perhaps the commission is not without dangers?"

"What matters it, if you avoid them?"

"Madame Bonacieux," said the mercer, "I refuse; intrigues terrify me."

"If you do not go, I will have you arrested by the queen's orders, and placed in the Bastille you dread so much."

Bonacieux weighed the two angers in his brain—that of the cardinal and that of the queen; that of the cardinal predominated enormously.

"Have me arrested on the part of the queen," said he, "and I will appeal to His Eminence."

At once Mme Bonacieux saw that she had gone too far.

"Well, be it so!" said she. "Perhaps you are right. In the long run, a man knows more about politics than a woman. And yet it is very hard," added she, "that a man upon whom I thought I might depend, will not comply with my fancies."

"That is because your fancies go too far," replied the triumphant Bonacieux.

"Well, I will give it up," said the young woman, sighing.

"At least you should tell me what I should have to do in London," replied Bonacieux, who remembered a little late that Rochefort had desired him to obtain his wife's secrets.

"It is of no use for you to know anything about it," said the young woman. "It was about one of those purchases that interest women."

But the more the young woman excused herself, the more important Bonacieux thought the secret. He resolved to hasten immediately to the Comte de Rochefort, and tell him that the queen was seeking a messenger to send to London.

"Pardon me for quitting you, my dear," said he, "but I made an engagement with a friend. Shall I see you again soon?"

"Next week I hope my duties will afford me a little liberty."

"I shall expect you." Bonacieux kissed his wife's hand, and set off.

At that moment, a rap on the ceiling made Madame Bonacieux raise her head, and a voice cried, "Dear Madame, I will come down to you."

EIGHTEEN

LOVER AND HUSBAND

"Madame," said d'Artagnan, "allow me to tell you that you have a bad sort of a husband."

"You have overheard our conversation?" asked Mme Bonacieux. "What did you understand?"

"Your husband is a fool; you are in trouble; the queen wants a brave, intelligent, devoted man to make a journey to London. I have at least two of the qualities you stand in need of."

Mme Bonacieux's heart beat with joy.

"What guarantee will you give me," asked she, "if I confide this message to you?"

"My love for you. Speak!"

"My God!" murmured the young woman. "Ought I to confide in you?"

"I see that you require someone to answer for me?"

"I admit that would reassure me greatly."

"Do you know Monsieur de Treville, captain of the Musketeers?"

"I have heard the queen speak of him as a brave and loyal gentleman."

"Reveal your secret to him, and ask whether you may confide it to me."

"This secret is not mine, and I cannot reveal it."

"You were about to confide it to Monsieur Bonacieux," said d'Artagnan, with chagrin.

"As one confides a letter to the hollow of a tree."

"And yet, you see plainly that I love you."

"You say so."

"I am a gallant fellow."

"I believe it."

"I am brave."

"I am sure of that!"

"Then, put me to the proof."

She found herself in circumstances where everything must be risked. The queen might be as much injured by reticence as by confidence; and—let us admit it—the sentiment that she felt for her young protector decided her to speak.

"Listen," said she. "If you betray me, I will kill myself, while accusing you of my death."

"I swear to you before God," said d'Artagnan, "that I will die sooner than compromise anyone."

Then the young woman confided in him. This was their mutual declaration of love.

D'Artagnan was radiant with joy.

"I go at once," said he. "A furlough is needful. I will go to Treville, whom I will request to ask this favor for me of his brother-in-law, Monsieur Dessessart."

"Then," replied Mme Bonacieux, opening a cupboard and taking from it the very bag that her husband had caressed so affectionately, "take this bag."

"The cardinal's?" cried d'Artagnan, breaking into a laugh.

"The cardinal's," replied Mme Bonacieux. "It makes a very respectable appearance."

"*Pardieu,*" cried d'Artagnan, "it will be amusing to save the queen with the cardinal's money!"

"You are a charming young man," said Mme Bonacieux. "You will not find Her Majesty ungrateful."

Then, "Silence!" said Mme Bonacieux, starting. "Someone is talking in the street."

"It is the voice of—"

"Of my husband!"

D'Artagnan ran to the door.

"He shall not come in before I am gone," said he.

"But I ought to be gone, too. And the disappearance of his money; how am I to justify it?"

"You must come up into my room."

Both, light as shadows, ascended the stairs, and entered d'Artagnan's chambers. Once there, he barricaded the door. They approached the window, and through a slit in the shutter, saw Bonacieux talking with a man in a cloak.

At sight of this man, d'Artagnan sprang toward the door. It was the man of Meung.

"What are you going to do?" cried Mme Bonacieux.

"I have sworn to kill that man!" said d'Artagnan.

"Your life is devoted from this moment. In the queen's name, I forbid you to throw yourself into any peril foreign to that of your journey."

"And do you command nothing in your own name?"

"In my name," said Mme Bonacieux, with great emotion, "I beg you! Listen; they speak of me."

M. Bonacieux had opened his door, and returned to the man in the cloak, whom he had left for an instant.

"She is gone," said he. "She must have returned to the Louvre."

"You are sure," replied the stranger, "she did not suspect the intentions with which you went out?"

"No," replied Bonacieux, "she is too superficial a woman."

"Let us return to your apartment."

"We shall hear no more," whispered Mme Bonacieux.

"On the contrary," said d'Artagnan, "we shall hear better."

D'Artagnan raised the three or four boards, spread a carpet on the floor, went upon his knees, and made a sign to Mme Bonacieux to stoop as he did toward the opening.

"You think your wife—" said the stranger.

"Has returned to the Louvre."

"Without speaking to anyone but yourself?"

"I am sure of it."

"That is an important point, you understand?"

"Then the news I brought you is of value?"

"The greatest, my dear Bonacieux. Are you sure that your wife mentioned no names?"

"No; she only told me she wished to send me to London to serve the interests of an illustrious personage."

"You were a fool not to have pretended to accept the mission," continued the man in the cloak. "You would be in possession of the letter. The state would be safe, and you—"

"And I?"

"The cardinal would have given you letters of nobility."

"Be satisfied," replied Bonacieux. "My wife adores me, and there is yet time."

"The ninny!" murmured Mme Bonacieux.

"I go to the Louvre," he continued. "I ask for Mme Bonacieux; I say that I have reflected; I obtain the letter, and I run directly to the cardinal."

"Go quickly!"

The stranger went out.

"Infamous!" said Mme Bonacieux.

A terrible howling interrupted these reflections. It was her husband, who had discovered the disappearance of the money-bag. Bonacieux called a long time; finding that nobody came, he went out continuing to call, his voice fainter and fainter.

"Now he is gone, it is your turn," said Mme Bonacieux. "Courage, my friend; above all, prudence. Think what you owe to the queen."

"To her and to you!" cried d'Artagnan.

A few seconds afterward, d'Artagnan went out enveloped in a cloak, which ill concealed the sheath of a long sword.

When he had turned the angle of the street, Mme Bonacieux fell on her knees. "Oh, God," cried she, "protect the queen, protect me!"

NINTEEN

D'Artagnan went straight to M. de Treville's. The heart of the young man overflowed with joy. There was glory to be acquired, money to be gained; and all this brought him into intimacy with a woman he adored.

All the way, d'Artagnan considered whether he should confide in M. de Treville. M. de Treville had always been so devoted to the king and queen, and hated the cardinal so cordially, that the young man resolved to tell him everything.

"Did you ask for me, my friend?" said M. de Treville.

"Yes, monsieur," said d'Artagnan, lowering his voice. "You will pardon me for having disturbed you when you know my business. It concerns nothing less than the honor, perhaps the life, of the queen. Chance has rendered me master of a secret—"

"Which you will guard, I hope, as your life."

"But which I must impart to you, monsieur, for you alone can assist me."

"Are you authorized by Her Majesty to communicate this secret to me?"

"No, monsieur, I am desired to preserve the profoundest mystery."

"Why, then, are you about to betray it?"

"Because I am afraid you will refuse me if you do not know why I ask this favor."

"Keep your secret, young man, tell me what you wish."

"I wish you to obtain for me leave of absence for fifteen days. I am going on a mission to London."

"Has anyone interest in preventing your arrival there?"

"The cardinal would give the world to prevent my success."

"And you are going alone? In that case you will be assassinated."

"I shall die in the performance of my duty."

"But your mission will not be accomplished," continued Treville. "In order that one may arrive, four must set out."

"You are right, monsieur," said d'Artagnan.

"I can send Athos, Porthos, and Aramis each a leave of absence for fifteen days—to Athos, whose wound still makes him suffer, to go to the waters of Forges; to Porthos and Aramis to accompany their friend."

M. de Treville assured him that by two o'clock in the morning the leaves of absence should be with the travelers.

"Have the goodness to send mine to Athos's residence. I should dread some disagreeable encounter if I were to go home."

"*Adieu*, and a prosperous voyage."

D'Artagnan saluted M. de Treville, who held out his hand; d'Artagnan pressed it with gratitude.

His first visit was to Aramis. After the two friends had been chatting a few moments, a servant from M. de Treville entered.

"The leave of absence monsieur has asked for," said the lackey.

"I have asked for no leave of absence."

"Hold your tongue and take it!" said d'Artagnan.

The lackey bowed and departed.

"What does this mean?" asked Aramis.

"Pack for a journey of a fortnight, and follow me."

"But I cannot leave Paris without knowing—"

Aramis stopped.

"Knowing what is become of her?" said d'Artagnan.

"Become of whom?" replied Aramis.

"The woman who was here—the woman with the embroidered handkerchief."

"Listen!" said Aramis. "Since you know so much, can you tell me what is become of that woman?"

"She has returned to Tours."

"Why did she return to Tours without telling me?"

"Because she was in fear of being arrested."

"Why has she not written to me?"

"Because she was afraid of compromising you."

"D'Artagnan, you restore me to life!" cried Aramis. "Since she has left Paris, I am ready to follow you. You say we are going—"

"To see Athos, make haste."

As they went out, Aramis placed his hand upon the arm of d'Artagnan. "You have not spoken of this lady?" said he.

"I have not breathed a syllable."

Tranquil on this point, Aramis continued with d'Artagnan, and they soon arrived at Athos's dwelling. They found him holding his leave of absence in one hand, and M. de Treville's note in the other.

"Can you explain this?" said the astonished Athos.

> *My dear Athos,*
> *I wish, as your health requires it, that you should rest for a fortnight. Go and take the waters of Forges, or any that may be agreeable to you, and recuperate yourself.*
> *—de Treville*

"Well, this leave of absence and letter mean that you must follow me, Athos."

At that moment Porthos entered. "Since when did they grant men leave of absence without their asking?" said he.

"Since," said d'Artagnan, "they have friends who ask it for them."

"Ah!" said Porthos. "It appears there's something fresh here."

"To London, gentlemen," said d'Artagnan.

"What the devil are we going to do in London?" cried Porthos.

"I am not at liberty to tell; you must trust me."

"In order to go to London," said Porthos, "money is needed; I have none."

"I have," replied d'Artagnan, pulling out his treasure. "Let each take seventy-five pistoles, enough to take us to London and back. Besides, we shall not all arrive at London."

"If we do risk being killed," said Porthos, "I should like to know what for."

"Is the king accustomed to give you reasons? No. He says, 'Gentlemen, go and fight,' and you go. You need give yourselves no more uneasiness about this."

"D'Artagnan is right," said Athos. "Here are our leaves of absence from Monsieur de Treville, and here are pistoles from I don't know where. Let us go and get killed. D'Artagnan, I am ready to follow you."

"I also," said Porthos.

"I also," said Aramis.

"When are we to go?" asked Athos.

"Immediately," replied d'Artagnan. "We have not a minute to lose."

TWENTY

Our adventurers left Paris. It was like the eve of a battle; the heart beat, the eyes laughed, and they felt that life was, after all, a good thing.

All went well till they arrived at Chantilly, about eight o'clock in the morning. They alighted at an *auberge* and placed themselves at a table. A gentleman seated at the same table drank to their good health, and the travelers returned his politeness.

The stranger proposed to Porthos to drink the health of the cardinal. Porthos replied that he asked no better if the stranger, in his turn, would drink the health of the king. The stranger cried that he acknowledged no king but His Eminence. Porthos called him drunk, and the stranger drew his sword.

"You have committed a piece of folly," said Athos, "but it can't be helped. Kill the fellow, and rejoin us as soon as you can."

They set out at a good pace, while Porthos was promising to perforate his adversary with all the thrusts known in the fencing schools.

"There goes one!" cried Athos.

"Why did that man attack Porthos rather than any of us?" asked Aramis.

"As Porthos was talking loudest, he took him for the chief," said d'Artagnan.

At Beauvais they stopped to wait for Porthos. At the end of two hours, as he did not come, they resumed their journey.

A league from Beauvais, where the road was between two high banks, they fell in with eight men who, taking advantage of the road being unpaved, appeared to be employed in filling up the ruts with mud.

Aramis, not liking to soil his boots, apostrophized them rather sharply. Then these men retreated as far as the ditch, from which each took a concealed musket; our travelers were outnumbered in weapons. Aramis received a ball through his shoulder. Wounded as he was, he seized the mane of his horse, which carried him on with the others.

"They'll kill poor Porthos when he comes up," said Aramis.

"If Porthos were on his legs, he would have rejoined us," said Athos.

At Crevecoeur, Aramis could proceed no farther. They lifted him off at the door of a cabaret, and set forward again in the hope of sleeping at Amiens.

"Reduced to two!" said Athos. "I will neither open my mouth nor draw my sword between this and Calais, I swear."

They arrived at Amiens at midnight, and alighted at the Auberge of the Golden Lily. The host wished to lodge each in a charming chamber, at opposite extremities of the hotel. D'Artagnan and Athos refused. The host replied that he had no other worthy of their excellencies; the travelers declared they would sleep in the common chamber.

The night was quiet. At four o'clock in the morning they wished to saddle the horses; but the horses were all used up. At the door stood two horses, fresh and fully equipped. They asked where their masters were, and were informed that they were settling their bill with the host.

Athos went down to pay the reckoning without the least mistrust. The host took the money that Athos offered, and turning it over in his hands, cried out that it was bad, and that he would have him and his companion arrested as forgers.

"You blackguard!" cried Athos. "I'll cut your ears off!"

At the same instant, four men, armed to the teeth, entered and rushed upon Athos.

"I am taken!" shouted Athos. "Go on, d'Artagnan!" and he fired two pistols.

D'Artagnan unfastened one of the horses waiting at the door, leaped upon it, and set off at full gallop.

"Brave Athos!" murmured d'Artagnan. "To think that I am compelled to leave him."

A hundred paces from the gates of Calais, d'Artagnan's horse gave out. He left it upon the road, and ran toward the dock. A gentleman who preceded him by about fifty paces inquired if he could cross over to England.

"Nothing would be easier," said the captain of a vessel, "but this morning came an order to let no one leave without permission from the cardinal."

"I have that permission," said the gentleman. "Here it is."

"Have it examined by the governor of the port," said the

shipmaster. "You may see his house from here—at the foot of that hill."

"Very well," said the gentleman. And he took the road to the governor's house.

D'Artagnan followed him and overtook him as he was entering a little wood.

"Monsieur, you appear to be in great haste?"

"No one can be more so, monsieur."

"I am sorry for that," said d'Artagnan, "for I wish to beg you to let me sail first."

"That's impossible," said the gentleman. "I have traveled sixty leagues in forty hours, and by tomorrow at midday I must be in London."

"I have performed that same distance in forty hours, and by ten o'clock in the morning I must be in London."

"Very sorry, monsieur; but I was here first, and will not sail second."

"I am sorry, too, monsieur; but I arrived second, and must sail first. I wish that order of which you are bearer."

"Let me pass!"

The gentleman drew his sword. In three seconds d'Artagnan had wounded him three times, exclaiming at each thrust, "One for Athos; one for Porthos; one for Aramis!" At the third hit the gentleman fell like a log. D'Artagnan believed him insensible, and went toward him to take the order; but the wounded man plunged the point of his sword into d'Artagnan's breast, crying, "One for you!"

"And one for me—the best for last!" cried d'Artagnan, nailing him to the earth with a fourth thrust through his body.

This time the gentleman fainted. D'Artagnan searched his pockets, and took the order for passage, in the name of Comte de Wardes.

Then, casting a glance on the handsome young man, whom he was leaving in his gore, perhaps dead, he gave a sigh for that destiny which leads men to destroy each other for the interests of people who often do not even know that they exist.

"And now," said d'Artagnan, "to the Governor's."

The Comte de Wardes was announced, and d'Artagnan was introduced.

"You have an order signed by the cardinal?" said the governor.

"Yes, monsieur," replied d'Artagnan. "Here it is."

"It is quite regular and explicit," said the governor. "It appears that His Eminence is anxious to prevent someone from crossing to England?"

"Yes; a certain d'Artagnan."

"You know him?" asked the governor. "Describe him to me."

And d'Artagnan gave, feature for feature, a description of the Comte de Wardes.

"We will keep a lookout for him; if we lay hands on him, His Eminence may be assured he will be reconducted to Paris."

"By doing so," said d'Artagnan, "you will deserve well of the cardinal."

The governor countersigned the passport. D'Artagnan bowed and departed. He set off as fast as he could, avoided the wood, and reentered the city by another gate.

The vessel was quite ready to sail, and the captain was waiting.

"Here is my pass countersigned," said d'Artagnan.

"And that other gentleman?

"He will not go today," said d'Artagnan.

They had scarcely sailed half a league, when d'Artagnan saw a flash and heard a detonation. It was the cannon that announced the closing of the port. He had now leisure to look to his wound. Fortunately, it was not dangerous.

D'Artagnan was worn out. A mattress was laid upon the deck for him. He threw himself upon it and fell asleep.

At ten o'clock the vessel cast anchor in the harbor of Dover, and at half past ten d'Artagnan placed his foot on English land. In a few hours, he was in the capital. He did not know a word of English, but wrote the name of Buckingham on a piece of paper, and everyone pointed the way to the duke's house.

The duke was at Windsor hunting with the king. D'Artagnan inquired for the valet of the duke, who spoke French well; he told him that he came from Paris and must speak with his master instantly. Patrick, this minister of the minister, ordered two horses saddled, and himself went as guide to the young Guardsman.

On their arrival at the castle, Patrick reached the duke, and announced that a messenger awaited him. Buckingham only took the time to inquire where the messenger was. Recognizing the uniform of the Guards, he rode straight to d'Artagnan.

"No misfortune has happened to the queen?" cried Buckingham, throwing all his love into the question.

"I believe she runs some great peril. Take this letter," said d'Artagnan.

"From Her Majesty!" said Buckingham, so pale that d'Artagnan feared he would faint. "What is this rent?" said he,

They had scarcely sailed half a league, when d'Artagnan saw a flash and heard a detonation.

showing d'Artagnan a place where the letter had been pierced through.

"Ah," said d'Artagnan, "the sword of the Comte de Wardes made that hole, when he gave me a good thrust in the breast."

"You are wounded?" asked Buckingham, as he opened the letter.

"Oh, nothing but a scratch," said d'Artagnan.

"What have I read?" cried the duke. "Patrick, tell His Majesty that an affair of the greatest importance recalls me to London. Come, monsieur!" and both set off at full gallop.

TWENTY-ONE

As they rode, the duke endeavored to discover what d'Artagnan knew. That which astonished him most was that the cardinal, interested in preventing this young man from setting foot in England, had not succeeded in arresting him. D'Artagnan related how, thanks to the devotion of his three friends, he had succeeded in coming off with a single sword thrust.

In a few minutes they were at the gates of London.

On entering the court of his hotel, Buckingham sprang from his horse. The duke walked so fast that d'Artagnan had some trouble in keeping up. They arrived at length in a bedchamber. In the alcove was a concealed door, which the duke opened with a little gold key. "Come in!" cried Buckingham. "If you have the good fortune to be admitted to Her Majesty's presence, tell her what you have seen."

They found themselves in a small chapel brilliantly lighted with a vast number of candles. Beneath a canopy of blue velvet was a full-length portrait of Anne of Austria. Beneath the portrait was the casket containing the diamond studs.

The duke knelt as a priest might before a crucifix. "There," said he, drawing from the casket a blue ribbon sparkling with diamonds, "are the precious studs. The queen gave them to me, the queen requires them again. Her will be done."

He began to kiss those studs with which he was about to part. All at once he uttered a terrible cry. "All is lost! Two of the studs are wanting."

"If they have been stolen, perhaps the person who stole them still has them."

"Wait!" said the duke. "The only time I have worn these studs was at a ball given by the king eight days ago at Windsor. The Comtesse de Winter, with whom I had quarreled, became reconciled to me at that ball. The woman is an agent of the cardinal."

"He has agents, then, throughout the world?" cried d'Artagnan.

"Oh, yes," said Buckingham. "He is a terrible antagonist. When is this ball to take place?"

"Monday next."

"Five days before us. Patrick!" cried the duke. His valet appeared.

"My jeweler and my secretary."

The secretary found Buckingham writing orders. "Mr. Jackson," said he, "go to the lord chancellor, and tell him that I charge him with the execution of these orders."

"If the lord chancellor interrogates me upon what led Your Grace to adopt such a measure, what shall I reply?"

"That I answer for my will to no man."

"Will that be the answer," replied the secretary, smiling, "he must transmit to His Majesty if His Majesty should wish to know why no vessel is to leave Great Britain?"

"He will say to the king that I am determined on war, and that this is my first act against France."

The secretary bowed and retired.

"We are safe on that side," said Buckingham, turning toward d'Artagnan. "If the studs are not yet gone to Paris, they will not arrive till after you."

D'Artagnan looked with stupefaction at a man who thus employed the unlimited power with which he was clothed by the confidence of a king. Buckingham smiled.

"Yes," said he, "Anne of Austria is my true queen. Upon a word from her, I would betray my country, I would betray my king, I would betray my God."

D'Artagnan was amazed to note by what threads the destinies of nations are suspended.

The goldsmith entered.

"Mr. O'Reilly," said the duke, "look at these diamond studs, and tell me what they are worth."

The goldsmith cast a glance at their elegant setting, calculated, and said, "Fifteen hundred pistoles each, my lord."

"How many days would it require to make two studs exactly like them?"

"Eight days, my lord."

"I will give you three thousand pistoles apiece if I can have them the day after tomorrow."

"My lord, they shall be yours."

"You are a jewel of a man. It must be done in the palace."

"Impossible, my lord! Nobody but myself can so execute them that one cannot tell the new from the old."

"Therefore, my dear Mr. O'Reilly, you are my prisoner. Name such of your workmen as you need, and the tools they must bring."

The goldsmith knew argument was useless. "May I inform my wife?" said he.

"You may even see her, Mr. O'Reilly. Here is, in addition to the price of the studs, an order for a thousand pistoles, to make you forget the annoyance I cause you."

D'Artagnan could not get over the surprise created in him by this minister, who thus openhanded sported with men and millions.

As to the goldsmith, he wrote to his wife, charging her to send him his most skillful apprentice, an assortment of diamonds, and the necessary tools. Buckingham conducted him to the chamber destined for him, which was transformed into a workshop.

The duke turned to d'Artagnan. "Now, my young friend," said he. "What do you desire?"

"A bed, my lord," replied d'Artagnan. "At present that is the thing I stand most in need of."

In one hour, the ordinance was published in London that no vessel bound for France should leave port. In the eyes of everybody, this was a declaration of war between the two kingdoms.

On the day after the morrow, the two diamond studs were finished, so perfectly alike that no one could tell the new from the old. Buckingham immediately called d'Artagnan. "Here," said he, "are the diamond studs that you came for; I have done all that human power can."

"Does Your Grace mean to give me the studs without the little rosewood box?"

"The box is the more precious from being all that is left to me. And now," resumed Buckingham, looking earnestly at the young man, "how shall I acquit myself of the debt I owe you?"

D'Artagnan blushed. The idea that the blood of his friends and himself was to be paid for with English gold was repugnant to him.

"Let us understand each other, my lord," replied d'Artagnan, "I am in the service of the king and queen of France. What I have done has been for the queen. At this moment when there is question of war, I see nothing in Your Grace but an enemy whom I should have much greater pleasure in meeting on the field of battle than in the corridors of the Louvre—which will not prevent me from executing my commission." D'Artagnan bowed to the duke, and was retiring.

"Are you going away in that manner? Where, and how?"

"I had forgotten that England was an island, and that you were the king of it."

"Go to the riverside, ask for the brig *Sund*, and give this letter to the captain; he will convey you to a little port ordinarily only frequented by fishermen."

"The name of that port?"

"St. Valery. When you have arrived there, go to a tavern. There is but one. Ask for the host, and repeat to him the word 'forward.' He will give you a horse and point out the road you ought to take. You will find, in the same way, four relays on your route. Your hand, young man. Perhaps we shall meet on the field of battle; in the meantime we shall part friends."

D'Artagnan bowed to the duke, made his way to the riverside, found the vessel, and delivered his letter to the captain, who made immediate preparations to sail.

Fifty vessels were waiting to set out. Passing alongside one, d'Artagnan fancied he perceived the woman whom the unknown gentleman had called Milady; his vessel passed so quickly that he had little more than a glimpse.

The next day about nine o'clock in the morning, he landed at St. Valery, went in search of the inn, advanced toward the host, and pronounced the word "forward." The host led him to the stable, where a saddled horse awaited him, and asked if he stood in need of anything else.

"I want to know the route I am to follow," said d'Artagnan.

"Go from hence to Neufchâtel. At the Tavern of the Golden Harrow, give the password to the landlord, and you will find a horse already saddled. Begone, and may God guide you!"

"Amen!" cried the young man, and set off at full gallop.

Four hours later he was in Neufchâtel. He followed the instructions he had received, and found a horse quite ready and awaiting him.

"Which route must I take?" demanded d'Artagnan.

"That of Rouen. Stop at the little village of Eccuis, at the Shield of France. You will find a horse in the stables quite as good as this."

At Eccuis, the same scene was repeated. At Pontoise he changed his horse for the last time, and at nine o'clock galloped into the yard of Treville's house. He had made nearly sixty leagues in little more than twelve hours.

TWENTY-TWO

Nothing was talked of in Paris but the ball, in which Their Majesties were to dance the favorite ballet of the king. At six in the evening the guests began to arrive.

At midnight loud acclamations were heard. It was the king passing through the streets that led to the hotel. The provost of the merchants made him the speech of welcome. Everybody noticed that the king looked dull and preoccupied.

Half an hour after the entrance of the king, fresh acclamations announced the arrival of the queen. Like the king, she looked weary.

At the moment she entered, the curtain of a small gallery was drawn and the cardinal appeared, dressed as a Spanish cavalier. His eyes were fixed upon the queen, and a smile passed over his lips; she did not wear her diamond studs.

The queen remained for a short time to receive the compliments of the city dignitaries. All at once the king appeared with the cardinal at one of the doors. He made his way to the queen, and said, "Why, madame, have you not thought proper to wear your diamond studs?"

The queen saw the cardinal behind, with a diabolical smile on his countenance.

"Sire," replied the queen, faltering, "in the midst of such a crowd, I feared some accident might befall them."

"You were wrong, madame. I made you that present so that you might adorn yourself." The voice of the king trembled with anger.

"Sire," said the queen, "I can send for them and Your Majesty's wishes will be complied with."

"Do so, madame."

The queen bent in submission. Everybody remarked that something had passed between the king and queen; but both had spoken so low that nobody had heard anything. The violins began to sound, but nobody listened.

The cardinal drew near to the king and placed in his hand a small box. The king opened it, and found two diamond studs.

"What does this mean?" demanded he.

"Nothing," replied the cardinal. "Only, if the queen has the studs, which I doubt, count them, sire. If you only find ten, ask Her Majesty who can have stolen the two that are here."

The king looked at the cardinal, but had not time to address any question—a cry of admiration burst from every mouth. The queen was without doubt the most beautiful woman in France. On her shoulder sparkled the diamonds.

The king trembled with joy and the cardinal with vexation.

Distant as they were from the queen, they could not count the studs.

At that moment the violins sounded the signal for the ballet. The king advanced toward Madame le President, with whom he was to dance. They took their places, and the ballet began.

The ballet lasted an hour, and ended amid applause, and everyone reconducted his lady to her place. The king advanced eagerly toward the queen.

"I thank you, madame," said he, "for your deference to my wishes, but I think you want two of the studs."

With these words he held out the studs the cardinal had given him.

"How, sire?" cried the young queen, affecting surprise. "You are giving me two more; I shall have fourteen."

The king counted; the twelve studs were all on Her Majesty's shoulder.

The king called the cardinal.

"What does this mean, Monsieur le Cardinal?" asked the king in a severe tone.

"This means, sire," replied the cardinal, "that I was desirous of presenting Her Majesty with these two studs, and adopted this means of inducing her to accept them."

"And I am the more grateful to Your Eminence," replied Anne of Austria, with a smile, "from being certain that these two studs have cost you as much as all the others cost His Majesty." The queen resumed her way to the chamber where she was to take off her costume.

The attention that we have been obliged to give these illustrious personages has diverted us from him to whom Anne of Austria owed her triumph over the cardinal—and who, in the crowd, looked on.

D'Artagnan was about to retire when he felt his shoulder touched. He turned and saw a young woman. Her face was covered with a black velvet mask, but he recognized the intelligent Mme Bonacieux.

On the evening before, they had scarcely seen each other. Her haste to convey to the queen the news of his return prevented them from exchanging more than a few words. D'Artagnan therefore followed Mme Bonacieux, moved by both love and curiosity. At length, Mme Bonacieux opened the door of a closet, which was entirely dark, and then a second door concealed by tapestry. This door disclosed a brilliant light, and she disappeared.

D'Artagnan remained motionless; soon a ray of light, together with the warm and perfumed air, the conversation of two of three ladies in language at once respectful and refined, and the word "Majesty" several times repeated, indicated that he was in a closet attached to the queen's apartment.

D'Artagnan soon distinguished the queen's voice, first by a slightly foreign accent, next by that tone of domination naturally impressed upon all royal words. He twice saw the shadow of a person intercept the light.

At length a hand and arm, beautiful in form, glided through the tapestry. D'Artagnan cast himself on his knees, seized the hand, and touched it respectfully with his lips. The hand was withdrawn, leaving in his a ring. The door closed, and d'Artagnan found himself again in complete darkness.

D'Artagnan placed the ring on his finger, and waited; all was not over. After the reward of his devotion, that of his love was to come.

The sound of voices diminished. The company was heard departing; then the door of the closet opened, and Mme Bonacieux entered.

"Silence!" said the young woman, placing her hand upon his lips.

"When shall I see you again?" cried d'Artagnan.

"A note which you will find at home will tell you. Begone!"

She pushed d'Artagnan out of the room.

TWENTY-THREE

At home, D'Artagnan found this letter from Mme Bonacieux:

Be this evening about ten o'clock at St. Cloud, in front of the pavilion which stands at the corner of the house of M. d'Estrées. —C.B.

D'Artagnan felt ready to dissolve at the very gate of that terrestrial paradise called Love! He kissed the lines traced by the hand of his beautiful mistress. At length he went to bed and had golden dreams.

At seven o'clock in the morning he arose and went out.

M. Bonacieux was at his door. He made so friendly a salutation that his tenant felt obliged to enter into conversation, which naturally fell upon the poor man's incarceration. "But," asked M. Bonacieux, "what has become of you? I have not seen you nor your friends."

"We have been on a little journey. We took Monsieur Athos to the waters of Forges, where my friends still remain."

"And you have returned?" replied M. Bonacieux, giving to his countenance a sly air. "A handsome young fellow like you does not obtain long leaves of absence from his mistress?"

"My faith!" said the young man, laughing. "I confess it."

A shade passed over the brow of Bonacieux, which d'Artagnan did not perceive.

"Since the robbery in my house, I am alarmed every time I hear a door open, particularly in the night."

"Well, don't be alarmed if I return at three o'clock in the morning; indeed, don't be alarmed if I do not come at all."

This time Bonacieux became so pale that d'Artagnan asked him what was the matter.

"Nothing," replied Bonacieux. "Since my misfortunes I have been subject to faintnesses. Pay no attention."

The young man departed, laughing.

"Amuse yourself well!" replied Bonacieux, in a somber tone.

But d'Artagnan was too far off to hear him.

He took his way toward the hotel of M. de Treville and found Treville in a joyful mood. He had thought the king and queen charming at the ball.

"Now," said Treville, lowering his voice, "let us talk about yourself; it is evident that your happy return has something to do with the joy of the king, the triumph of the queen, and the humiliation of His Eminence. You must look out."

"What have I to fear," replied d'Artagnan, "if I enjoy the favor of Their Majesties?"

"Everything, believe me. The cardinal is not the man to forget a mystification."

"Do you believe that the cardinal knows that I have been to London?"

"Was it from London you brought that beautiful diamond that glitters on your finger? A present from an enemy is not a good thing."

"This diamond does not come from an enemy, monsieur," replied d'Artagnan. "It comes from the queen. She gave it to me herself, giving me her hand to kiss."

"You have kissed the queen's hand?" said M. de Treville, looking earnestly at d'Artagnan.

"Her Majesty did me the honor to grant me that favor. Be satisfied; nobody saw her," replied d'Artagnan, and he related to M. de Treville how the affair came to pass.

"Oh, the women!" cried the old soldier. "Everything that savors of mystery charms them. So you would meet the queen, and she would not know who you are?"

"No; but thanks to this diamond," replied the young man.

"Shall I give you the counsel of a friend?" asked M. de Treville. "Off to the nearest goldsmith's, and sell that diamond for the highest price you can get."

"Sell a ring which comes from my sovereign? Never!" said d'Artagnan.

"The cardinal will repay you by some ill turn. If anyone seeks a quarrel with you, shun it. If you cross a bridge, feel every plank with your foot, lest one give way beneath you. Mistrust everybody, your friend, your brother, your mistress—your mistress above all."

D'Artagnan blushed.

"My mistress above all," repeated he, "why her?"

"Because a mistress is one of the cardinal's favorite means. A woman will sell you for ten pistoles."

D'Artagnan thought of the appointment Mme Bonacieux had made with him for that very evening; but the bad opinion M. de Treville entertained of women did not inspire him with the least suspicion of his pretty hostess.

"But," resumed M. de Treville, "what has become of your companions?"

"I left them on my road—Porthos with a duel on his hands; Aramis with a ball in his shoulder; and Athos detained by an accusation of coining."

"How the devil did you escape?" asked M. de Treville.

"By a miracle, monsieur, with a sword thrust in my breast, and by nailing the Comte de Wardes like a butterfly on a tapestry."

"De Wardes, one of the cardinal's men! In your place, while His Eminence was seeking me in Paris, I would make inquiries concerning my companions."

"The advice is good, monsieur; tomorrow I will set out."

D'Artagnan called at the abodes of Athos, Porthos, and Aramis. Nothing had been heard of them.

TWENTY-FOUR

Just before ten o'clock, d'Artagnan arrived in front of the pavilion. It was situated in a very private spot. A high wall, at the angle of which was the pavilion, ran along one side of the lane; on the other was a little garden connected with a poor cottage.

As no signal had been given by which to announce his presence, he waited. At the end of a few minutes the belfry of St. Cloud let fall ten sonorous strokes.

His eyes were fixed upon the little pavilion. All the windows were closed, except one on the first story. Through this window shone a mild light. There could be no doubt that behind this little window, which threw forth such friendly beams, the pretty Mme Bonacieux expected him.

Wrapped in this sweet idea, d'Artagnan waited.

The belfry of St. Cloud sounded half past ten. Without knowing why, d'Artagnan felt a cold shiver run through his veins. The idea seized him that he had read incorrectly, and that the appointment was for eleven o'clock. He drew near to the window, so that a ray of light should fall upon the letter, and read again; the appointment was for ten o'clock. He resumed his post, rather uneasy.

Eleven o'clock sounded.

D'Artagnan began to fear that something had happened to Mme Bonacieux. He clapped his hands three times—the ordinary signal of lovers; but nobody replied. He thought that perhaps the young woman had fallen asleep. The tree was easy to climb. In an instant he was among the branches, and his keen eyes plunged into the interior of the pavilion.

It was a strange thing to find that this soft light enlightened a scene of fearful disorder. One window was broken, the door of the chamber hung on its hinges. A table, which had been covered with an elegant supper, was overturned. Everything gave evidence of a desperate struggle. D'Artagnan hastened to descend, a frightful beating at his heart, to see if he could find other traces of violence.

The little soft light shone on. D'Artagnan perceived that the ground presented confused traces of men and horses. The wheels of a carriage, which appeared to have come from Paris, had made a deep impression, and turned again toward Paris.

D'Artagnan's heart was oppressed by a horrible anguish. And yet, Mme Bonacieux had made an appointment with him before the pavilion, not in the pavilion; she might have been detained in Paris.

Reason was overthrown by that feeling of intimate pain which, on certain occasions, cries that some great misfortune is hanging over us.

Then d'Artagnan ran along the high road, and reaching the ferry, interrogated the boatman. About seven o'clock in the evening, the boatman had taken over a woman, who appeared to be very anxious not to be recognized; the boatman had paid attention and discovered that she was young and pretty. D'Artagnan did not doubt that it was Mme Bonacieux.

He read the billet of Mme Bonacieux once again, and satisfied himself that he had not been mistaken: the appointment was at St. Cloud, before the d'Estrées pavilion.

He ran back to the château. The lane was still deserted, and the same calm light shone through the window.

D'Artagnan thought of that silent cottage that had no doubt seen all. No one answered his first knocking. He knocked again.

He heard a slight noise within. Then d'Artagnan prayed with an accent so full of anxiety, that his voice was of a nature to reassure the most fearful. At length a shutter was pushed ajar, but closed as soon as the light shone upon the baldric, sword belt, and pistol pommels of d'Artagnan.

"In the name of heaven!" cried he. "Listen; I have been waiting for someone who has not come. I am dying with anxiety."

The window was again opened slowly, and an old man appeared. D'Artagnan told how he had a rendezvous with a young woman before that pavilion, and how, not seeing her come, had climbed the linden tree and seen the disorder of the chamber.

The old man listened attentively, and when d'Artagnan had ended, shook his head. "Oh, monsieur!" he said. "If I dared tell you what I have seen, no good would befall me."

"In the name of heaven, tell me! I pledge that not one of your words shall escape from my heart."

The old man read so much grief in the face of the young man that he made him a sign to listen, and repeated: "It was scarcely nine o'clock when somebody endeavored to open my door. I opened the gate and saw three men. In the shadow was a carriage with two horses, and some saddle horses. 'Ah, my worthy gentlemen,' cried I, 'what do you want?' 'You must have a ladder?' said the leader of the party. 'Yes, monsieur.' 'Lend it to us, and go into your house again. If you speak a word of what you may see or hear, you are lost.' He threw me a crown and took the ladder. After shutting the gate behind them, I went out a back door and gained yonder clump of elder, from which I could hear and see everything. The three men brought the carriage up quietly and took out of it a little man, elderly and commonly dressed, who ascended the ladder carefully, looked in at the window, came down, and whispered, 'It is she!' Immediately, he who had spoken to me approached the door of the pavilion, opened it, and disappeared, while the other two men ascended the ladder. All at once cries resounded in the pavilion, and a woman came to the window; as soon as she perceived the men, she fell back and they went into the chamber. I saw no more; but I heard the noise of breaking furniture. The men appeared, bearing the woman in their arms, and carried her to the carriage, into which the little old man got after her. The leader closed the window, came out by the door, sprang into his saddle; the carriage went off, and all was over."

D'Artagnan, overcome by this terrible story, remained motionless and mute.

"My good gentleman," resumed the old man, upon whom this

mute despair produced a greater effect than tears would have done, "do not take on so; they did not kill her."

"Can you guess," said d'Artagnan, "who headed this infernal expedition?"

"A tall, dark man, with a black mustache, dark eyes, and the air of a gentleman."

"That's the man!" cried d'Artagnan. "He is my demon, apparently. And the other? The short one."

"Oh, he was not a gentleman, he did not wear a sword, and the others treated him with small consideration."

"Some lackey," murmured d'Artagnan. "Oh, if I had my friends here," cried he, "I should have some hopes of finding her; but who knows what has become of them?"

TWENTY-FIVE

Instead of returning home, d'Artagnan alighted at the door of M. de Treville. As M. de Treville saw the queen almost daily, he might be able to draw from Her Majesty some intelligence of the poor young woman.

M. de Treville listened seriously. When d'Artagnan had finished, he said, "All this savors of His Eminence."

"What is to be done?" said d'Artagnan.

"Nothing at present but quitting Paris. I will relate to the queen the details of the disappearance of this poor woman. On your return, I shall perhaps have some good news to tell you."

D'Artagnan bowed to M. de Treville, full of gratitude.

Determined to put his advice in practice, d'Artagnan directed his course toward the rue des Fossoyeurs, to supervise the packing of his valise. On approaching the house, he perceived M. Bonacieux standing at his threshold.

"Well, young man," said M. Bonacieux, "seven o'clock in the morning! You come home when other people are going out."

"No one can reproach you for anything of the kind, Monsieur Bonacieux," said the young man. "When a man possesses a young and pretty wife, he has no need to seek happiness elsewhere."

Bonacieux grinned a ghastly smile. "Where were you gladding last night, young master?" asked he. "It does not appear to be very clean in the crossroads."

D'Artagnan glanced down at his boots, covered with mud. That same glance fell upon the shoes of the mercer; it might have been said they had been dipped in the same mud heap. A sudden idea struck d'Artagnan. That elderly man, treated without ceremony by the men wearing swords, was Bonacieux himself. A terrible inclination seized d'Artagnan to grasp the mercer by the throat and strangle him; but he restrained himself.

"Pardon, my dear Monsieur Bonacieux," said d'Artagnan, "but nothing makes one so thirsty as want of sleep. Allow me to take a glass of water in your apartment."

Without waiting for permission, d'Artagnan went into the house, and cast a glance at the bed. It had not been used. Bonacieux had not been abed. He had only been back an hour or two; he had accompanied his wife to the place of her confinement, or at least to the first relay.

"Thanks, Monsieur Bonacieux," said d'Artagnan, emptying his glass, "that is all I wanted of you."

Then he directed his steps, for the last time, toward the residences of his three friends. No news had been received of them; only a letter, perfumed and of an elegant writing, had come for Aramis. D'Artagnan took charge of it.

He arrived at Chantilly without accident, and alighted at the tavern at which they had stopped on their first journey. D'Artagnan commended the horses to the care of his lackey, entered a small room, and desired the host to bring him a bottle of his best wine and two glasses.

"My faith, my good host," said d'Artagnan, filling the two glasses, "I hate drinking by myself, drink with me. Let us drink to the prosperity of your establishment."

"Your Lordship does me much honor," said the host, "and I thank you."

"There is more selfishness in my toast than you may think," said d'Artagnan. "It is only in prosperous establishments that one is well received. I wish to see all innkeepers making a fortune."

"It seems to me," said the host, "that this is not the first time I have had the honor of seeing monsieur."

"Why, I was here only ten or twelve days ago. I was conducting some friends, Musketeers, one of whom had a dispute with a stranger."

"Exactly," said the host. "It is Monsieur Porthos who your lordship means?"

"Yes, that is my companion's name. Has anything happened to him?"

"Your lordship must have observed that he could not continue his journey."

"Why, to be sure, he promised to rejoin us, and we have seen nothing of him."

"He has done us the honor to remain here; we are a little uneasy of certain expenses he has contracted."

"Can I see Porthos?"

"Certainly, monsieur. Go up the first flight and knock at number one. Only warn him that it is you, or Monsieur Porthos may imagine you belong to the house and run his sword through you."

"What have you done to him?"

"We have asked him for money."

"Ah, it is a demand that Porthos takes very ill."

"As we make out our bills every week, at the end of eight days we presented our account; but at the first word on the subject, he sent us to the devil. He had been playing the day before."

"The foolish fellow lost all he had? That's Porthos all over," murmured d'Artagnan.

"As we seemed not likely to come to an understanding," continued the host, "I hoped he would have the kindness to grant the favor of his custom to the host of the Golden Eagle; but Monsieur Porthos replied that, my house being the best, he should remain where he was. I confined myself to begging him to give up his chamber, which is the handsomest in the hotel, and to be satisfied with a room on the third floor; but he took one of his pistols, laid it on his table, and said that at the first word spoken to him about leaving he would blow out the brains of the person who meddled with the matter."

"Has he been wounded?"

"He had boasted that he would perforate the stranger with whom you left him in dispute; on the contrary, the stranger quickly threw him on his back. Monsieur Porthos insists that nobody shall know he has received this wound."

"It is a wound that confines him to his bed?"

"A master stroke, I assure you. Your friend's soul must stick tight to his body."

"Were you there?"

"Monsieur, I followed them, so that I saw the combat without the combatants seeing me. The stranger made a feint and a lunge; Monsieur Porthos had three inches of steel in his breast. He immediately fell backward. The stranger placed the point of his sword at his throat; and Monsieur Porthos acknowledged himself conquered. The stranger asked his name, and learning that it was Porthos, and not d'Artagnan, assisted him to rise, brought him back to the hotel, mounted his horse, and disappeared."

"So it was with Monsieur d'Artagnan this stranger meant to quarrel?"

"It appears so."

"Very well. Porthos's chamber is number one?"

"Yes, monsieur, the handsomest in the inn—a chamber I could have let ten times over."

"Never mind; I will answer for it. Continue to take all the care that his situation requires." D'Artagnan went upstairs, leaving his host better satisfied.

Upon the most conspicuous door of the corridor was traced in black ink a gigantic number one. D'Artagnan knocked, and entered.

Porthos was in bed, a spit loaded with partridges turning before the fire; on each side of the chimneypiece were boiling two stewpans, from which exhaled a double odor of rabbit and fish stews. In addition, the top of a wardrobe was covered with empty bottles.

At the sight of his friend, Porthos uttered a cry of joy.

"Is that you?" said Porthos to d'Artagnan. "You are right welcome. Excuse my not coming to meet you; but," added he, looking at d'Artagnan with uneasiness, "you know what has happened to me?"

"No, I asked after you, and came up as soon as I could."

Porthos seemed to breathe more freely.

"What has happened, my dear Porthos?" continued d'Artagnan.

"On making a thrust at my adversary, whom I had already hit three times, I slipped, and strained my knee. Luckily for the rascal, for I should have left him dead on the spot."

"What has become of him?"

"I don't know; he had enough, and set off."

"So this strain of the knee," continued d'Artagnan, "my dear Porthos, keeps you in bed?"

"That's all. I shall be about in a few days."

"Why did you not have yourself conveyed to Paris?"

"As I was cruelly bored, I invited a gentleman who was traveling this way to walk up, and proposed a cast of dice. He accepted my challenge, and my seventy-five pistoles passed from my pocket to his. But let us speak of you. I confess I began to be very uneasy on your account."

D'Artagnan related how Aramis was obliged to stop at Crevecoeur, how he had left Athos fighting at Amiens, and how he had been forced to run the Comtes de Wardes through in order to reach England. But there d'Artagnan stopped.

As d'Artagnan was anxious to obtain news of his other friends, he held out his hand to the wounded man. As he reckoned upon returning by the same route, if Porthos were still at Chantilly, he would call for him.

Porthos replied that in all probability his sprain would not permit him to depart yet a while. D'Artagnan, having paid his bill, resumed his route.

TWENTY-SIX

Absorbed in thought, d'Artagnan traveled the leagues that separated Chantilly from Crevecoeur. There he perceived the cabaret at which he had left Aramis. This time it was a cheerful hostess who received him. "My good dame," asked d'Artagnan, "can you tell me what has become of my friend, whom we were obliged to leave here about a dozen days ago?"

"A handsome young man, amiable, and well made?"

"That is he—wounded in the shoulder."

"He is still here."

"My dear dame," said d'Artagnan, "where? I am in a hurry to see him again."

"Pardon, monsieur, but I doubt whether he can see you at this moment."

"Has he a lady with him?"

"What do you mean by that? No, monsieur, he has not a lady with him. He is with the curate of Montdidier and the superior of the Jesuits of Amiens."

"Good heavens!" cried d'Artagnan. "Is the poor fellow worse, then?"

"No, monsieur; after his illness he determined to take orders."

"That's it!" said d'Artagnan. "I had forgotten that he was only a Musketeer for a time."

"Monsieur has only to knock at number five on the second floor."

D'Artagnan found the door marked number five. Aramis, in a black gown, was seated before a table covered with enormous volumes in folio. At his right hand was placed the superior of the Jesuits, and on his left the curate of Montdidier. At the noise made by d'Artagnan in entering, Aramis lifted his head.

"Good day, dear d'Artagnan," said Aramis. "I am glad to see you."

"So am I delighted to see you," said d'Artagnan, "although I am not sure that it is Aramis I am speaking to."

"What makes you doubt it?"

"I was afraid I had found my way into the apartment of some churchman. Then, on seeing you in company with these gentlemen, I was afraid you were dangerously ill."

The two men in black darted him a glance.

Aramis colored. "Quite the contrary, dear friend; I am rejoiced to see you safe. This gentleman, who is my friend, has just escaped from a serious danger," continued Aramis, addressing the two ecclesiastics.

"Praise God, monsieur," replied they, bowing together.

"I have not failed to do so," replied the young man, returning their salutation.

The two men in black rose, bowed to Aramis and d'Artagnan, and advanced toward the door. Aramis conducted them to the foot of the stairs, and came up again. When left alone, the two friends at first kept an embarrassed silence. It became necessary for one of them to break it, and Aramis said, "You see that I am returned to my fundamental ideas. You have often heard me speak of them, my friend?"

"Yes; but I always thought you jested."

"With such things! Oh, d'Artagnan!"

"Let us not theologize, Aramis. I confess I have eaten nothing since ten o'clock this morning, and I am devilish hungry."

"We will dine directly, my friend; only you must remember that this is Friday. On such a day I can neither eat flesh nor see it eaten. If you can be satisfied with my dinner—it consists of cooked tetragones and fruits."

"What do you mean by tetragones?" asked d'Artagnan, uneasily.

"I mean spinach," replied Aramis, "but on your account I will add some eggs, a serious infraction of the rule—for eggs are meat, since they engender chickens."

"This feast is not very succulent; but I will put up with it for the sake of remaining with you."

"I am grateful to you for the sacrifice," said Aramis, "but if your body be not greatly benefited by it, be assured your soul will."

"And so, Aramis, you are going into the Church? What will Monsieur de Treville say? They will treat you as a deserter."

"I deserted the Church when I became a Musketeer. The moment has come for me to reenter the bosom of the Church.

This wound, my dear d'Artagnan, has been a warning to me from heaven."

"Bah, it is nearly healed, and I am sure it is not that which gives you the most pain. You have one at heart more painful—a wound made by a woman."

The eye of Aramis kindled in spite of himself.

"Ah," said he, with a slight tone of bitterness, "all ties which attach him to life break in the hand of man."

"Alas, my dear Aramis," said d'Artagnan, heaving a profound sigh, "that is my story! A woman I love has been torn from me by force. She is perhaps a prisoner; she is perhaps dead!"

"Yes, but you have at least this consolation, she has not quit you voluntarily; while I—"

D'Artagnan made no answer.

Aramis continued, "And yet, while I belong to the earth, I wish to speak of our friends."

"And on my part," said d'Artagnan, "I wished to speak of you, but I find you so completely detached! To love you cry, 'Fie! The world is a sepulchre!' Let us say no more about it, and burn this letter."

"What letter?" cried Aramis, eagerly.

"A letter which was sent to your abode in your absence."

"From whom is that letter?"

"I must have lost it," said the young man maliciously. "But fortunately the world is a sepulchre; and love is a sentiment to which you cry, 'Fie!"

"D'Artagnan," cried Aramis, "you are killing me!"

"Well, here it is!" said d'Artagnan, as he drew the letter, sealed with the coronet of a duchess, from his pocket.

Aramis made a bound, seized the letter, devoured it, his countenance radiant.

"Thanks, d'Artagnan, thanks!" cried Aramis, almost in a state of delirium. "She was forced to return to Tours; she is not faithless; she loves me! Come, my friend, let me embrace you!"

The two friends began to dance.

"Let us drink, my dear d'Artagnan!" exclaimed Aramis. "While we do so, tell me a little of what is going on in the world."

TWENTY-SEVEN

"Now to search for Athos," said d'Artagnan, when they had shared an excellent dinner.

"Do you think any harm can have happened to him?" asked Aramis. "Athos is so cool, and handles his sword so skillfully."

"Nobody has a higher opinion of Athos than I have; but I like better to hear my sword clang against lances than against staves. I fear lest Athos should have been beaten down by serving men."

"I will try to accompany you," said Aramis.

The next morning, the two young men descended, and Aramis sprang into the saddle with his usual grace, but soon turned pale and became unsteady in his seat. D'Artagnan assisted him to his chamber.

"That's all right, my dear Aramis," said he. "I will go alone in search of Athos. How do you mean to pass your time till I come back?"

Aramis smiled. "I will make verses," said he.

"Yes, I dare say; verses perfumed with the odor of the billet from Madame de Chevreuse."

In ten minutes, d'Artagnan was trotting along in the direction of Amiens. How was he going to find Athos?

That distinguished air of Athos, that equality of temper which made him the most pleasant companion in the world, that bravery which was the result of the rarest coolness—such qualities attracted more than the friendship of d'Artagnan; they attracted his admiration.

Etiquette had no minutiae unknown to Athos. He was profoundly versed in hunting and falconry, and had one day when conversing on this art astonished Louis XIII himself.

And yet in his hours of gloom, his brilliant side disappeared into profound darkness. His head hanging down, his eye dull, Athos would look for hours together at his bottle.

For the present he had no anxiety. He shrugged his shoulders when people spoke of the future. His secret was in the past. This rendered still more interesting the man who never revealed anything, however skillfully questions were put to him.

"Well," thought d'Artagnan, "poor Athos is perhaps at this moment dead."

About eleven o'clock in the morning he perceived Amiens, and at half past eleven was at the door of the cursed inn. D'Artagnan had often meditated against the host a hearty vengeance. He entered the hostelry with his left hand on the pommel of his sword, cracking his whip with his right hand.

"Do you remember me?" said he to the host. "What have you done with that gentleman against whom you had the audacity, about twelve days ago, to make an accusation of passing false money?"

The host became as pale as death. "Ah, monseigneur!" he cried, in the most pitiable voice imaginable. "How dearly have I paid for that fault!"

"That gentleman, what has become of him?"

"Here is the story, monseigneur," resumed the trembling host. "I had been warned that a celebrated coiner would arrive at my inn, with several companions, all disguised as Guards or Musketeers. I was furnished with a description of your horses, your countenances—nothing was omitted."

"Go on!" said d'Artagnan, who understood whence such an exact description had come.

"I took such measures as I thought necessary to get possession of the pretended coiners. Your friend defended himself desperately. Having disabled two men with his pistols, he retreated fighting with his sword, with which he disabled one of my men, and stunned me with a blow of the flat side of it. While retreating, he found the door of the cellar stairs behind him, and barricaded himself inside. As we were sure of finding him there, we left him alone."

"Yes," said d'Artagnan, "you wished to imprison him."

"He imprisoned himself. He made rough work of it; one man was killed on the spot, and two others severely wounded. As for myself, when I recovered my senses I went to Monsieur the Governor and asked what to do with my prisoner. Monsieur the Governor told me that the orders I had received did not come from him."

"But Athos!" cried d'Artagnan. "Where is he?"

"In the cellar, monsieur."

"You scoundrel! You kept him in the cellar all this time?"

"Merciful heaven! We keep him in the cellar! If you could persuade him to come out, monsieur, I should owe you the gratitude of my whole life! We every day pass through the air hole some bread and meat; but alas! It is not bread and meat of which he makes the greatest consumption. I once endeavored to go down; but he flew into a terrible rage. Upon this I went and complained to the governor, who replied that it would teach me to insult honorable gentlemen who took up their abode in my house."

"So since that time—" replied d'Artagnan, unable to refrain from laughing.

"From that time, monsieur," continued the latter, "we have led the most miserable life; all our provisions are in the cellar. The wine, the beer, the oil, the spices, the bacon, and sausages. We are forced to refuse food and drink to the travelers who come to the house. If your friend remains another week in my cellar, I shall be a ruined man."

"And not more than justice, you ass!"

"Yes, monsieur, you are right," said the host. "Hark! There he is!"

"Somebody has disturbed him," said d'Artagnan.

"But he must be disturbed," cried the host. "Here are two English gentlemen just arrived. The English like good wine. My wife has requested permission of Monsieur Athos to go into the cellar; and he has refused."

D'Artagnan rose, and preceded by the host, approached the scene of action.

The two gentlemen were exasperated; they had had a long ride, and were dying with hunger and thirst.

"This is tyranny!" cried one of them, in very good French. "This madman will not allow these people access to their own wine!"

"Good!" cried Athos, from the other side of the door. "Let them come in, and we shall see!"

The two English gentlemen looked at each other; at length the angrier one descended the steps that led to the cellar, and gave a kick against the door.

"Ah, gentlemen, you want battle; you shall have it," said d'Artagnan, cocking his pistols.

"Good God!" cried the voice of Athos. "I can hear d'Artagnan."

"Yes," cried d'Artagnan."I am here, my friend."

"Good," replied Athos, "we will teach them, these door breakers!"

The gentlemen hesitated; but pride prevailed, and a second kick split the door from bottom to top.

"Stand aside, d'Artagnan," cried Athos. "I am going to fire!"

"Gentlemen," exclaimed d'Artagnan, "let me conduct your business and my own. You shall soon have something to drink; I give you my word."

"If there is any left," grumbled the jeering voice of Athos.

"'If there is any left!'" murmured the host.

"There must be plenty left," replied d'Artagnan. "He cannot have drunk all the cellar. Gentlemen, return your swords to their scabbards."

The Englishmen sheathed their swords. The history of Athos's imprisonment was related to them; and as they were really gentlemen, they pronounced the host in the wrong.

"Now, gentlemen," said d'Artagnan, "go up to your room; in ten minutes, you shall have all you desire."

The Englishmen bowed and went upstairs.

"Now I am alone, dear Athos," said d'Artagnan. "Open the door, I beg of you."

"Instantly," said Athos.

The pale face of Athos appeared, and took a survey of the surroundings. D'Artagnan embraced him tenderly. He tried to draw him from his abode, but perceived that Athos staggered.

"You are wounded," said he.

"No, I am dead drunk. I must at least have drunk a hundred and fifty bottles."

The friends took possession of the best apartment in the house. The host and his wife hurried down into the cellar, where a frightful spectacle awaited them. They found, swimming in puddles of oil and wine, the bones and fragments of all the hams, while a heap of broken bottles filled the whole left-hand corner of the cellar. Of fifty large sausages, suspended from the joists, scarcely ten remained. Their lamentations pierced the vault of the cellar. Athos did not even turn his head.

To grief succeeded rage. The host armed himself with a spit, and rushed into the chamber.

"Some wine!" said Athos, on perceiving the host.

"Some wine!" cried the stupefied host. "Why, you have drunk more than a hundred pistoles' worth! I am a ruined man!"

"Triple ass!" said Athos, rising, but sank down again immediately. D'Artagnan came to his relief with his whip in his hand.

The host burst into tears.

"My dear friend," said d'Artagnan, "if you annoy us in this manner, we will both go and shut ourselves up in your cellar."

"Oh, gentlemen," said the host, "I have been wrong! Have pity on me."

"If you speak in that way," said Athos, "you will break my heart, and the tears will flow from my eyes as the wine flowed from the cask. Let us talk."

The host approached with hesitation.

"Let us inquire further," said d'Artagnan. "Athos's horse, where is that?"

"In the stable."

"It's worth eighty pistoles. Take it, and there ends the matter. Let us drink."

"What?" asked the host, quite cheerful again.

"Some of that at the bottom. There are twenty-five bottles left. Bring six of them."

"Why, this man is a cask!" said the host, aside. "If he remains here a fortnight, and pays for what he drinks, I shall soon reestablish my business."

"And don't forget," said d'Artagnan, "to bring up four bottles for the two English gentlemen."

"And now," said Athos, "while they bring the wine, tell me, d'Artagnan, what has become of the others!"

D'Artagnan related how he had found Porthos in bed with a strained knee, and Aramis at a table between two theologians. As he finished, the host entered with the wine.

"That's well!" said Athos, filling their glasses. "Here's to Porthos and Aramis! But what has happened to you?"

D'Artagnan related his adventure with Mme Bonacieux.

Athos listened to him without a frown, and said, "Trifles!"

"You always say *trifles,* my dear Athos!" said d'Artagnan. "And that comes very ill from you, who have never loved."

The drink-deadened eye of Athos flashed, but only for a moment. "Love is a lottery you are very fortunate to have lost, believe me, my dear d'Artagnan," he said quietly. "I should like to know what you would say if I were to relate to you a tale of love!"

Athos was at that period of intoxication in which vulgar drinkers fall on the floor and go to sleep. He kept himself upright and dreamed, without sleeping. This somnambulism of drunkenness had something frightful in it.

"One of my friends—please observe, not myself," said Athos with a melancholy smile, "at twenty-five years of age fell in love with a girl of sixteen. She lived with her brother, a curate. They came nobody knew whence; but seeing her so lovely and her brother so pious, nobody thought of asking. My friend married her. The fool!"

"How so, if he love her?" asked d'Artagnan.

"Wait," said Athos. "He took her to his château, and made her the first lady in the province; she supported her rank becomingly."

"Well?" asked d'Artagnan.

"One day," continued Athos, "she fell from her horse and fainted. The count flew to her, and as she appeared oppressed by her clothes, he ripped them open with his poniard, and in so doing laid bare her shoulder. D'Artagnan," said Athos, "guess what she had on her shoulder."

"How can I tell?" said d'Artagnan.

"A *fleur-de-lis,*" said Athos. "She was branded. The angel was a demon; the girl had stolen the sacred vessels from a church. The count had on his estates the rights of high and low tribunals. He tied her hands behind her and hanged her on a tree."

"Heavens, Athos, a murder?" cried d'Artagnan.

"No less," said Athos; he seized the last bottle and emptied it at a single draught, as he would have emptied an ordinary glass.

Then he let his head sink upon his hands, while d'Artagnan stood before him, stupefied.

"She is dead?" stammered d'Artagnan. "And her brother?"

"I inquired after him to hang him likewise; but he had quit the curacy the night before. He was doubtless the lover of the fair lady, and had pretended to be a curate for the purpose of getting his mistress married."

"My God!" cried d'Artagnan, quite stunned. He could no longer endure this conversation. Allowing his head to sink upon his hands, he pretended to sleep.

"These young fellows can none of them drink," said Athos, looking at him with pity, "and yet this is one of the best!"

TWENTY-EIGHT

Many things appeared very obscure in this revelation. It had been made by a man quite drunk to one who was half drunk; yet d'Artagnan, the following morning, had all the words of Athos present to his memory. He went into his friend's chamber determined to renew the conversation; but the Musketeer broached the matter first.

"I was drunk yesterday, d'Artagnan," said he. "I wager that I uttered a thousand extravagances."

While saying this, he looked at his friend with an earnestness that embarrassed him.

"No," replied d'Artagnan, "if I recollect, nothing out of the common way."

"Ah, you surprise me. I thought I had told you a most lamentable story." And he looked at the young man as if he would read the bottom of his heart.

"My faith," said d'Artagnan, "I remember nothing of the kind."

"You cannot have failed to remark, my dear friend, that everyone has his particular kind of drunkenness. My mania is to relate all the lugubrious stories which my foolish nurse inculcated into my brain." Athos spoke this in so natural a manner that d'Artagnan was shaken.

"I remember as we remember a dream," replied the young man. "We were speaking of hanging."

"Ah, you see," said Athos, attempting to laugh. "The hanging of people is my nightmare."

"Yes," replied d'Artagnan. "I remember; it was a woman."

"That's it," replied Athos, becoming almost livid, "my story of the fair lady. When I relate that, I must be very drunk."

"A woman who was hanged by her husband."

"You see how a man may compromise himself," replied Athos, shrugging his shoulders. "I certainly never will get drunk again, d'Artagnan; it is a bad habit."

They were soon on the road to Crevecoeur, where Aramis joined them, and they set forward to join Porthos. The four friends returned to Paris.

TWENTY-NINE

A few days after returning to Paris, D'Artagnan saw, stepping into a carriage, a very handsome lady, attended by a maidservant. He recognized the lady of Meung, whom the man with the scar had saluted by the name of Milady. D'Artagnan heard her order the coachman to drive to St. Germain.

It was useless to try to keep pace on foot with a carriage drawn by two powerful horses. D'Artagnan therefore returned to the rue Ferou, where Athos was emptying a bottle of wine, and described how he had found that lady who, with the seigneur with the scar near his temple, filled his mind constantly.

"That is to say, you are as in love with this lady as you were with Madame Bonacieux," said Athos, shrugging his shoulders.

"Not at all!" said d'Artagnan. "I am curious to unravel the mystery. I love my poor Constance; but all my searches have been useless. I must divert my attention!"

"Amuse yourself with Milady, my dear d'Artagnan; I wish

you may with all my heart."

On horseback, D'Artagnan took the road to St. Germain. Milady had spoken to the man in the black cloak; therefore she knew him. It was certainly the man in the black cloak who had carried off Mme Bonacieux. By going in search of Milady he at the same time went in search of Constance.

Thinking all this, d'Artagnan arrived at St. Germain. He rode up a quiet street, looking to see if he could catch any vestige of his beautiful Englishwoman, when from the ground floor of a pretty house he saw the face of the Comte de Wardes—he whom d'Artagnan had taken such good care of at Calais, on the road to the governor's house! D'Artagnan watched from behind a hedge.

At the end of an instant's observation, he heard Milady's carriage stop opposite. He could not be mistaken; Milady was in it. D'Artagnan leaned upon the neck of his horse, in order that he might see without being seen.

Milady put her charming blond head out at the window, and gave her orders to her maid.

The latter—a pretty girl—took her way toward the house at which d'Artagnan had perceived de Wardes. D'Artagnan followed the chambermaid with his eyes and saw her leave a billet in the garden, then run back to the carriage, which drove off.

D'Artagnan picked up the letter and read these words:

> *A person who takes more interest in you than she is willing to confess wishes to know on what day it will suit you to walk in the forest? Tomorrow, at the Hotel of the Cloth of Gold, a lackey in red will wait for your reply.*

He jumped onto his horse, intending to intercept the carriage. At the end of five minutes he perceived it drawn up by the roadside; a cavalier, richly dressed, was close to the door.

The conversation between Milady and the cavalier was so animated that d'Artagnan stopped on the other side of the carriage without anyone perceiving his presence.

It took place in English—a language that d'Artagnan could not understand; but he saw that the beautiful Englishwoman was in a great rage. She terminated the conversation by a blow with her fan, applied with such force that the little feminine weapon flew into a thousand pieces. The cavalier laughed.

D'Artagnan approached the door, and taking off his hat, said, "Madame, this cavalier has made you angry. Speak, and I will punish him for his want of courtesy."

Milady turned, looking at the young man with astonishment; she said in very good French, "Monsieur, I should with confidence place myself under your protection if the person with whom I quarrel were not my brother."

"What is that stupid fellow troubling himself about?" cried the cavalier whom Milady had designated as her brother. "Why does not he go about his business?"

"Stupid fellow yourself!" said d'Artagnan. "I do not go on because it pleases me to stop here."

The cavalier addressed some words in English to his sister.

"I speak to you in French," said d'Artagnan. "Be kind enough to reply in the same language. You are madame's brother, but you are not mine."

It might be thought that Milady would have interposed in order to prevent the quarrel from going too far; on the contrary,

D'Artagnan approached the door.

she called out coolly to the coachman, "Go on—home!"

The carriage went, and left the two men facing each other. The cavalier made a movement to follow the carriage, but d'Artagnan caught at his bridle.

"Well, monsieur," said he, "you forget there is a quarrel to arrange."

"You see plainly that I have no sword," said the Englishman. "Do you wish to play the braggart with an unarmed man?"

"I hope you have a sword at home. If you like, I will throw with you for one."

"Needless," said the Englishman. "I am well furnished with such playthings."

"Very well," replied d'Artagnan, "show one to me this evening behind the Luxembourg."

"I will be there."

"You have probably one or two friends?"

"I have three, who would be honored by joining in the sport with me."

"Three? Just my number!"

"Now, who are you?" asked the Englishman.

"I am Monsieur d'Artagnan, serving in the king's Guards. And you?"

"I am Lord de Winter, Baron Sheffield."

"I am your servant, Monsieur Baron," said d'Artagnan.

He cantered back to the residence of Athos, and related all that had passed, except the letter to M. de Wardes. Athos was delighted to find he was going to fight an Englishman.

They immediately sent for Porthos and Aramis.

THIRTY

The hour having come, they went behind the Luxembourg. Then, according to foreign custom, the presentations took place. The Englishmen were all men of rank; consequently, the odd names of their adversaries were a matter of annoyance.

"After all," said Lord de Winter, when the three friends had been named, "we cannot fight with such names; they are names of shepherds."

"Therefore your lordship may suppose they are assumed names," said Athos.

"Which only gives us a greater desire to know the real ones," replied the Englishman. "One fights only with equals."

"That is just," said Athos, and took aside the Englishman with whom he was to fight and communicated his name in a low voice. Porthos and Aramis did the same.

"Does that satisfy you?" said Athos to his adversary. "Do you find me of sufficient rank to cross swords with me?"

"Yes, monsieur," said the Englishman, bowing.

"You would have acted more wisely if you had not required me to make myself known. I am believed to be dead, and have reasons for wishing nobody to know I am living; I shall be obliged to kill you."

The Englishman believed that he jested, but Athos did not jest.

Eight swords glittered in the rays of the setting sun, and the combat began. Athos fenced as calmly as if he had been practicing in a fencing school. Porthos, abated of his too-great confidence by his adventure at Chantilly, played with prudence. Aramis, who had a poem to finish, behaved like a man in haste.

Athos killed his adversary first. He hit him once; the sword pierced his heart. Second, Porthos stretched his upon the grass with a wound through his thigh. Aramis pushed his so vigorously that the man took to his heels, and disappeared.

As to d'Artagnan, when he saw his adversary fatigued, he sent his sword flying. The baron fell backward.

D'Artagnan said, sword to his throat, "My lord, I spare your life for the sake of your sister."

The Englishman paid a thousand compliments to the three Musketeers.

"And now, my young friend," said Lord de Winter, "this evening I will present you to my sister, Milady Clarik; she is not in bad odor at court and may someday speak a word that will prove useful to you." On quitting d'Artagnan, he gave him his sister's address, and undertook to call that evening and take d'Artagnan to introduce him.

This introduction to Milady Clarik occupied our Gascon

greatly. According to his conviction, she was some creature of the cardinal, and yet he felt drawn toward her. Athos recommended prudence.

"You have just lost one woman, whom you call perfect," he said, "and here you are, running after another."

D'Artagnan felt the truth of this reproach. "I loved Madame Bonacieux with my heart, while I only love Milady with my head," said he. "My principal object is to ascertain what part she plays at court."

"Her part! She is some emissary of the cardinal, who will draw you into a snare. I mistrust women—particularly fair women. Milady is fair?"

"She has the most beautiful light hair imaginable!"

"My poor d'Artagnan!" said Athos.

Lord de Winter arrived at the appointed time. They were soon at the Place Royale. Milady's house was remarkably sumptuous. While most English had quit France on account of the war, Milady had been laying out money upon her residence.

"You see," said Lord de Winter, presenting d'Artagnan to his sister, "a young gentleman who has held my life in his hands, and not abused his advantage, although it was I who insulted him and I am an Englishman. Thank him, madame, if you have any affection for me."

Milady frowned slightly; a peculiar smile appeared upon her lips. The brother did not perceive this; he had turned round to play with Milady's favorite monkey.

"You are welcome, monsieur," said Milady, in a voice whose sweetness contrasted with the symptoms of ill humor that d'Artagnan had remarked. "You have today acquired eternal rights to my gratitude."

The Englishman described the combat. Milady listened with attention, but her little foot worked impatiently beneath her robe.

Lord de Winter perceived nothing of this. He filled two glasses, and invited d'Artagnan to drink. D'Artagnan took the second glass. In a mirror, he perceived the change that came over Milady. Now that she believed herself no longer observed, ferocity animated her countenance.

That pretty little chambermaid came in. She spoke, in English, to Lord de Winter, who requested d'Artagnan's permission to retire, referring to urgent business.

D'Artagnan returned to Milady. Her countenance had recovered its gracious expression; but little red spots on her handkerchief indicated that she had bitten her lips till the blood came.

Milady told d'Artagnan that Lord de Winter was her brother-in-law, not her brother. She had married his brother, who had left her a widow. After a half hour's conversation d'Artagnan was convinced that Milady was his compatriot; she spoke French with an elegance that left no doubt.

D'Artagnan came again on the morrow. Lord de Winter was not at home; Milady did all the honors. She asked him whence he came, who were his friends, and whether he had not sometimes thought of attaching himself to the cardinal.

D'Artagnan remembered his suspicions regarding Milady. He launched into a eulogy of His Eminence, and said that he should have entered into the Guards of the cardinal instead of the king's Guards if he had not happened to know M. de Treville.

Milady asked d'Artagnan in the most careless manner if he had ever been in England. D'Artagnan replied that he had been sent by M. de Treville to bargain for a supply of horses.

At the same hour as on the preceding evening, d'Artagnan retired.

D'Artagnan came again on the morrow and the day after that, and each day Milady gave him a more gracious reception.

THIRTY-ONE

CHAMBERMAID AND MISTRESS

D'Artagnan became hourly more in love with Milady. One day, light at heart as a man who awaits a shower of gold, he found the chambermaid under the gateway of the hotel.

"Good!" thought d'Artagnan. "She is charged with some message from her mistress."

"I wish to speak to you," stammered the chambermaid. "If Monsieur le Chevalier would follow me?"

"Where you please, my dear."

Kitty led him up a little staircase and opened a door. "Here, Monsieur le Chevalier," said she. "We shall be alone."

"Whose room is this, my dear?"

"Mine, Monsieur Chevalier; it communicates with my mistress's by that door."

D'Artagnan cast a glance around. The little apartment was charming; but his eyes were directed to that door which led to Milady's chamber.

Kitty heaved a sigh. "You love my mistress, Monsieur le Chevalier?" said she. "Alas, that is too bad."

"What the devil is so bad in it?" said d'Artagnan.

"Because, monsieur," replied Kitty, "my mistress loves you not at all. Out of the regard I have for you, I have resolved to tell you so."

"Much obliged, my dear Kitty; but we have always some difficulty in believing such things, if only from self-love."

"What do you think of this?" Kitty drew a note from her bosom.

"For me?" said d'Artagnan, seizing the letter.

"For Monsieur Le Comte de Wardes."

As quick as thought, he tore open the letter and read:

You have not answered my first note. Have you forgotten the glances you favored me with at the ball of Mme de Guise? You have an opportunity, Count; do not allow it to escape.

D'Artagnan became very pale.

"Poor dear Monsieur d'Artagnan," said Kitty.

"You pity me, little one?" said d'Artagnan.

"With all my heart; for I know what it is to be in love."

"Then assist me in avenging myself on your mistress. I would triumph over her, and supplant my rival."

"I will never help you in that, Monsieur le Chevalier," said Kitty, warmly.

"Why not?" demanded d'Artagnan.

"For two reasons. The first is that my mistress will never love you."

"And the second?"

"I will never confess but to the man who should read to the bottom of my soul!"

D'Artagnan looked at Kitty. The young girl had a freshness and beauty that many duchesses would have purchased with their coronets. "Kitty," said he, "I will read to the bottom of your soul whenever you like." And he gave her a kiss, at which the poor girl became as red as a cherry.

"Oh, no," said Kitty, "it is my mistress you love."

"Does that hinder you from letting me know the second reason?"

"The second reason, Monsieur le Chevalier," replied Kitty, emboldened by the kiss, "is that in love, everyone for herself!"

Then d'Artagnan remembered the languishing glances of Kitty; absorbed by his desire to please the great lady, he had disdained the chambermaid. Our Gascon saw the advantage to be derived from Kitty's love: the interception of letters addressed to the Comte de Wardes, news on the spot, entrance to Kitty's chamber, contiguous to her mistress's.

"Well," said he to the young girl, "are you willing that I should give you proof of that love I am ready to feel toward you? Shall I this evening pass with you the time I generally spend with your mistress?"

"Oh, yes," said Kitty, clapping her hands.

"Then come here, my dear," said d'Artagnan, establishing himself in an easy chair. "Let me tell you that you are the prettiest chambermaid I ever saw!"

And he did tell her, so well that the poor girl believed him.

Midnight sounded, and the bell was rung in Milady's chamber.

"There is my mistress calling me!" cried Kitty. "Go directly!"

D'Artagnan rose, then, opening the door of a large closet, buried himself amid the dressing gowns of Milady.

"What are you doing?" cried Kitty.

D'Artagnan shut himself in the closet.

"Well," cried Milady, opening the door. "Are you asleep, that you don't answer when I ring?"

Both went into the bedroom, and d'Artagnan could hear Milady scolding her maid. At length the conversation turned.

"Well," said Milady, "I have not seen our Gascon this evening."

"What, Milady!" said Kitty.

"He must have been prevented by Monsieur Dessessart. I have this one safe."

"What will you do with him, madame?"

"There is something that he is ignorant of: he nearly made me lose credit with His Eminence. I will be revenged!"

"I believed that madame loved him."

"I detest him! An idiot, who held the life of Lord de Winter in his hands and did not kill him, by which I missed three hundred thousand livres' income."

D'Artagnan shuddered at hearing this creature reproach him for not having killed a man whom he had seen load her with kindnesses.

"For this," continued Milady, "I should have revenged myself if the cardinal had not requested me to conciliate him."

"Madame has not conciliated that little woman he was so fond of."

"The mercer's wife? He has already forgotten she existed."

A cold sweat broke from d'Artagnan's brow. This woman was a monster!

"That will do," said Milady. "Tomorrow endeavor to get me an answer to that letter."

D'Artagnan heard the door close. Kitty turned the key of the lock, and d'Artagnan opened the closet door.

"Silence!" said Kitty. "There is nothing but a wainscot between my chamber and Milady's; every word that is uttered in one can be heard in the other."

"That's exactly the reason I won't go," said d'Artagnan. He drew Kitty to him.

It was a movement of vengeance upon Milady. With a little more heart, he might have been contented with this new conquest; but the principal features of his character were ambition and pride. The first use he made of his influence over Kitty was to try and find out what had become of Mme Bonacieux; but the poor girl was ignorant—only she believed she was not dead.

As to the cause near making Milady lose credit with the cardinal, Kitty knew nothing; d'Artagnan suspected it was on account of the diamond studs.

What was clearest was that the hatred of Milady was increased by his not having killed her brother-in-law.

D'Artagnan came the next day to Milady's, and finding her in ill humor, had no doubt that it was lack of answer from M. de Wardes that provoked her. Toward the end of the evening, the beautiful lioness became milder; she listened to d'Artagnan's soft speeches and gave him her hand to kiss.

He found Kitty at the gate. Milady could not comprehend the silence of the Comte de Wardes, and ordered Kitty to come in the morning to take a third letter. D'Artagnan made Kitty promise to bring him that letter.

As on the night before, d'Artagnan concealed himself; Milady called, undressed, sent away Kitty, and shut the door. As before, d'Artagnan did not return home till five o'clock in the morning.

At eleven o'clock Kitty came to him. She held a fresh billet from Milady.

D'Artagnan opened the letter and read:

This is the third time I have written to tell you that I love you. Beware that I do not write again to tell you that I detest you.

If you repent of the manner in which you have acted, the young girl who brings you this will tell you how a man of spirit may obtain his pardon.

D'Artagnan colored several times in reading this billet.

"You love her still," said Kitty.

"No, Kitty, but I will avenge myself for her contempt."

D'Artagnan took a pen and wrote:

Madame, I could not believe that it was to me your first two letters were addressed, so unworthy did I feel of such an honor; besides, I was so seriously indisposed that I could not have replied to them.

Now I am forced to believe in your kindness, since not only your letter but your servant assures me that I have the good fortune to be beloved by you.

She has no occasion to teach me the way in which a man of spirit may obtain his pardon. I will come and ask mine at eleven o'clock this evening.

From him whom you have rendered the happiest of men,
Comte de Wardes

D'Artagnan's plan was simple. By Kitty's chamber he could gain that of her mistress. He would triumph over her. In eight days the campaign against the Huguenots at la Rochelle would open, and he would leave Paris; d'Artagnan had no time for a prolonged love siege.

"There," said d'Artagnan, handing Kitty the letter, "give that to Milady."

Poor Kitty became as pale as death; she suspected what the letter contained.

"Listen, my dear," said d'Artagnan, "Milady may discover that I have opened the others which ought to have been opened by de Wardes. You know she is not the woman to limit her vengeance."

"Alas!" said Kitty. "For whom have I exposed myself?"

Although Kitty cried before transmitting the letter to her mistress, she did so, which was all d'Artagnan wished.

THIRTY-TWO

D'Artagnan presented himself at Milady's at nine o'clock, and found her in a charming humor. At ten o'clock she began to appear restless. She looked at the clock, rose, and smiled at d'Artagnan with an air that said, "You would be charming if you would only depart."

D'Artagnan rose and took his hat; Milady gave him her hand to kiss. The young man felt her press his hand, and comprehended that this gratitude was because of his departure.

"She loves him devilishly," he murmured.

This time Kitty was nowhere waiting for him. Alone, d'Artagnan found the little chamber. She heard him enter, but did not raise her head.

On receiving his letter, Milady joyfully had told her servant everything, and had given Kitty a purse. Returning to her room, Kitty had thrown the purse into a corner, where it lay disgorging gold pieces. D'Artagnan was touched by her sorrow, but held too tenaciously to his projects to change the program he had laid out.

Presently they heard Milady retire to her room. The bell sounded. Kitty went to her mistress; the partition was so thin that one could hear all that passed between the women.

Milady seemed overcome with joy, and made Kitty repeat the smallest details of the pretended interview with de Wardes. To all these questions poor Kitty responded in a stifled voice.

As the hour approached, Milady had everything darkened, and ordered Kitty to return to her own chamber. Hardly had d'Artagnan seen that the whole apartment was in obscurity, than he slipped out of his concealment.

"It is I," said d'Artagnan in a subdued voice, "the Comte de Wardes."

"Well," said Milady, in a trembling voice, "you know that I wait for you."

D'Artagnan slipped into the chamber.

If rage or sorrow ever torture the heart, it is when a lover receives protestations of love addressed to his rival. Jealousy gnawed d'Artagnan's heart.

"Count," said Milady, pressing his hand, "I love you. That you may not forget me, take this!" She slipped a ring from her finger onto d'Artagnan's. "Keep that ring for love of me. In accepting it," she added, in a voice full of emotion, "you render me a much greater service than you imagine."

"This woman is full of mysteries," murmured d'Artagnan. He opened his mouth to tell Milady who he was; but she added, "Poor angel, whom that monster of a Gascon barely failed to kill. Be tranquil, I will avenge you!"

It took some time for d'Artagnan to resume this dialogue. This woman exercised over him an unaccountable power; he hated and adored her at the same time. He would not have believed that two sentiments so opposite could dwell together.

Poor Kitty hoped to speak to d'Artagnan when he passed through her chamber; but Milady herself reconducted him through the darkness, and only quit him at the staircase.

The next morning d'Artagnan ran to find Athos. He was engaged in an adventure so singular that he wished for counsel.

"Your Milady," said Athos, "appears to be an infamous creature, but you have done wrong to deceive her." While speaking, Athos regarded the sapphire that had taken on d'Artagnan's finger the place of the queen's ring.

"You notice my ring?" said the Gascon, proud to display so rich a gift.

"Yes," said Athos, "it reminds me of a family jewel. I did not think two sapphires of such fine water existed."

"It is a gift from my beautiful Englishwoman, or rather Frenchwoman—for I am convinced she is French. She gave it me last night," replied d'Artagnan, taking it from his finger.

Athos tried it on; it fit his finger as if made for it.

"It is impossible," said he. "How could this ring come into the hands of Milady Clarik?" He returned the ring without ceasing to look at it. "Pray, d'Artagnan," said Athos, after a minute, "either take off that ring or turn the mounting inside; I shall have no head to converse. Let me look at that sapphire again; the one I mentioned had one of its faces scratched."

D'Artagnan took off the ring, giving it to Athos.

Athos started. "Look," said he, "is it not strange?" and pointed out the scratch he had remembered.

"But from whom did this ring come, Athos?"

"As I told you, it is an old family jewel."

"And you—sold it?" asked d'Artagnan, hesitatingly.

"No," replied Athos. "I gave it away, as it has been given to you."

D'Artagnan became pensive. He took back the ring, but put it in his pocket and not on his finger.

"D'Artagnan," said Athos, taking his hand, "I love you; if I had a son I could not love him better. Take my advice, renounce this woman."

"You are right," said d'Artagnan. "I own that she terrifies me."

"In truth, you will act rightly," said Athos. "God grant that this woman, who has scarcely entered into your life, may not leave a terrible trace in it!"

On reaching home d'Artagnan found Kitty waiting for him. Her mistress wished to know when her lover would meet her. The counsels of his friend, joined to the cries of d'Artagnan's own heart, made him determine not to see Milady. He wrote the following letter:

> *Since my convalescence I have so many affairs of this kind that I am forced to regulate them. When your turn comes, I shall inform you. I kiss your hands.*
> *—Comte de Wardes*

D'Artagnan gave the letter to Kitty, who became wild with joy on reading it. She ran back to the Place Royale as fast as her legs could carry her. Milady opened the letter with eagerness equal to Kitty's in bringing it; but at the first words became livid. She crushed the paper in her hand, and cried, "Impossible! It is impossible a gentleman could have written such a letter." Then all at once she cried, "My God! Can he have—" She tried to go toward the window, but her legs failed her, and she sank into an armchair. Kitty, fearing she was ill, was beginning to open her dress; but Milady started up. "What do you want?" said she. "Why do you place your hand on me?"

"I thought that madame was ill," responded the maid, frightened at the expression on her mistress's face.

"When I am insulted I do not faint; I avenge myself!"

THIRTY-THREE

Milady gave orders that M. d'Artagnan should be admitted; but he did not come. The next day Kitty related all that had passed. D'Artagnan smiled; this jealous anger of Milady was his revenge.

That evening Milady was more impatient. As before, she expected d'Artagnan in vain.

The next morning, when Kitty presented herself at d'Artagnan's, she was no longer joyous. D'Artagnan asked what was the matter; she drew a letter from her pocket, addressed to M. d'Artagnan.

He read:

> *Dear M. d'Artagnan,*
> *It is wrong thus to neglect your friends, particularly as you are about to leave them. We expected you yesterday and the day before, but in vain. Will it be the same this evening?*
> *—Milady Clarik*

"Will you go?" asked Kitty.

"Listen to me, my dear," said the Gascon, who sought an excuse for breaking the promise he had made Athos. "It would be impolite not to accept. Milady might suspect; who could say how far the vengeance of such a woman would go?"

"Oh!" said Kitty. "You know how to represent things in such a way that you are always in the right. If you succeed in pleasing her in your own name, it will be much worse."

D'Artagnan desired Kitty to tell her mistress that he would be obedient to her orders. He did not dare to write for fear of not being able to disguise his writing sufficiently.

At nine o'clock, d'Artagnan was at the Place Royale. Milady looked fatigued. D'Artagnan approached her with his usual gallantry. She made an effort to receive him, but never did a more distressed countenance give the lie to a more amiable smile.

To the questions that d'Artagnan put concerning her health, she replied, "Bad, very bad."

"Then," replied he, "my visit is ill timed; I will withdraw."

"No!" said Milady. "Stay, Monsieur d'Artagnan; your company will divert me."

"Oh, oh!" thought d'Artagnan. "She has never been so kind. En garde!"

Milady conversed with more than her usual brilliancy. D'Artagnan's love, which he believed to be extinct, awoke again in his heart. Milady smiled, and he felt that he could damn himself for that smile.

Milady asked d'Artagnan if he had a mistress.

"Alas!" said d'Artagnan, with the most sentimental air he

could assume. "Can you be cruel enough to put such a question to me—who, from the moment I saw you, have only breathed for you?"

"Then you love me?" said she. "You know the more hearts are worth the capture, the more difficult they are to win."

"Difficulties do not affright me," said d'Artagnan. "I shrink before nothing but impossibilities."

"Nothing is impossible," replied Milady, "to true love."

"The devil!" thought d'Artagnan. "Is she going to fall in love with me? Will she give me another sapphire like that which she gave me for de Wardes?"

D'Artagnan drew his seat nearer to Milady's.

"Let us talk a little seriously," said Milady, in turn drawing her armchair nearer to d'Artagnan. She remained thoughtful for a moment, then said, "I have an enemy."

"You, madame!" said d'Artagnan, affecting surprise. "Is that possible?"

"An enemy who has insulted me so cruelly that between us it is war. May I reckon on you as an auxiliary?"

D'Artagnan at once perceived the ground that the vindictive creature wished to reach.

"You may, madame," said he, with emphasis. "My arm and my life belong to you."

"Then," said Milady, "since you are as generous as you are loving—"

"Well?" demanded d'Artagnan.

"Well," replied Milady, after a moment of silence, "from the present time, cease to talk of impossibilities."

"Do not overwhelm me with happiness," cried d'Artagnan,

covering her hands with kisses.

"Avenge me of that infamous de Wardes," said Milady, between her teeth, "and I shall soon get rid of you—you idiot, you animated sword blade!"

"Fall into my arms, hypocritical and dangerous woman," said d'Artagnan, likewise to himself, "and I will laugh at you with him whom you wish me to kill." D'Artagnan lifted up his head.

"I am ready," said he.

"You have understood me, Monsieur d'Artagnan," said Milady. "You would employ for me your arm, which has already acquired so much renown?"

"Instantly!"

"How should I repay such a service?" said Milady.

"You know the only reply that I desire," said d'Artagnan. And he drew nearer to her. "Ah," he cried, "my happiness appears so impossible that I pant to make a reality of it. Only name to me the man that has brought tears into your beautiful eyes!"

"Who told you that I wept?" said she. "Such women as I never weep."

"So much the better! Come, tell me his name!"

"You know him."

"Surely not one of my friends?" replied d'Artagnan, affecting hesitation.

"If it were one of your friends you would hesitate?" cried Milady.

"Not if it were my own brother!" cried d'Artagnan, as if carried away by his enthusiasm.

"I love your devotedness," said Milady.

"Do you love nothing else in me?" asked d'Artagnan.

"I love you!" said she, taking his hand. D'Artagnan trembled.

"You love me!" cried he. "Oh, if that were so, I should lose my reason!"

And he folded her in his arms. Her lips were cold; it appeared to d'Artagnan that he had embraced a statue. He was not the less electrified by love. He almost believed in the tenderness of Milady; he almost believed in the crime of de Wardes. If de Wardes had at that moment been under his hand, he would have killed him.

"His name is—" said Milady.

"De Wardes; I know," cried d'Artagnan.

"How do you know?" asked Milady, seizing his hands.

D'Artagnan felt he had committed an error. "How do I know?" he said. "I know because yesterday Monsieur de Wardes, in a saloon where I was, showed a ring which he had received from you."

"Wretch!" cried Milady.

"I will avenge you," replied d'Artagnan.

"Thanks, my brave friend!" cried Milady. "And when shall I be avenged?"

"Would it be just," he asked, "to allow me to go to a possible death without having given me something more than hope?"

Milady answered by a glance that said, "Is that all?" And then, "That is just," said she, tenderly. "Silence! I hear my brother. Go out this way," opening a small private door, "and come back at eleven o'clock."

"It appears that these appointments are all made for eleven

o'clock," thought d'Artagnan. "That's a settled custom."

Milady held out to him her hand, which he kissed.

"But," said he, as he retired, "this woman is certainly a great liar. I must take care."

THIRTY-FOUR

MILADY'S SECRET

D'Artagnan loved Milady like a madman, and she did not love him at all. The best way in which he could act would be to confess that he and de Wardes were, up to the present moment, absolutely the same, and that consequently he could not undertake to kill the Comte de Wardes. But he wished to subdue this woman in his own name.

He walked round the Place Royale, turning to look at the light in Milady's apartment through the blinds. At length the light disappeared. With a beating heart and a brain on fire, he reentered the house.

Kitty wished to delay him; but Milady heard d'Artagnan, and opening the door, said, "Come in."

This was of such immodesty that d'Artagnan could scarcely believe what he saw or heard. He darted quickly toward Milady.

D'Artagnan gained the summit of his wishes. It was no longer a rival who was beloved; it was himself who was apparently beloved. A voice whispered that he was but an instrument of vengeance; but self-love silenced this voice.

Milady was no longer that woman who had terrified him; she was an ardent mistress, abandoning herself to love. Two hours glided away. When the transports of the two lovers were calmer, Milady asked the young man if the encounter between him and de Wardes were arranged in his mind. D'Artagnan answered that it was too late to think about duels and sword thrusts. Milady's questions became more pressing.

Then d'Artagnan, who had never seriously thought of this impossible duel, endeavored to turn the conversation. He advised Milady to renounce, by pardoning de Wardes, the projects she had formed.

The young woman exclaimed, "Are you afraid, Monsieur d'Artagnan?"

"You cannot think so!" replied d'Artagnan. "But suppose Comte de Wardes were less guilty than you think?"

"At all events," said Milady, seriously, "from the moment he deceived me, he merited death."

"He shall die, then!" said d'Artagnan, in so firm a tone that it appeared to Milady a proof of devotion.

We cannot say how long the night seemed to Milady, but d'Artagnan believed it to be hardly two hours before daylight peeped through the window blinds. Seeing d'Artagnan about to leave, Milady recalled his promise to avenge her on the Comte de Wardes.

"I am quite ready," said d'Artagnan, "but I should like to be certain of one thing: whether you really love me."

"I have given you proof of that."

"If you love me as much as you say," replied d'Artagnan, "do you not entertain fear that I may be killed?"

"Impossible!" cried Milady. "You are such an expert swordsman."

"You would not, then, prefer a method," resumed d'Artagnan, "which would avenge you while rendering combat useless?"

Milady looked at him in silence. The pale light of the first rays of day gave to her clear eyes a strange expression. "Really," said she, "I believe you hesitate."

"No, but I pity poor Comte de Wardes. A man must be so punished by the loss of your love that he needs no other chastisement."

"Who told you that I loved him?" asked Milady, sharply.

"At least, I am now at liberty to believe that you love another," said the young man, in a caressing tone, "and I am really interested for the count."

"You?" asked Milady. "Why?"

"Because I know that he is far from being so guilty as he appears."

"Indeed!" said Milady. "Explain yourself."

"I am a man of honor," said d'Artagnan, "and a confession weighs on my mind. If I had the least doubt of your love I would not make it, but you love me, do you not?"

D'Artagnan tried to touch his lips to Milady's, but she evaded him.

"This confession," said she, "what is it?"

"You gave de Wardes a meeting on Thursday last in this very room, did you not?"

"No!" said Milady, with a countenance so unchanged, that if d'Artagnan had not been in perfect possession of the fact, he would have doubted.

"Do not lie, my angel," said d'Artagnan, smiling. "It is useless. De Wardes cannot boast of anything."

"How is that? You told me yourself that that ring—"

"That ring I have! The Comte de Wardes of Thursday and the d'Artagnan of today are the same person."

Pale and trembling, Milady repulsed d'Artagnan's embrace by a violent blow on the chest as she sprang out of bed.

It was almost broad daylight.

D'Artagnan detained her by her nightdress to implore her pardon. The cambric was torn from her beautiful shoulders; and d'Artagnan recognized, with astonishment, the *fleur-de-lis*—that indelible mark imprinted by the hand of the executioner.

"Great God!" cried d'Artagnan, loosing his hold.

Milady felt herself denounced. She flew to a little box upon the dressing table, drew from it a small poniard with a sharp thin blade, and threw herself upon d'Artagnan. He was terrified at those terribly dilated pupils and bleeding lips, recoiled as from a serpent, and drew his sword from the scabbard. Milady endeavored to get near enough to stab him, and did not stop till she felt the sword's point at her throat.

She tried to seize the sword; but d'Artagnan, presenting the point sometimes at her eyes, sometimes at her breast, compelled her to glide behind the bedstead, while he retreated toward Kitty's apartment. Milady continued to strike at him. As this bore some resemblance to a duel, d'Artagnan began to recover.

"Beautiful lady," said he, "if you don't calm yourself, I will design a second *fleur-de-lis* upon one of those pretty cheeks!"

"Scoundrel!" howled Milady.

The *fleur-de-lis*—that indelible mark imprinted by the hand of the executioner.

At the noise they made, Kitty opened the door. With one spring d'Artagnan flew into her chamber, slammed the door, and placed his weight against it, while Kitty pushed the bolts.

Milady stabbed the door with her poniard, the point glittering through the wood.

"Quick, Kitty!" said d'Artagnan. "Let me get out of the house."

THIRTY-FIVE

D'Artagnan did not stop till he came to Athos's door. Athos came out of his apartment in a dressing gown.

"Are you wounded?"

"Are you alone?"

"Whom do you expect to find with me at this hour?"

D'Artagnan rushed into Athos's chamber.

"Speak!" said the latter, closing the door. "Is the king dead? Have you killed the cardinal?"

"Athos," said d'Artagnan, "prepare to hear an incredible story."

Lowering his voice, he said, "Milady has a *fleur-de-lis* upon her shoulder!"

"Ah!" cried the Musketeer, as if he had received a ball in his heart.

"Are you *sure* that the *other* is dead?"

"*The other?*" said Athos, in a stifled voice.

"Yes, she of whom you told me at Amiens."

Athos let his head sink on his hands. "Fair," said he. "Blue eyes, of a strange brilliancy, with black eyebrows?"

"Yes."

"The *fleur-de-lis* is small, rosy in color, and looks as if efforts had been made to efface it?"

"Yes."

"But you say she is English?"

"She is called Milady, but Lord de Winter is only her brother-in-law."

"I will see her!"

"Beware, Athos. You tried to kill her; she is a woman to return you the like, and not to fail. I am afraid I have drawn a terrible vengeance on both of us!"

D'Artagnan related all.

"You are right," said Athos. "Fortunately, the day after tomorrow we leave Paris. We are going to la Rochelle, and once gone—"

"She will follow you to the end of the world, Athos, if she recognizes you."

"Of what consequence is it if she kills me?" said Athos. "Do you think I set any great store by life?"

"This woman is one of the cardinal's spies, I am sure."

"If the cardinal does not hold you in high admiration for the affair of London, he entertains great hatred for you; take care of yourself. If you go out, do not go out alone. Mistrust everything, even your own shadow."

"All this will be only necessary till after tomorrow evening," said d'Artagnan, "for once with the army, we shall have only men to dread."

"In the meantime," said Athos, "wherever you go, I will go. Fortunately, you have the sapphire."

"The jewel is yours! Did you not tell me it was a family jewel?"

"Yes, my grandfather gave two thousand crowns for it. My mother gave it to me, and I, fool as I was, gave it to this wretch."

"Then take back this ring."

"I take back the ring, after it has passed through the hands of that infamous creature? Never; that ring is defiled, d'Artagnan."

"Pledge it, then; you can borrow at least a thousand crowns on it. When you are full of money again, you can take it back cleansed, as it will have passed through the hands of usurers."

Athos smiled. "You are a capital companion, d'Artagnan," said he. "Let us pledge the ring, upon one condition: take half the sum advanced, or I will throw it into the Seine."

The two arrived without accident at the rue des Fossoyeurs. Bonacieux was standing at the door, and looked at d'Artagnan hatefully.

"Make haste," said he. "There is a pretty girl waiting."

"Kitty!" said d'Artagnan, and darted into the passage.

He found the poor girl crouching against the door, all in a tremble. As soon as she perceived him, she cried, "You have promised your protection!"

"Yes, Kitty," said d'Artagnan. "Be at ease. What happened after my departure?"

"How can I tell!" said Kitty. "She was mad with passion. I took what money I had and got away."

"Poor dear girl! What can I do? I am going away the day after tomorrow."

"Help me out of Paris; help me out of France!"

"I cannot take you to the siege of la Rochelle," said d'Artagnan.

"Place me in one of the provinces with some lady of your acquaintance—in your own country, for instance."

"In my country the ladies do without chambermaids. But stop! I can manage your business," he said, and sent his valet for Aramis.

"I do not care where I live," said Kitty, "provided nobody knows where I am. I shall always love you."

"And I," said d'Artagnan, "shall always love you. But now answer me. Did you never hear talk of a young woman who was carried off one night?"

"Oh, Monsieur le Chevalier, do you love that woman still?"

"It is my friend who loves her—Monsieur Athos here."

"I?" cried Athos, with the accent of a man who perceives he is about to tread upon an adder.

"You, to be sure!" said d'Artagnan, pressing Athos's hand. "You understand, my dear girl," he continued, "she is the wife of that frightful baboon you saw at the door as you came in."

"You remind me of my fright! If he should have known me!"

"Know you? Did you ever see that man before?"

"He came twice to Milady's. Yesterday evening he came again, just before you came."

"My dear Athos, we are enveloped in a network of spies. Do you believe he knew you, Kitty?"

"I pulled down my hood when I saw him, but perhaps it was too late."

"Go down, Athos, and see if he be still at his door."

Athos went down and returned immediately. "He has gone," said he, "and the house door is shut."

"He has gone to make his report."

At that moment Aramis entered. The matter was explained, and the friends gave him to understand that among his high connections he must find a place for Kitty.

Aramis reflected for a minute. "Very well. If you can answer for Mademoiselle—"

"Oh, monsieur, be assured that I shall be entirely devoted to the person who will give me the means of quitting Paris."

"Then," said Aramis, "this falls out very well." He placed himself at the table and wrote a little note, which he sealed with a ring and gave to Kitty.

"And now, my dear girl," said d'Artagnan, "let us separate. We shall meet again."

"Whenever we find each other," said Kitty, "you will find me loving you as I love you today."

Aramis returned home, and Athos and d'Artagnan busied themselves pledging the sapphire.

THIRTY-SIX

At four o'clock the friends were assembled. D'Artagnan's valet entered, bringing him two letters: one genteelly folded, with a pretty seal in green wax; the other a large square epistle, resplendent with the arms of His Eminence the cardinal duke.

At the sight of the little letter the heart of d'Artagnan bounded, for he believed he recognized the handwriting. He opened it eagerly.

Be, from six to seven o'clock in the evening, on the road to Chaillot, and look carefully into the carriages that pass; if you have any consideration for those who love you, do not make a movement which may lead anyone to believe you have recognized her who exposes herself for the sake of seeing you for an instant.

"That's a snare," said Athos. "Don't go."

"Suppose we all go," said d'Artagnan. "They won't devour all four!"

"If a woman writes," said Aramis, "and desires not to be seen, you compromise her, d'Artagnan."

"We will remain in the background," said Porthos, "and he will advance alone."

"A pistol shot is easily fired from a carriage."

"Bah!" said d'Artagnan. "They will miss me; if they fire, we will ride after the carriage and exterminate those in it."

"As you please," said Athos.

"Gentlemen," said d'Artagnan, "it is half past four, and we have scarcely time to be on the Chaillot road by six."

"But this second letter," said Athos, "I think of more consequence than the little piece of wastepaper you have slipped into your bosom."

D'Artagnan blushed.

"Well," said he, "let us see what His Eminence commands," and d'Artagnan read:

M. d'Artagnan, of the king's Guards, is expected at the Palais-Cardinal this evening at eight o'clock.

"The devil!" said Athos. "Here's a rendezvous more serious."

"I will go to the second after attending the first," said d'Artagnan. "There will be time."

"I would not go at all," said Aramis. "A gallant knight cannot decline a rendezvous with a lady; but a prudent gentleman may excuse himself from waiting on His Eminence."

"I am of Aramis's opinion," said Porthos.

"Gentlemen," replied d'Artagnan, "I will go."

"But the Bastille?" said Aramis.

"You will get me out if they put me there," said d'Artagnan.

"To be sure we will," replied Aramis and Porthos, with admirable promptness, "but you would do better not to risk it."

"Let each of us wait at a gate of the palace with three Musketeers behind him," said Athos. "If we see a closed carriage come out, let us fall upon it. It is a long time since we have had a skirmish with the Guards of Monsieur le Cardinal."

"To a certainty, Athos," said Aramis, "you were meant to be a general!"

"Well," said Porthos, "I will engage our comrades; the rendezvous, the Place du Palais-Cardinal."

All put themselves in their saddles. Near the Louvre they met M. de Treville, who assured d'Artagnan that if on the morrow he did not appear, M. de Treville himself would undertake to find him.

A short gallop brought them to the Chaillot road. D'Artagnan, at some distance from his friends, darted a glance into every carriage that appeared, but saw no face with which he was acquainted.

At twilight, a carriage appeared, coming at a quick pace. His heart beat violently. A female head was put out at the window, with two fingers placed upon her mouth, either to enjoin silence or to send him a kiss. D'Artagnan uttered a cry of joy; this was Mme Bonacieux. In a few strides, he overtook the carriage; but the window was closed, the vision had disappeared. D'Artagnan stopped, trembling for the poor woman who had evidently exposed herself to great danger. The carriage pursued its way at a great pace, dashed into Paris, and disappeared. If it was Mme Bonacieux returning to Paris, why this fugitive rendezvous? If it was not she—for the little light that remained rendered a mistake easy—might it be some plot against him?

His companions joined him. All had seen a woman's head appear at the window, but only Athos knew Mme Bonacieux. His opinion was that it was she; he had fancied he saw a second head inside the carriage.

"If that be the case," said d'Artagnan, "they are doubtless transporting her from one prison to another. How shall I ever meet her again?"

"Friend," said Athos, gravely, "it is the dead alone whom we are not likely to meet again. If your mistress is alive, you will meet her again some day. And perhaps," added he, with that misanthropic tone peculiar to him, "sooner than you wish."

Half past seven sounded. D'Artagnan's friends reminded him that he had a visit to pay, but that there was yet time to retract.

But d'Artagnan was curious. He had made up his mind that he would learn what His Eminence had to say.

In the Place du Palais-Cardinal they found the invited Musketeers and explained to them the matter in hand. Athos divided them into three groups, assumed the command of one, gave the second to Aramis, and the third to Porthos; each group took their watch near an entrance.

D'Artagnan entered boldly at the principal gate.

Although he felt himself ably supported, the young man was uneasy. His conduct toward Milady bore a strong resemblance to treachery. Further, de Wardes, whom he had treated so ill, was one of the tools of His Eminence; His Eminence was terrible to his enemies, but strongly attached to his friends.

"If de Wardes has related all to the cardinal, I may consider myself a condemned man," said d'Artagnan, shaking his head. "Milady has laid her complaints against me, and this last offense has made the cup overflow.

"Fortunately," added he, "my friends will not allow me to be carried away without a struggle. Nevertheless, Monsieur de Treville's company of Musketeers cannot maintain a war against the cardinal. D'Artagnan, the women will ruin you!"

He came to this melancholy conclusion as he entered the antechamber. In this waiting room were six of the cardinal's Guards, who looked upon him with smiles of singular meaning.

As our Gascon was not easily intimidated, he placed himself haughtily in front of Messieurs' Guards, and waited, hand on hip. The usher made a sign to d'Artagnan to follow him. He entered a library, and found himself in the presence of the cardinal.

THIRTY-SEVEN

The cardinal looked at the young man for a moment. D'Artagnan felt this glance run through his veins like a fever.

"Monsieur," said the cardinal, "you set out eight months ago to seek your fortune in the capital?"

"Yes, monseigneur."

"You came through Meung, where something befell you."

"Monseigneur," said d'Artagnan, "what happened—"

"Never mind!" resumed the cardinal, with a smile. "You were recommended to Monsieur de Treville, who placed you in the company of Monsieur Dessessart, leaving you to hope that one day you should enter the Musketeers."

"Monseigneur is correctly informed," said d'Artagnan.

"Since that time many things have happened. You were walking one day behind the Chartreux, when it would have been better if you had been elsewhere. You took with your friends a journey to the waters of Forges; they stopped on the road, but you continued. Very simple: you had business in England."

"Monseigneur," said d'Artagnan, "I went—"

"On your return you were received by an august personage, and you preserve the souvenir she gave you."

D'Artagnan placed his hand upon the queen's diamond and turned the stone inward; too late.

"I have heard nothing of you for some time," continued the cardinal. "I wished to know what you were doing. You are brave, Monsieur d'Artagnan; you are prudent. But you have powerful enemies."

"Alas, monseigneur!" replied the young man. "They are well supported, while I am alone."

"Yes, you have need to be guided; you came to Paris with the idea of making your fortune."

"I am at the age of extravagant hopes, monseigneur," said d'Artagnan.

"There are no extravagant hopes but for fools, monsieur. What would you say to an ensign's commission in my Guards?"

"Monseigneur," replied d'Artagnan, with an embarrassed air. "I am in His Majesty's Guards. I have no reason to be dissatisfied."

"It appears to me that my Guards are also His Majesty's Guards; whoever serves in a French corps serves the king."

"Monseigneur, Your Eminence has ill understood my words."

"You want a pretext, do you? You have this excuse: advancement, opportunity—so much for the world. For yourself, the need of protection; I have received serious complaints against you."

D'Artagnan colored.

"In fact," said the cardinal, placing his hand upon a bundle of papers, "I have here a whole pile which concerns you. Come; reflect and decide."

"Your goodness confounds me, monseigneur," replied d'Artagnan. "All my friends are in the king's Musketeers and Guards, my enemies are in the service of Your Eminence; I should be ill received here and ill regarded there if I accepted what monseigneur offers me."

"Do you happen to entertain the haughty idea that I have not made you an offer equal to your value?" asked the cardinal, with a smile of disdain.

"Monseigneur, on the contrary, I think I have not proved myself worthy of your goodness. The siege of la Rochelle is about to be resumed, monseigneur. If I have the good fortune to conduct myself in such a manner as merits your attention, then I shall have the right of giving myself; at present I shall appear to sell myself."

"That is, you refuse to serve me, monsieur," said the cardinal. "I don't wish you ill; but it is trouble enough to defend our friends. We owe nothing to our enemies; take care of yourself, Monsieur d'Artagnan."

"I will try to do so, monseigneur," replied the Gascon.

"Remember, if any mischance should happen to you," said Richelieu, significantly, "I did all in my power to prevent it."

"I shall entertain, whatever may happen," said d'Artagnan, bowing, "eternal gratitude toward Your Eminence."

"We shall see each other again. Young man," said Richelieu, "if I shall be able to say to you at another time what I have said today, I promise to do so."

This last expression of Richelieu's alarmed d'Artagnan more

than a menace, for it was a warning. He opened his mouth to reply, but with a haughty gesture the cardinal dismissed him.

D'Artagnan went out, but at the door his heart almost failed him. Then the noble countenance of Athos crossed his mind; if he made the compact with the cardinal, Athos would no more give him his hand.

D'Artagnan found the Musketeers waiting. One ran to inform the other sentinels that it was useless to keep guard longer; d'Artagnan had come out safe. Athos, Aramis, and Porthos inquired eagerly the cause of the strange interview; but d'Artagnan confined himself to telling them that M. de Richelieu proposed to him to enter into his Guards, and that he had refused.

"And you were right," cried Aramis and Porthos.

Athos said, "You have done that which you ought to have done; but perhaps you have been wrong." D'Artagnan sighed, for this responded to a secret voice of his soul, which told him that great misfortunes awaited him.

The whole of the next day was spent in preparations for departure. At the first sound of the morning trumpet the friends separated, the Musketeers hastening to the house of M. de Treville, the Guards to that of M. Dessessart. Each captain led his company to the Louvre, where the king held his review.

The king appeared ill. He had, nonetheless, decided upon setting out that same evening. The review over, the Guards set forward alone on their march, the Musketeers waiting for the king.

Arriving at the Faubourg St. Antoine, d'Artagnan turned to look at the Bastille, but did not observe Milady, who designated him to two men who came close up to the ranks to take notice of him. The two men followed the company.

THIRTY-EIGHT

The Siege of la Rochelle was one of the great events of the reign of Louis XIII, and one of the great enterprises of the cardinal. Richelieu, as everyone knows, had loved the queen. Buckingham had the advantage over him, and in two or three circumstances, particularly that of the diamond studs, had thanks to the devotedness of the three Musketeers and the courage and conduct of d'Artagnan, cruelly mystified him. Richelieu knew that in triumphing over England he triumphed over Buckingham, that in humiliating England in the eyes of Europe he humiliated Buckingham in the eyes of the queen. The cardinal had ordered all the troops he could dispose of to march toward the theater of war. It was of this detachment that d'Artagnan formed a part.

The king was to follow, but was attacked by fever and forced to stop. Whenever the king halted, the Musketeers halted. It followed that d'Artagnan found himself separated from Athos, Porthos, and Aramis.

The Guards, under the command of M. Dessessart, took up their quarters; d'Artagnan had formed but few friendships among his comrades, and felt himself isolated. His reflections were not cheerful. From his arrival in Paris, his affairs had made no great progress, either in love or fortune. Mme Bonacieux had disappeared. He had made an enemy of the cardinal, and another enemy: Milady. He had acquired the goodwill of the queen; but the favor of the queen was at the present time an additional cause of persecution.

What he had gained was the diamond, but since he could not part with it, even this had no more value than the gravel under his feet.

We say the gravel under his feet, for d'Artagnan made these reflections while walking along a road that led from the camp to the village. By the last ray of the setting sun, he saw the barrel of a musket glitter from behind a hedge.

D'Artagnan comprehended that he who bore it had not concealed himself with any friendly intentions. On the opposite side of the road, he perceived another musket.

The first musket was leveled in his direction; he threw himself upon the ground. At the same instant the gun was fired, and he heard the whistling of a ball pass over his head.

D'Artagnan sprang up with a bound. The ball from the other musket tore up the gravel on the very spot on the road where he had thrown himself.

D'Artagnan was not one of those foolhardy men who seek a ridiculous death in order that it may be said they did not retreat a single step. He took to his heels; the first who fired, having had time to reload, fired again, this time striking d'Artagnan's hat, and carrying it ten paces from him.

As he had no other hat, he picked up this as he ran, and arrived at his quarters out of breath. He sat down and began to reflect.

This event might have three causes:

It might be an ambush of the Rochellais, not sorry to kill one of His Majesty's Guards. D'Artagnan took his hat, examined the hole, and shook his head. The ball was not a musket ball—it was a harquebus ball. This could not be a military ambush.

This might be a kind remembrance of Monsieur le Cardinal. But d'Artagnan again shook his head. His Eminence had rarely recourse to such means.

It might be a vengeance of Milady; that was most probable.

D'Artagnan passed a very bad night. Nevertheless, day dawned without darkness having brought any accident. At nine o'clock, the Duc d'Orleans visited the posts. D'Artagnan took his place in the midst of his comrades. M. Dessessart made him a sign to approach. He left the ranks, and advanced to receive orders.

"Monsieur is about to ask for some men for a dangerous mission; hold yourself in readiness."

"Thanks, my captain!" replied d'Artagnan, who wished for nothing better than to distinguish himself.

The Rochellais had retaken a bastion. The matter was to ascertain how the enemy guarded this bastion. Monsieur raised his voice and said, "I want for this mission three or four volunteers, led by a man who can be depended upon."

"As to the man to be depended upon, I have him, monsieur," said M. Dessessart, pointing to d'Artagnan. "As to the volunteers, Monsieur has but to make his intentions known."

"Four men who will risk being killed with me!" said d'Artagnan, raising his sword.

Two of his comrades of the Guards immediately sprang forward, and two other soldiers joined them. D'Artagnan set out with his companions; the two Guards marched abreast with him, and the two soldiers followed behind.

They arrived, screened by the lining of the trench, within a hundred paces of the bastion. There, d'Artagnan perceived that the two soldiers had disappeared.

D'Artagnan and his men found themselves within sixty paces of the bastion. The three Guards were deliberating whether to proceed when a dozen balls came whistling around them. They knew all they wished to know; the bastion was guarded. D'Artagnan and his companions retreated.

On arriving at the angle of the trench, one fell. A ball had passed through his breast. The other continued toward camp. D'Artagnan, not willing to abandon his companion, stooped to raise him; at this moment two shots were fired. One struck the head of the already wounded Guard; the other passed within two inches of d'Artagnan.

This attack could not have come from the bastion, which was hidden by the angle of the trench. He resolved this time to know with whom he had to deal, and fell as if dead.

The two soldiers appeared. As he might be only wounded, they came up to him to make sure. Deceived by d'Artagnan's trick, they neglected to reload their guns.

When they were within ten paces, d'Artagnan, who had not let go his sword, sprang up. One assassin used his gun as a club,

aiming a blow at d'Artagnan, who avoided it by springing to one side. The assassin darted toward the bastion. The Rochellais who guarded the bastion fired upon him, and he fell.

Meantime, d'Artagnan had thrown himself upon the other soldier. The sword of the Guardsman slipped along the barrel of the gun and passed through the thigh of the assassin. D'Artagnan placed the point of his sword at his throat.

"Do not kill me!" cried the bandit. "I will tell you all."

"Is your secret of enough importance to spare your life for it?" asked the young man. "Speak quickly! Who employed you to assassinate me?"

"A woman called Milady. It was with my comrade she agreed; he has in his pocket a letter from her."

"I grant you my pardon, upon one condition: that you fetch me the letter your comrade has in his pocket."

"But," cried the bandit, "that is only another way of killing me. How can I fetch that letter under fire from the bastion?"

"Get it, or die by my hand."

"Pardon, monsieur! In the name of that young lady you love!" cried the bandit, leaning upon his hand—for he began to lose his strength with his blood.

"How do you know whom I love?" asked d'Artagnan.

"By that letter which my comrade has in his pocket."

"I must have that letter," said d'Artagnan. "No more delay." He made so fierce a gesture that the wounded man sprang up.

"Stop!" cried he, regaining strength by force of terror. "I will go!"

It was a frightful thing to see this wretch, leaving a long track of blood on the ground, trying to drag himself to the body of his accomplice. Terror was so strongly painted on his face that d'Artagnan took pity, and casting upon him a look of contempt, "Stop," said he. "I will show you a man of courage. Stay where you are; I will go myself."

And, taking advantage of the accidents of the ground, d'Artagnan reached the second soldier. He lifted the assassin onto his shoulders at the moment the enemy fired. A convulsion of agony proved that the would-be assassin had saved his life.

D'Artagnan regained the trench, and threw the corpse beside the wounded man. A leather pocketbook, a purse, a dice box and dice completed the possessions of the dead man. He left the box and dice where they fell, threw the purse to the wounded man, opened the pocketbook, and found the following letter:

Since you have lost sight of that woman and she is now in safety in the convent, try not to miss the man. If you do, you shall pay very dearly for the hundred louis you have from me.

No signature. Nevertheless, it was plain the letter came from Milady. He began to interrogate the wounded man, who confessed that he had undertaken with his comrade to carry off a young woman, but had missed the carriage by ten minutes.

"What were you to do with that woman?" asked d'Artagnan, with anguish.

"Convey her to a house in the Place Royale," said the wounded man.

"Milady's own residence!" murmured d'Artagnan. He comprehended how well Milady must be acquainted with the affairs of the court, since she had discovered all. He also perceived that the queen must have discovered the prison in which poor Mme Bonacieux was, and freed her; her passage along the Chaillot road was explained. It became possible to find Mme Bonacieux, and a convent was not impregnable.

He turned toward the wounded man, and holding out his arm, said, "I will not abandon you. Let us return to the camp."

"To have me hanged?" asked the man.

"You have my word," said he. "For the second time I give you your life."

The wounded man sank upon his knees, to kiss the feet of his preserver.

D'Artagnan explained the sword wound of his companion by a sortie that he improvised. The whole army talked of this expedition for a day. D'Artagnan believed that he might be tranquil, as one of his enemies was killed and the other devoted to his interests.

This tranquillity proved that d'Artagnan did not know Milady.

THIRTY-NINE

THE ANJOU WINE

D'Artagnan's only uneasiness was at not hearing from his friends. But everything was explained by this letter:

M. d'Artagnan,
MM. Athos, Porthos, and Aramis, after having had an entertainment at my house, created such a disturbance that the provost of the castle has ordered them to be confined for some days; I accomplish their order by forwarding to you a dozen bottles of my Anjou wine. I have done this, and am, monsieur, with great respect,
Your obedient servant,
Godeau, Purveyor of the Musketeers

"That's well!" cried d'Artagnan. "I will drink to their health, but I will not drink alone."

And d'Artagnan went among those Guardsmen with whom

he had formed intimacy, to invite them to enjoy with him this present of delicious wine. One of the two Guardsmen was engaged that evening, and another the next, so the meeting was fixed for the day after that.

D'Artagnan sent the wine to the refreshment room of the Guards. Assisting at the banquet would be the false soldier who had tried to kill d'Artagnan and who had entered into his service.

The hour of the banquet came, the two Guards arrived, and the dishes were arranged on the table. Brisemont, which was the name of the convalescent, poured the wine carefully into decanters. Of this wine, the first bottle being a little thick at the bottom, Brisemont poured the lees into a glass, and d'Artagnan desired him to drink it, for the poor devil had not yet recovered his strength.

The guests were about to lift the first glass to their lips, when the cannon sounded. The Guardsmen sprang to their swords, and all ran out to their posts.

Scarcely were they out of the room before cries of "Live the king! Live the cardinal!" resounded on every side. The king had arrived, with his Musketeers. D'Artagnan, in line with his company, saluted his three friends. The four were soon in one another's arms.

"You could not have arrived in better time," cried d'Artagnan. "The dinner cannot have had time to get cold!"

"It appears we are feasting!" said Porthos.

"Is there any drinkable wine in your tavern?" asked Athos.

"Well, there is yours, my friend," replied d'Artagnan.

"Our wine!" said Athos, astonished.

"Yes, that you sent me."

"We have sent you some wine?" said Porthos.

"Did you send this wine, Aramis?" said Athos.

"No; you, Porthos?"

"No; you, Athos?"

"No!"

"If it was not you, it was your purveyor," said d'Artagnan.

"Our purveyor!"

"Yes, the purveyor of the Musketeers, Godeau."

"Never mind where it comes from," said Porthos, "let us taste it."

"No," said Athos. "Don't drink wine from an unknown source."

"You are right, Athos," said d'Artagnan. "Did none of you charge your purveyor to send me some wine? Here is his letter," and he presented the note to his comrades.

"A false letter altogether," said Porthos. "We have not been disciplined."

"D'Artagnan," said Aramis, in a reproachful tone, "how could you believe that we had made a disturbance?"

D'Artagnan grew pale. "Can this be another vengeance of that woman?" he cried.

He rushed toward the refreshment room, the three Musketeers and the two Guards following.

Brisemont was stretched upon the ground, rolling in horrible convulsions. "Ah!" cried he, perceiving d'Artagnan. "You pretend to pardon me, and you poison me!"

"I!" cried d'Artagnan. "What do you say?"

"I say that it was you who gave me the wine. You wished to

avenge yourself on me!"

"Do not think so, Brisemont," said d'Artagnan. "I swear—"

"God will punish you! God, grant that he one day suffer what I suffer!" cried the soldier, and he expired amid horrible tortures.

"Frightful!" murmured Athos, while Porthos broke the bottles and Aramis gave orders, a little late, that a confessor should be sent for.

"Oh, my friends," said d'Artagnan, "you come to save my life, and that of these gentlemen. Gentlemen," continued he, addressing the Guardsmen, "I request you will be silent with regard to this adventure. Put off the party till another day, I beg."

The Guardsmen accepted d'Artagnan's excuses, and retired.

When the young Guardsman and the three Musketeers were without witnesses, they looked at one another.

"In the first place," said Athos, "let us leave this chamber; the dead are not agreeable company."

The host gave them another chamber, and served them fresh eggs and some water. In a few words, Porthos and Aramis were posted as to the situation.

"The fact is, one cannot remain with a sword hanging over his head," said Athos. "You must say to her: 'Peace or war! My word never to do anything against you; on your side, an oath to remain neutral to me. If not, I will apply to the king, I will denounce you as branded, I will bring you to trial; if you are acquitted, I will kill you as I would a mad dog.'"

"But how to meet with her?" said d'Artagnan.

"Time brings round opportunity."

"But to wait surrounded by assassins."

"Bah!" said Athos. "God will preserve us."

"It is our lot to risk our lives; but Constance?" asked d'Artagnan.

"Madame Bonacieux!" said Athos. "I had forgotten you were in love."

"Well," said Aramis, "have you not learned that she is in a convent? One may be very comfortable in a convent."

"As soon as the siege is over, we'll carry her off," said Porthos.

"We must first learn what convent she is in."

"I take upon myself to obtain intelligence of her by the queen's almoner, to whom I am very intimately allied," said Aramis, coloring.

On this assurance, the four friends separated.

FORTY

The English, who require good living in order to be good soldiers, had many invalids in their camp. Beaten in all encounters, they were obliged to reembark. The cardinal was left free to carry on the siege.

An envoy of the Duke of Buckingham was taken, and proof obtained of a league between the German empire, Spain, and England against France. In Buckingham's lodging, papers were found that strongly compromised Mme de Chevreuse and the queen.

If the league that threatened France triumphed, all the cardinal's influence would be lost. The king, obeying him like a child, hated him as a child hates his master, and would abandon him to the vengeance of the queen.

Courtiers succeeded one another, day and night, in the little house in which the cardinal had established his residence. There were also less agreeable visits and reports spread that the cardinal had nearly been assassinated. These attempts did not prevent the cardinal from making nocturnal excursions, sometimes to have an interview with a messenger whom he did not wish to see at home.

One evening when d'Artagnan, who was in the trenches, was not able to accompany them, Athos, Porthos, and Aramis were returning from a drinking place called the Red Dovecot, when they heard horses approaching. As the moon broke from behind a cloud, they saw two horsemen. Athos cried, "Who goes there?"

"Beware of what you are about, gentlemen!" said a clear voice.

"It is some superior officer making his night rounds," said Athos. "What do you wish, gentlemen?"

"Who are you?" said the same voice, in the same commanding tone.

"King's Musketeers," said Athos.

"Advance, and account for what you are doing here."

The three companions advanced rather humbly, convinced that they had to do with someone more powerful than themselves.

"Your name?" said the officer, who covered a part of his face with his cloak.

"But yourself, monsieur," said Athos, "give me proof that you have the right to question me."

"Your name?" repeated the cavalier, letting his cloak fall.

"Monsieur le Cardinal!" cried the stupefied Musketeer.

"Your name?" cried His Eminence, for the third time.

"Athos," said the Musketeer.

The cardinal made a sign to his attendant. "These Musketeers shall follow us," said he. "I am not willing it should be known I have left the camp."

“Monsieur le Cardinal!” cried the stupefied Musketeer.

"We are gentlemen, monseigneur," said Athos. "We can keep a secret."

The cardinal fixed his piercing eyes on this courageous speaker.

"You have a quick ear, Monsieur Athos," said the cardinal. "It is not from mistrust that I request you to follow, but for my security. Your companions are no doubt Messieurs Porthos and Aramis."

"Yes, Your Eminence," said Athos.

"I know you are not quite my friends, but are brave and loyal gentlemen," said the cardinal. "Do me the honor to accompany me."

"Upon my honor," said Athos, "Your Eminence is right in taking us with you; we have seen several ill-looking faces on the road."

The three Musketeers passed behind His Eminence. They soon arrived at the silent, solitary inn. No doubt the host knew what illustrious visitor was expected, and had sent intruders out of the way.

Ten paces from the door the cardinal made a sign to his esquire and the Musketeers to halt. A saddled horse was fastened to the window shutter. A man, enveloped in a cloak, came out and exchanged some words with the cardinal, after which he mounted the horse and set off in the direction of Paris.

The cardinal alighted; the three Musketeers did likewise. The host stood at the door.

"Have you any chamber where these gentlemen can wait near a fire?" said the cardinal.

The host opened the door of a large room, in which an old

stove had been replaced by a large and excellent chimney.

"I have this," said he.

"That will do," replied the cardinal. "Gentlemen, be kind enough to wait for me."

While the Musketeers entered the room, the cardinal ascended the staircase.

FORTY-ONE

THE UTILITY OF STOVEPIPES

Porthos called the host and asked for dice. Porthos and Aramis began to play. Athos walked about. While walking, Athos passed the pipe of the stove; every time he passed he heard a murmur of words. Athos made a sign to his friends to be silent, his ear directed toward the stovepipe.

"Listen, Milady," said the cardinal, "the affair is important."

"Milady!" murmured Athos.

"I listen with great attention," replied a female voice that made the Musketeer start.

"A vessel awaits you. Two men, whom you will find at the door on going out, will serve you as escort. You will allow me to leave first; after half an hour, you can go."

"Yes, monseigneur. And the mission with which you wish to charge me?"

There was an instant of silence. It was evident that the cardinal was weighing his words. Athos took advantage of this moment to tell his two companions to come and listen.

"You will go to London," continued the cardinal, "and seek Buckingham."

"I must beg Your Eminence to observe," said Milady, "since the affair of the diamond studs, His Grace distrusts me."

"This time," said the cardinal, "present yourself frankly as a negotiator. Go to Buckingham and tell him I am acquainted with the preparations he has made; but that at the first step he takes I will ruin the queen. Tell him I will publish the interview the duke had with the queen on the evening Madame the Constable gave a masquerade. Tell him that he came there in the costume which the Chevalier de Guise was to have worn."

"Is that all, monseigneur?"

"Tell him I am acquainted with the details of the adventure at Amiens; that I will have a little romance made of it, with portraits of the principal actors in that nocturnal romance."

"I will tell him."

"Tell him that I hold Montague in my power; that torture may make him tell much of what he knows, and even what he does not know. Add that His Grace left behind a letter from Madame de Chevreuse which singularly compromises the queen, as it proves that Her Majesty can conspire with the enemies of France."

"But," resumed Milady, "if the duke does not give way?"

"The duke is in love to folly," replied Richelieu. "If he becomes certain that this war will cost the honor, and perhaps the liberty, of his lady love, he will look twice."

"And yet," said Milady, "if he persists?"

"The only thing to be sought is some woman who has cause of quarrel with the duke," said the cardinal.

"No doubt," said Milady, coolly, "such a woman may be found."

"Well, such a woman, who would place the knife in the hands of a fanatic, would save France."

"I require an order which would ratify beforehand all that I should do for the good of France."

"But this woman must be found who is desirous of avenging herself upon the duke."

"She is found," said Milady.

"Then the fanatic must be found who will serve as an instrument of God's justice."

"He will be found."

"Well," said the cardinal, "then it will be time to claim the order which you require."

"Your Eminence is right," replied Milady. "The mission with which you honor me is to announce to His Grace that you are acquainted with the disguise by means of which he succeeded in approaching the queen during the fete of Madame the Constable; that you have ordered a little romance written upon the adventures of Amiens; that Montague is in the Bastille, and torture may make him say things he remembers, and even things he has forgotten; that you possess a certain letter from Madame de Chevreuse which singularly compromises her in whose name it was written. Then, if he persists, I shall have nothing to do but to pray a miracle for the salvation of France. That is it, monseigneur?"

"That is it," replied the cardinal, dryly.

"And now," said Milady, "that I have received instruction as concerns your enemies, monseigneur will permit me to say a few words of mine?"

"Have you enemies?" asked Richelieu.

"In the first place, there is little Bonacieux."

"She is in the prison of Nantes."

"The queen has had her conveyed to a convent," said Milady. "Your Eminence will find out in what convent she is?"

"I can see nothing inconvenient in that," said the cardinal.

"I have an enemy much more to be dreaded," cried Milady. "It is he who in an encounter with your Guards decided victory in favor of the king's Musketeers; he who wounded de Wardes and caused the affair of the diamond studs to fail; he who, knowing I had Madame Bonacieux carried off, has sworn my death. I mean d'Artagnan."

"I must have," said the cardinal, "a proof of his connection with Buckingham, then I will send him to the Bastille. Ah, if it were as easy for me to get rid of my enemy—"

"Monseigneur," replied Milady, "life for life; give me one, I will give you the other."

"I don't know what you mean," replied the cardinal,"but see nothing out of the way in giving what you demand—as you tell me d'Artagnan is a libertine and a traitor."

There was a moment of silence. Athos led his companions to the other end of the room. "Hush!" he said. "I must be gone."

"You must be gone!" said Porthos. "If the cardinal asks for you, what answer can we make?"

"Tell him I am gone lookout, because certain expressions of our host have given me reason to think the road is not safe."

Porthos and Aramis resumed their places by the stovepipe.

Athos went out, in four words convinced the attendant of the necessity of a vanguard for their return, and took the road to camp.

FORTY-TWO

It was not long before the cardinal came down.

"What has become of Monseigneur Athos?" asked he.

"Monseigneur," replied Porthos, "he has gone as a scout; some words of our host made him believe the road was not safe. We are at Your Eminence's orders."

The attendant confirmed to the cardinal what the two Musketeers had said with respect to Athos. The cardinal made an approving gesture, and retraced his route.

Let us return to Athos.

When out of sight, he came back to watch the passage of the little troop, waited till the horsemen had turned the angle of the road, and returned at a gallop to the inn. He ascended the stairs with his lightest step, entered the chamber, and closed the door behind him. At the noise he made pushing the bolt, Milady turned round. On seeing his figure, mute and immovable as a statue, Milady was frightened.

"Who are you? What do you want?" cried she.

"It is certainly she!" murmured Athos. Raising his hat, he advanced toward Milady.

"The Comte de la Fère!" murmured Milady, drawing back till the wall prevented her from going any farther.

"Yes, Milady," replied Athos, "the Comte de la Fère in person, who comes from the other world for the pleasure of paying you a visit."

Milady, under the influence of inexpressible terror, sat down without uttering a word.

"You certainly are a demon sent upon the earth!" said Athos. "I thought I had crushed you, madame; but hell has resuscitated you!"

Milady hung down her head with a groan.

"Hell has given you another name, but it has neither effaced the stains from your soul nor the brand from your body. Our position is a strange one," continued Athos, laughing. "We have only lived because we believed each other dead."

"But," said Milady, in a faint voice, "what brings you back to me?"

"I wish to tell you that I have not lost sight of you. It was you who cut the diamond studs from the shoulder of the Duke of Buckingham; who had Madame Bonacieux carried off; who, thinking to pass the night with de Wardes, opened the door to Monsieur d'Artagnan; who, believing that de Wardes had deceived you, wished to have him killed by his rival; who, when this rival discovered your secret, wished to have him killed by assassins; who sent poisoned wine with a forged letter. It was you who have made an engagement with Cardinal Richelieu to cause the Duke of Buckingham to be assassinated, in exchange for the promise he has made to allow you to assassinate d'Artagnan."

Milady was livid. "You must be Satan!" cried she.

"Perhaps," said Athos. "Listen well. Assassinate the Duke of Buckingham, I care little! But do not touch a hair of d'Artagnan, or that crime shall be your last."

"Monsieur d'Artagnan has insulted me," said Milady, in a hollow tone. "Monsieur d'Artagnan shall die!"

Athos arose, drew forth a pistol, and cocked it. Milady endeavored to cry out, but could utter no more than a hoarse sound like the rattle of a wild beast.

Athos stretched out his arm so that the weapon almost touched Milady's forehead, and then, in a voice the more terrible from having the calmness of resolution, "Madame," said he, "you will deliver to me the paper the cardinal signed; or I will blow your brains out."

Milady reached her hand quickly to her bosom and drew out a paper. "Take it," said she, "and be accursed!"

Athos took the paper and read:

> *It is for the good of the state that the bearer of this has done what has been done.*
> *—Richelieu*

"I have drawn your teeth, viper," said Athos. "Bite if you can." And he left the chamber.

Athos set out across the fields, stopping occasionally to listen. In one of those halts he heard the steps of horses. He had no doubt it was the cardinal and his escort, and immediately placed himself across the road.

"That is our brave Musketeer, I think," said the cardinal. "Monsieur Athos, receive my thanks for the good guard you have kept. Gentlemen, we are arrived."

Saying these words, the cardinal saluted the three friends and took the right hand, followed by his attendant.

"Well!" said Porthos and Aramis, as soon as the cardinal was out of hearing. "He signed the paper!"

"I know," said Athos, coolly. "Here it is."

Milady, on finding the men that awaited her, made no difficulty in following them. She thought it best to discreetly accomplish her mission, then come to the cardinal and claim her vengeance.

FORTY-THREE

The next morning the Musketeers and d'Artagnan arrived at the Inn of the Parpaillot, ordered breakfast, and went into a room in which the host said they would not be disturbed.

Unfortunately, the hour was badly chosen for a private conference. Dragoons, Swiss, Guardsmen, Musketeers, and light-horsemen succeeded one another with a rapidity that agreed badly with the views of the four friends.

"D'Artagnan, tell us what sort of a night you have had," said Athos. "We will describe ours afterward."

"Ah, yes," said a light-horseman, M. de Busigny, with a glass of brandy in his hand. "I hear you gentlemen of the Guards have been in the trenches tonight."

"Have you not taken a bastion?" said a Swiss.

"Yes, monsieur," said d'Artagnan, bowing. "We introduced a barrel of powder under one of the angles, which in blowing up made a very pretty breach. As the bastion was not built yesterday, the rest of the building was badly shaken."

"What bastion is it?" asked a dragoon.

"The bastion St. Gervais," replied d'Artagnan. "We lost five men, and the Rochellais eight or ten."

"But it is probable," said the light-horseman, "that they will send pioneers this morning to repair the bastion."

"Gentlemen," said Athos, "a wager! I will bet you that my three companions and myself breakfast in the bastion St. Gervais and remain an hour, whatever the enemy do to dislodge us."

Porthos and Aramis looked at each other.

"But," said d'Artagnan, in the ear of Athos, "you are going to get us all killed."

"I take it," said M. de Busigny. "Let us fix the stake."

"You are four gentlemen," said Athos, "and we are four; an unlimited dinner for eight. Will that do?"

"Capitally," replied M. de Busigny.

"The breakfast for these gentlemen is ready," said the host. "Where are you going to eat it?"

"What matter, if you are paid for it?" said Athos, and he threw two pistoles majestically on the table.

The young men took the road to the bastion St. Gervais. As long as they were within the camp, they did not exchange one word. Once they found themselves in the open plain, d'Artagnan thought it time to demand an explanation.

"And now, my dear Athos," said he, "tell me where we are going?"

"Why, we are going to the bastion, to breakfast there."

"But why did we not breakfast at the Parpaillot?"

"Because we have very important matters to communicate, and it was impossible to talk without being annoyed by all those fellows. Here at least," said Athos, pointing to the bastion, "they will not disturb us."

"It appears to me," said d'Artagnan, "that we could have found some retired place on the seashore."

"Where we should have been seen conferring, so that the cardinal would have been informed that we were holding a council. We have made a wager, of which I defy anyone to divine the true cause. Either we shall be attacked, or not. If we are not, we shall have time to talk; if we are, we will talk just the same."

"We ought to have brought our muskets."

"You are stupid, Porthos. Why should we load ourselves with a useless burden?"

"I don't find a good musket useless in the face of an enemy."

"Well," replied Athos, "have you not heard what d'Artagnan said? In the attack last night eight or ten Frenchmen were killed, and as many Rochellais. We shall find their muskets."

"Oh, Athos!" said Aramis. "Truly you are a great man."

FORTY-FOUR

As Athos had foreseen, the bastion was only occupied by corpses.

"As there is no longer any fear of being overheard," said d'Artagnan, "I hope you are going to let me into your secret."

"The secret is," said Athos, "that I saw Milady last night." D'Artagnan was lifting a glass to his lips; but at the name his hand trembled so, he was obliged to put it down.

"I am lost," said d'Artagnan.

"Not yet," replied Athos, "for by this time she must have quit the shores of France." D'Artagnan breathed again.

"But after all," asked Porthos, "who is Milady?"

"A charming woman!" said Athos, sipping a glass of sparkling wine, "who entertained kind views toward our friend d'Artagnan. She tried to revenge herself a month ago by having him killed by musket shots, a week ago by poisoning him, and yesterday by demanding his head of the cardinal."

"Demanding my head of the cardinal?" cried d'Artagnan, pale with terror. "I may as well blow my brains out."

"That's the last folly to be committed," said Athos. "It is the only one for which there is no remedy. Approaching is a troop of about twenty men."

Swallowing the contents of his glass, Athos arose carelessly, took the musket next to him, and drew near to one of the loopholes. Porthos, Aramis, and d'Artagnan followed his example. Approaching were twenty fellows armed with pickaxes and shovels, accompanied by soldiers and a brigadier armed with muskets.

"I must confess I feel a great repugnance to fire on these civilians," said Aramis.

"Aramis is right," said Athos. Mounting on the breach, he said, bowing courteously: "Gentlemen, we are about to breakfast. We request you wait till we have finished, unless you come and drink with us to the health of the king of France."

"Take care, Athos!" cried d'Artagnan. "Don't you see they are aiming?"

"Yes, yes," said Athos, "but they are civilians, who will not hit me." Four shots were fired, and the balls flattened against the wall around Athos, but not one touched him.

Four shots replied almost instantaneously; three soldiers fell dead, and one of the pioneers was wounded. The rest of the troop took flight.

"We will go on with breakfast," said Athos.

"You were saying," said d'Artagnan, "that after having demanded my head of the cardinal, Milady quit the shores of France. Whither goes she?"

"England," said Athos, "with the view of assassinating the Duke of Buckingham. Let her do what she likes with the duke. What engaged my attention was getting from this woman a *carte blanche* that she had extorted from the cardinal, by means of which she could with impunity get rid of you and of us."

"This *carte blanche,*" said d'Artagnan, "does it remain in her hands?"

"Here it is," said Athos; and he took the paper from the pocket of his uniform. D'Artagnan read:

> *It is for the good of the state that the bearer of this has done what has been done.*
> *—Richelieu*

"That paper must be torn to pieces," said d'Artagnan, who read in it his sentence of death.

"On the contrary," said Athos. "I would not give it up if covered with as many gold pieces."

"What will she do?" asked the young man.

"Why," replied Athos, carelessly, "she will write to the cardinal that a Musketeer, named Athos, has taken her safe-conduct; she will advise him to get rid of Aramis and Porthos at the same time. Some fine morning he will arrest d'Artagnan, and send us to keep him company in the Bastille."

"Fortunately, she is far off," said Porthos. "She would worry me if she were here."

"She worries me in England as well as in France," said Athos.

"She worries me everywhere," said d'Artagnan.

"But when you held her in your power, why did you not

strangle her?" said Porthos. "The dead do not return."

"You think so, Porthos?" replied the Musketeer, with a smile that d'Artagnan alone understood.

"I have an idea," said d'Artagnan.

"To arms!" cried Athos suddenly. This time a troop advanced. "As soon as the enemy are within shot, fire upon them. If those who remain persist, allow the besiegers to get as far as the ditch, and then push down that strip of wall which keeps perpendicular by a miracle."

"Bravo!" cried Porthos. "Decidedly, Athos, you were born to be a general."

The four muskets made one report; four men fell. The shots were repeated, aimed with the same accuracy. Nevertheless, the Rochellais continued to advance.

Arrived at the foot of the bastion, there were still more than a dozen of the enemy.

"Now," said Athos, "finish them at a blow. To the wall!"

The four friends pushed with the barrels of their muskets an enormous sheet of the wall, which fell with a crash into the ditch. A cloud of dust mounted toward the sky.

"Can we have destroyed them all?" said Athos.

"No," cried Porthos, "there go three or four, limping away." The Musketeers reseated themselves.

"You had an idea," said Athos.

"I will go to England and find Buckingham," said d'Artagnan.

"You shall not, d'Artagnan," said Athos, coolly. "We are at war. What you would do amounts to treason."

"I will ask leave of absence," said Porthos. "Milady does not know me; I will get access to her and strangle her."

"For shame!" said Aramis. "Kill a woman? I have the true idea. We must inform the queen."

"Ah, yes!" said Porthos and d'Artagnan, at the same time.

"As to remitting a letter to Her Majesty," said Aramis, coloring, "I will take that upon myself. I know a clever person at Tours—"

Aramis stopped on seeing Athos smile.

"But," objected Porthos, "the queen would save Monsieur de Buckingham, but take no heed of us."

"Gentlemen," said d'Artagnan, "what Porthos says is full of sense."

"What's going on in the city yonder?" said Athos.

"The drum draws near," said d'Artagnan.

"Let it come," said Athos. "It is a quarter of an hour's journey from the city, time enough to devise a plan. My friends," pointing to the bodies under the wall of the bastion, "let us set those gentlemen up against the wall, put their hats upon their heads, and their guns in their hands."

"Oh!" cried d'Artagnan. "I comprehend."

"You comprehend?" said Porthos. "I should like to comprehend."

"Athos's idea!" cried Aramis and d'Artagnan, at the same time.

"This Milady has a brother-in-law, you told me, d'Artagnan?"

"Lord de Winter. He returned to London at the first sound of war."

"Just the man we want," said Athos. "We will have him informed that his sister-in-law is on the point of having someone assassinated, and beg him not to lose sight of her."

"Look out!" cried d'Artagnan. "It is a veritable army!"

"Faith, yes," said Athos. "See the sneaks come, without drum or trumpet."

The Musketeers had arranged a dozen bodies in the most picturesque attitudes. Some carried arms, others seemed to be taking aim, and the remainder appeared sword in hand.

"All very well," said Porthos, "but I should like to understand."

"Let us decamp first; you will understand afterward."

"My faith," said Athos, "I have nothing to say against a retreat. We bet upon one hour, and we have stayed an hour and a half. Let us be off, gentlemen!"

They heard a furious fusillade.

"What's that?" asked Porthos. "What are they firing at?"

"At the corpses," replied Athos.

"But the dead cannot return their fire."

"By the time they have found out the pleasantry, we shall be out of range."

"Oh, I comprehend now," said the astonished Porthos.

"These Rochellais are bungling fellows," said Athos. "How many have we killed of them—a dozen?"

"Or fifteen."

"How many did we crush under the wall?"

"Eight or ten."

"And in exchange for all that not even a scratch!"

The fusillade continued; but the four friends were out of reach, and the Rochellais only fired to appease their consciences.

"Here we are at the camp. They are coming to meet us. We shall be carried in triumph."

The whole camp was in motion. Nothing was heard but cries

of "Live the Musketeers! Live the Guards!" There was no end to laughter at the Rochellais. The tumult became so great that the cardinal sent his captain of the Guards to inquire.

"Well?" asked the cardinal, seeing the captain return.

"Monseigneur," replied the latter, "three Musketeers and a Guardsman laid a wager they would go and breakfast in the bastion St. Gervais; they held it for two hours against the enemy, and have killed many Rochellais."

"Did you inquire the names of those three Musketeers?"

"Messieurs Athos, Porthos, and Aramis."

"My three brave fellows!" murmured the cardinal. "And the Guardsman?"

"D'Artagnan."

"My young scapegrace. Positively, they must be on my side."

The same evening the cardinal spoke to M. de Treville, who had received the account of the adventure from the mouths of the heroes and related it to His Eminence.

"When four men are so much attached to one another," said the cardinal, "it is fair they should serve together. Take d'Artagnan into your company."

That same evening M. de Treville announced this good news to the three Musketeers. D'Artagnan was beside himself with joy. The three friends were likewise delighted.

"My faith," said d'Artagnan to Athos, "you had a triumphant idea! We have acquired glory, and were enabled to carry on a conversation of the highest importance."

"Which we can resume without anybody suspecting us, for we shall pass for cardinalists."

FORTY-FIVE

D'Artagnan would have been at the height of his wishes if he had not constantly seen Milady like a dark cloud on the horizon. There only remained three things to decide—what they should write to Milady's brother, what they should write to the clever person at Tours, and whose lackeys to carry the letters.

"To reach England"—Athos lowered his voice—"all France must be crossed. A passport must be obtained, and the party must be acquainted with English in order to ask the way to London. I think the thing very difficult."

"Not at all," cried d'Artagnan. "It would be difficult, if we write to Lord de Winter about affairs of vast importance—"

"Speak lower!" said Athos.

"—of secrets of state," continued d'Artagnan, complying. "But we only write concerning a family affair, to entreat that when Milady arrives in London he will put it out of her power to injure us."

"Let us see," said Athos, assuming a critical look.

"Monsieur and dear friend—"

"Ah, yes! 'Dear friend' to an Englishman," interrupted Athos, "well commenced!"

"Well, I will say 'monsieur.'"

"You may even say 'my lord,'" replied Athos.

"My lord, do you remember the little pasture of the Luxembourg?"

"Good! One might believe this an allusion to the queen mother! Ingenious," said Athos.

"Well, then: My lord, do you remember a certain enclosure where your life was spared?"

"My dear d'Artagnan, a man of spirit is not to be reminded of such services."

"The devil!" said d'Artagnan. "I renounce the task."

"And you do right. Handle the musket and the sword, my dear fellow; but pass the pen to Monsieur Abbé."

"So be it," said d'Artagnan. "Draw up this note, Aramis."

"I ask no better," said Aramis. "Let me be properly acquainted with the subject. I have heard that this sister-in-law was a hussy. I have obtained proof of it by listening to her conversation with the cardinal."

"Lower," said Athos.

"But," continued Aramis, "the details escape me."

D'Artagnan and Athos looked at each other. At length Athos made a sign of assent.

"This is what you have to say," said d'Artagnan. "My lord, your sister-in-law wished to have you killed that she might inherit your wealth; she could not marry your brother, being already married in France, and having been—" D'Artagnan looked at Athos.

"Repudiated by her husband," said Athos.

"Because she had been branded," continued d'Artagnan.

"Impossible!" cried Porthos. "She wanted to have her brother-in-law killed?"

"Yes."

"She was married?" asked Aramis.

"Yes."

"And her husband found she had a *fleur-de-lis* on her shoulder?" cried Porthos.

"Yes." These three yeses had been pronounced by Athos, each with a sadder intonation.

"Who has seen this *fleur-de-lis?*" inquired Aramis.

"D'Artagnan and I," replied Athos.

"Does the husband of this frightful creature still live?" said Aramis.

"I am he."

There was a moment of silence.

"This time," said Athos, breaking the silence, "d'Artagnan has given us an excellent program. The letter must be written at once."

"Be silent, I will write," said Aramis.

He took the quill, wrote, then read the following:

My lord,

The person who writes these lines had the honor of crossing swords with you in the enclosure of the rue d'Enfer. As you have declared yourself the friend of that person, he thinks it his duty to send you important information. Twice you have nearly been the victim of a relative you believe to be your heir because you are ignorant that before she contracted a marriage in England she was already married in France. But the third time, which is the present, you may succumb. Your relative left la Rochelle for England during the night. Watch her arrival, for she has great and terrible projects. If you require to know positively what she is capable of, read her past history on her left shoulder.

"That will do wonderfully," said Athos. "Lord de Winter will be upon his guard if the letter should reach him; if it falls into the hands of the cardinal, we shall not be compromised."

"But, gentlemen," said d'Artagnan, "we do not think of the queen. Let us take some heed of the welfare of Buckingham. That is the least we owe her."

"True," said Athos, "but that concerns Aramis."

"Well," replied the latter, blushing, "what must I say?"

"Oh, that's simple enough!" replied Athos. "Write a letter for that clever personage who lives at Tours."

Aramis wrote the following lines.

My dear cousin,

His Eminence, the cardinal, whom God preserve for the happiness of France, is on the point of putting an end to the rebellion of la Rochelle. It is probable that the English fleet will never even arrive in sight of the place. I am certain M. de Buckingham will be prevented from setting out by some great event. His Eminence would extinguish the sun if the sun incommoded him. I have dreamed that the unlucky

Englishman was dead. I cannot recollect whether it was by steel or by poison; only I have dreamed he was dead, and you know my dreams never deceive me. Be assured, then, of seeing me soon return.

"Capital!" cried Athos. "You are the king of poets, dear Aramis."

"Now," said Aramis, "only my valet can carry this letter to Tours."

"Very well," said d'Artagnan. "If arrangements at Tours are yours, Aramis, those of London are mine. I request my valet may be chosen."

The next morning, as his valet was mounting his horse, d'Artagnan, who felt at heart a partiality for the duke, took him aside.

"Listen," said he. "When you have given the letter to Lord de Winter, say to him: 'Watch over Lord Buckingham, for they wish to assassinate him.'"

Aramis's valet set out the next day for Tours.

The four friends, during these two absences, had the eye on the watch and the ear on the hark. More than once an involuntary trembling seized them when called upon for some unexpected service. Milady was a phantom that did not allow them to sleep quietly.

On the morning of the eighth day, Aramis's valet entered as the friends were sitting down to breakfast, saying, as had been agreed upon: "Monsieur Aramis, the answer from your cousin."

Aramis, blushing, took the letter, read, and passed it to Athos.

Athos read aloud:

My cousin,
My sister and I are skillful in interpreting dreams, and even entertain great fear of them; but of yours it may be said, I hope, every dream is an illusion. Adieu! Take care of yourself, and act so that we may hear you spoken of.

As they awaited their second messenger, D'Artagnan forgot the necessary slowness of navigation; he exaggerated to himself the power of Milady. At the least noise, he imagined himself about to be arrested. This anxiety became so great that it extended to Aramis and Porthos. Athos alone remained unmoved.

"You are children," said Athos, "to let a woman terrify you so! What does it amount to? To be imprisoned. We should be taken out of prison. To be decapitated? Why, every day in the trenches we risk worse—I am convinced a surgeon would give us more pain cutting off a thigh than an executioner cutting off a head. Wait quietly."

"If he does not come?" said d'Artagnan.

"If he does not come, it will be because he has been delayed. Sit down and drink. Nothing makes the future look so bright as surveying it through a glass."

"I am tired of fearing that the wine may come from Milady's cellar," replied d'Artagnan.

At half past seven the retreat was sounded.

Athos went out, followed by d'Artagnan. Aramis came behind, giving his arm to Porthos. A shadow appeared in the darkness, and a well-known voice said, "Monsieur, I have brought your cloak; it is chilly this evening."

At the same time d'Artagnan felt a note slipped into his hand.

D'Artagnan felt an inclination to embrace his valet, but feared lest this mark of affection might appear extraordinary to passersby, and restrained himself.

"I have the note," said he to his friends.

"That's well," said Athos, "let us go home and read it."

At length they reached the tent, and d'Artagnan, with a trembling hand, opened the letter.

It contained half a line, in a hand perfectly British:

Thank you; be easy.

Athos took the letter, set fire to the paper, and did not let go till it was reduced to a cinder.

FORTY-SIX

Milady entered the English port in triumph. All the city was agitated by an extraordinary movement. Four large vessels, recently built, had just been launched. At the end of the jetty, his clothes glittering with diamonds and precious stones, Buckingham was seen surrounded by a staff almost as brilliant.

As Milady's vessel drew near, a little cutter, formidably armed, approached and dropped into the sea a boat, which directed its course to the ladder. This boat contained an officer, a mate, and eight rowers. The officer went on board, where he was received with all the deference inspired by the uniform.

The officer inquired the point of the brig's departure, its route, and its landings. Then the officer began to review the people, stopping when he came to Milady. He said a few words to the captain, and the vessel resumed its course, still escorted by the little cutter.

When they entered the port, it was already night. The fog

increased the darkness, and the air they breathed was heavy, damp, and cold. Milady shivered in spite of herself.

"Who are you, sir," asked she, "who troubles yourself on my account? Is it the custom for the officers in the English navy to place themselves at the service of their female compatriots?"

"Madame, it is the custom that in time of war foreigners should be conducted to particular houses, in order that they may remain under the eye of the government." These words were pronounced with exact politeness.

"But I am not a foreigner, sir," said she. "My name is Lady Clarik—"

"This measure is general, madame; you will seek in vain to evade it."

Accepting the hand of the officer, she began the descent to the boat. In five minutes they gained the land. A carriage was waiting.

"Is this carriage for us?" asked Milady.

"Yes, madame," replied the officer.

"The house, then, is far away?"

"At the other end of the town."

"Very well," said Milady, and entered the carriage. The officer took his place and shut the door. Immediately the coachman set off at a rapid pace.

At the end of a quarter of an hour, Milady leaned forward to see whither she was being conducted. Houses were no longer to be seen; trees appeared in the darkness like great black phantoms chasing one another. Milady shuddered.

"We are no longer in the city, sir," said she.

The young officer preserved silence.

"I will go no farther unless you tell me whither you are taking me."

This threat brought no reply.

"Oh, this is too much," cried Milady. "Help! Help!"

The carriage continued to roll on. The young man remained immovable.

Milady tried to open the door in order to throw herself out.

"Take care, madame," said the young man, coolly. "You will kill yourself in jumping."

Milady reseated herself. The officer looked at her, and the artful creature at once collected her features and said: "In the name of heaven, sir, tell me if it is to you I am to attribute the violence that is done me?"

"No violence will be offered to you, madame. What happens is the result of a very simple measure which we are obliged to adopt with all who land in England."

"Then you have no cause of hatred against me?"

"None, I swear."

There was so much serenity in the voice of the young man that Milady felt reassured.

At length, the carriage stopped before an isolated castle. Milady could hear the noise of the sea dashing against some steep cliff. The door of the carriage was opened; the young man sprang out and presented his hand to Milady, who alighted with tolerable calmness.

"Then I am a prisoner," said Milady, looking around and bringing back her eyes with a gracious smile to the young officer. "But I feel assured it will not be for long."

The officer, with the same calm politeness, invited his prisoner to enter. She took his arm, and passed with him under a low arched door, which led to a stone staircase. They then came to a massive door, which after the introduction into the lock of a key that the young man carried with him turned heavily upon its hinges, and disclosed the chamber destined for Milady.

It was a chamber whose furniture was appropriate for a prisoner or a free man; bars at the windows decided the question in favor of the prison.

All Milady's strength of mind abandoned her; she sank into a large easy chair, head lowered, expecting every instant to see a judge enter to interrogate her. But no one entered.

At length Milady could hold out no longer. "In the name of heaven, sir," cried she, "if I am a prisoner, what crime have I committed?"

"I received orders to conduct you to this castle. The rest concerns another person."

"Who is that other person?" asked Milady.

At the moment a jingling of spurs was heard on the stairs.

"He is here, madame," said the officer, drawing himself up in an attitude of respect.

A man appeared on the threshold. He carried a sword and flourished a handkerchief in his hand. As he advanced, Milady involuntarily drew back. Then when she had no longer any doubt, she cried, "What, my brother, is it you?"

"Yes, fair lady!" replied Lord de Winter, making a bow. "It is I. Let us sit down and chat quietly, as brother and sister ought to do."

Seeing that the young officer was waiting for his orders, he said. "All is well; leave us, Mr. Felton."

FORTY-SEVEN

Milady knew her brother-in-law to be by no means remarkable for his skill in intrigues. How had he discovered her arrival? Why did he detain her?

Athos had dropped some words that proved that the conversation she had had with the cardinal had fallen into outside ears, but she could not suppose that he had dug a countermine so promptly. Buckingham might have guessed that it was she who had cut off the two studs, and avenged that little treachery. She congratulated herself upon having fallen into the hands of her brother-in-law, with whom she reckoned she could deal easily.

"Yes, let us chat, brother," said she, with cheerfulness.

"You decided to come to England," said Lord de Winter, "in spite of the resolutions you expressed in Paris never to set foot on British ground?"

Milady replied with another question. "How are you aware of the day, the hour, and the port at which I should arrive?"

"Tell me, my dear sister," replied he, "what makes you come to England?"

"I come to see you," replied Milady, without knowing how she aggravated the suspicions of her brother-in-law.

"To see me?" said de Winter. "What tenderness!"

"Am I not your nearest relative?" demanded Milady, with touching ingenuousness.

"And my only heir?" said Lord de Winter, fixing his eyes on those of Milady.

Milady could not help starting. "I do not understand, my lord," said she, in order to gain time. "Is there any secret meaning concealed beneath your words?"

"My God, no!" said Lord de Winter, with apparent good nature. "You wish to see me, and you come to England. In order to spare you all the fatigues of landing, I send one of my officers to bring you here. What is there astonishing in all this?"

"What I think astonishing is that you should expect my coming."

"The simplest thing in the world, my sister. The captain of your vessel sent forward the register of his voyagers. I am commandant of the port. They brought me that book."

"My brother," continued she, "was that Lord Buckingham whom I saw on the jetty this evening?"

"Ah, the sight of him struck you," replied Lord de Winter. "You came from a country where he must be very much talked of. I know he greatly engages the attention of your friend the cardinal."

"My friend the cardinal!" cried Milady, seeing that Lord de Winter seemed well instructed.

"Is he not your friend?" replied the baron, negligently. "Let us not depart from the sentimental turn our conversation had taken. You came to see me?"

"Yes."

"Well, we shall see each other every day."

"Am I to remain here eternally?" demanded Milady, with a certain terror.

"Do you find yourself badly lodged, sister? Tell me on what footing your household was established by your first husband, and I will arrange one similar."

"My first husband!" cried Milady.

"Yes, your French husband. If you have forgotten, I can write to him and he will send me information."

A cold sweat burst from the brow of Milady. "Indeed, sir," she said, "you must be either drunk or mad. Leave the room, and send me a woman."

"Women are indiscreet, my sister. Cannot I serve you as a waiting maid? All our secrets will remain in the family."

"Insolent!" cried Milady, and bounded toward the baron, who awaited her attack with one hand on the hilt of his sword.

"Come!" said he. "I know you are accustomed to assassinate people; but I shall defend myself."

"You are cowardly enough to lift your hand against a woman," said Milady.

"I have an excuse, for mine would not be the first hand placed upon you."

And the baron pointed, with an accusing gesture, to the left shoulder of Milady.

Milady uttered a shriek, and retreated to a corner of the room.

"Oh, growl as much as you please," cried Lord de Winter, "but don't try to bite. I have judges who will quickly dispose of a woman so shameless as to glide, a bigamist, into the bed of my brother. I can understand that it would be very agreeable to be my heir; but if you kill me, not a penny will pass into your hands. Were you not already rich enough? Could you not stop your fatal career? In ten days I shall set out for la Rochelle with the army; on the eve of my departure a vessel will convey you to our colonies in the south. Be assured that you shall be accompanied by one who will blow your brains out at your first attempt to return."

Milady listened with attention.

"At present," continued Lord de Winter, "you remain in this castle. The walls are thick, the doors strong, and the bars solid. A step, a word, on your part, denoting an effort to escape, and you are to be fired upon. You are saying to yourself: 'Ten days? Before that is expired some idea will occur to me. I shall be away from here.' Try it!"

Milady, finding her thoughts betrayed, dug her nails into her flesh to subdue every expression except agony.

Lord de Winter continued: "The officer who commands here in my absence you have seen. Could a statue of marble have been more impassive? You have already tried the power of your seductions upon many men; I give you leave to try them upon this one."

He went toward the door and opened it.

"Call Mr. Felton," said he.

A slow and regular step was heard. The young lieutenant stopped at the threshold.

"Come in, John," said Lord de Winter, "and shut the door."

The young officer entered.

"Look at this woman," said the baron. "She is young and beautiful. She is a monster guilty of many crimes. Her voice prejudices hearers in her favor; her beauty serves as bait to her victims; her body even pays what she promises. She will try to seduce you. I have extricated you from misery, Felton; I saved your life. This woman has come into England to conspire against my life. I say to you: Felton, guard me, and yourself, against her!"

"My lord," said the young officer, "all shall be done as you desire."

"She is not to leave this chamber," continued the baron. "She is to speak to no one. Now, madame, make your peace with God, for you are judged by men!" Lord de Winter went out, making a sign to Felton, who followed him.

Milady remained for some minutes in the same position, for they might be examining her through the keyhole; she then ran to the door to listen, and returning to her armchair, reflected.

FORTY-EIGHT

Meanwhile, the cardinal looked anxiously for news from England. He knew that, whether acting for or against him, his emissary would not remain motionless without great impediments; but whence did these impediments arise? Yet he reckoned on Milady. He had divined in the past of this woman terrible things and felt she could look only to himself for a support superior to the danger that threatened her.

During this time, the royal army led a joyous life. To take spies and hang them, to make hazardous expeditions, to imagine wild plans and execute them coolly—such were the pastimes that made the army find these days short which were long to the Rochellais, prey to famine and anxiety, and to the cardinal, who blockaded them closely.

One day, the cardinal strolled along the beach with two lackeys. He perceived, reclining on the sand, four men surrounded by empty bottles. They were our Musketeers, preparing to listen to a letter.

The cardinal was in low spirits; nothing increased his depression so much as gaiety in others. He alighted from his horse and went toward these merry companions, hoping to catch their conversation. At ten paces he recognized the talkative Gascon; he did not doubt that the others were Athos, Porthos, and Aramis.

He had not been able to catch more than a few syllables before the Musketeers were on their feet, saluting with respect.

"If we are so fortunate as to have some duty to perform for Your Eminence, we are ready to obey. Your Eminence may perceive," declared Athos, "that we have not come out without our arms."

And he showed the cardinal, with his finger, four muskets.

The cardinal bit his mustache, and even his lips a little. "Do you know what you look like?" he said. "Conspirators."

"Monseigneur," said Athos, "we do conspire, against the Rochellais."

"Ah, you gentlemen!" replied the cardinal, knitting his brow. "Many unknown things might be found in your brains, if we could read them as you read that letter which you concealed when you saw me coming."

The color mounted to the face of Athos. "One might think you suspected us, monseigneur. Your Eminence has but to question us, and we are ready to reply."

"What was that letter you were about to read, Monsieur Aramis?"

"A woman's letter, monseigneur."

"I see," said the cardinal. "We must be discreet with this sort of letter."

He turned as if to give an order. Athos saw the movement; he made a step toward the muskets. The cardinalists were three; the Musketeers, four. By one of those rapid turns which he always had at command, all the cardinal's anger faded away into a smile.

"Well!" said he. "You are brave young men, proud in daylight, faithful in darkness. We can find no fault with you for watching over yourselves, when you watch so carefully over others. If there were any danger to be apprehended on the road, I would request you accompany me; as there is none, finish your bottles, your game, and your letter. Adieu, gentlemen!"

Remounting his horse, he saluted them, and rode away.

The four young men looked at one another with terror, for they perceived that the cardinal went away with rage in his heart.

"Would you have given up the letter, Aramis?" said d'Artagnan.

"If he insisted upon the letter being given up," said Aramis, "I would have presented it with one hand, and with the other run my sword through his body."

"My dear Aramis, nevertheless we were in the wrong."

"How, in the wrong?" said Athos. "The cardinal fancies the world belongs to him. You are in love with a woman whom he has shut up, and you wish to get her out of his hands. That's a match you are playing; this letter is your game. Why should you expose your game to your adversary?"

"Very sensible, Athos," said d'Artagnan.

"Let Aramis resume the letter."

"You had only read a line or two," said d'Artagnan. "Read the letter again from the commencement."

"Willingly," said Aramis.

My dear cousin,

I think I shall set out for Bethune, where my sister has placed our little servant in the convent of the Carmelites; this poor child is quite resigned, as she knows she cannot live elsewhere without her soul being in danger. Nevertheless, if affairs are arranged as we hope they will be, I believe she will return to those she regrets, particularly as she knows they are thinking of her. My sister thanks you for your remembrance. She has experienced much anxiety; but is now a little reassured, having sent her secretary away in order that nothing may happen unexpectedly.

Adieu, my dear cousin. I embrace you.

"Oh, what I owe you, Aramis!" said d'Artagnan. "Dear Constance! She is in safety; she is at Bethune!"

FORTY-NINE

CAPTIVITY: THE FIRST DAY

Let us return to Milady. D'Artagnan has deceived her in love, humbled her in pride, thwarted her in ambition, and now deprives her of liberty. D'Artagnan turned aside the tempest with which Richelieu threatened Buckingham. D'Artagnan passed himself upon her as de Wardes. D'Artagnan knows that terrible secret that she has sworn no one shall know without dying. The moment she obtained from Richelieu a *carte blanche* to take vengeance, this precious paper is torn from her hands, and d'Artagnan holds her prisoner.

How many magnificent projects of vengeance she conceives against Mme Bonacieux, against Buckingham, but above all against d'Artagnan.

"Violence is the proof of weakness," she said. "Let me fight like a woman."

As if to render an account of the changes she could place upon her countenance, she made it take all expressions from that of passionate anger to that of the sweetest smile. Then her hair assumed, under her skillful hands, all the undulations she thought might assist the charms of her face. At length she murmured, "Come, nothing is lost; I am still beautiful."

It was nearly eight o'clock in the evening. They could not long delay bringing her a repast. A light appeared under the door. Milady threw herself into the armchair, her head back, her hair disheveled, her bosom half-bare beneath her lace.

The bolts were drawn. Steps sounded in the chamber.

"Place that table there," said the voice of Felton. "Bring lights. Ah! She is asleep. When she wakes she can sup."

"Lieutenant," said a soldier, "this woman is not asleep. She has fainted."

"You are right," said Felton, looking at Milady. "Go tell Lord de Winter."

The soldier went out. Felton sat down upon an armchair. Milady possessed that art of looking through her eyelashes without appearing to open the lids. She looked at Felton for nearly ten minutes, and he never turned round once.

She raised her head, opened her eyes, and sighed deeply. At this sigh Felton turned round.

"Ah, you are awake, madame," he said. "If you want anything, you can ring."

"How I have suffered!" said Milady, in that harmonious voice that charmed all whom she wished to destroy. And she assumed a still more graceful and abandoned position.

Felton arose. "You will be served three times a day," said he. "At nine o'clock, at one o'clock, and at eight."

"Am I to remain alone in this dismal chamber?" asked Milady.

"A woman of the neighborhood has been sent for, who will

return as often as you desire."

Felton made a slight bow, and directed his steps toward the door. As he was about to go out, Lord de Winter appeared in the corridor.

"Is this corpse come to life already?" said he, jeeringly. "Felton, did you not perceive that the first act was being performed of a comedy?"

"I thought so, my lord," said Felton, "but I wish to pay the prisoner the attention that every man of gentle birth owes to a woman, if not on her account, at least on my own."

"So," replied de Winter, laughing, "that beautiful hair, that white skin, that languishing look, have not yet seduced you?"

"No, my lord," replied the impassive young man. "It requires more than the coquetry of a woman to corrupt me."

"In that case, my brave lieutenant, let us leave Milady. Be easy! The second act of the comedy will not delay its steps after the first."

At these words Lord de Winter led Felton out, laughing.

"Oh, I will be a match for you!" murmured Milady, between her teeth.

"By the way," resumed de Winter, stopping at the threshold, "you must not, Milady, let this take away your appetite. I have a very good cook, and he is not to be my heir; I have perfect confidence in him. Adieu, dear sister!"

This was all that Milady could endure. The moment she was alone, a fit of despair seized her. She cast her eyes upon the table, saw the glittering of a knife, and clutched it; but the blade was round, and of flexible silver.

A burst of laughter resounded, and the door reopened.

"Ha!" cried Lord de Winter. "That knife was for you, my lad; she would have killed you. If I had listened to you, the knife would have been pointed and of steel. She would have cut your throat, and everybody else's."

In fact, Milady still held the harmless weapon in her clenched hand.

"You were right, my lord," said Felton, with a tone of disgust, "and I was wrong."

Both left the room. Milady listened as their steps died away.

"I am lost," murmured she. "I am in the power of men upon whom I have no more influence than upon statues of bronze. It is impossible that this should end as they have decreed!"

Milady ate, drank a little wine, and felt her resolution return. Before she went to bed she pondered the words, the steps, the gestures, and even the silence of her interlocutors; the result was that Felton appeared the more vulnerable of her persecutors.

"If I had listened to you," Lord de Winter had said. Felton had spoken in her favor.

"Weak or strong," repeated Milady, "that man has a spark of pity in his soul; of that spark I will make a flame that shall devour him."

And Milady fell asleep with a smile upon her lips.

FIFTY

Milady dreamed she was present at d'Artagnan's execution; it was the sight of his blood that spread that charming smile upon her lips.

In the morning, she stayed in bed. Felton brought the woman of whom he had spoken the evening before. Milady was pale. "I am in a fever," said she. "All I ask is permission to remain abed."

"Go and fetch Lord de Winter," said Felton.

"Oh, no!" cried Milady. "Do not call him. I am well." Turning her beautiful head round upon her pillow, she burst into tears. Felton surveyed her, then went out. The woman followed, and Lord de Winter did not appear.

"I begin to see my way," murmured Milady.

Two hours passed.

"Now the malady should be over," said she. "Let me obtain some success this very day."

In the morning they had brought her breakfast. They could not long delay coming to clear the table, and Felton would reappear.

Milady was not deceived. Felton reappeared, and made a sign that the table should be carried out of the room. He held a book in his hand.

Milady, reclining in an armchair near the chimney, beautiful, pale, and resigned, looked like a holy virgin awaiting martyrdom.

Felton said, "Lord de Winter, a Catholic like yourself, madame, has consented that you should read every day your Mass; here is a book which contains the ritual."

At the manner in which Felton laid the book upon the table, Milady looked attentively at the officer. By that plain arrangement of the hair, by that costume of extreme simplicity, she recognized one of those gloomy Puritans. With the rapidity of intelligence peculiar to her, this reply presented itself to her lips:

"I?" said she, with an accent of disdain. "Lord de Winter knows that I am not of his religion!"

"Of what religion are you, madame?" asked Felton, with astonishment.

"I will tell it," cried Milady, with feigned exultation, "on the day when I shall have suffered sufficiently for my faith."

Felton took the book and retired pensively.

Lord de Winter came toward five o'clock in the evening. "It appears," said the baron, seating himself, "we have made a little apostasy!"

"What do you mean, sir!"

"Since we last met you have changed your religion. You have not by chance married a Protestant for a third husband, have you?"

"Explain yourself, my lord," replied the prisoner. "Though I hear your words, I do not understand them."

"Then you have no religion at all; I like that best," replied Lord de Winter, laughing.

"Oh, you need not avow religious indifference, my lord; your debaucheries vouch for it."

"What, you talk of debaucheries! You are shameless!"

"You only speak thus because you are overheard," coolly replied Milady. "You wish to interest your jailers against me."

"My jailers! The comedy of yesterday turns to a tragedy this evening. Calm yourself, Madame Puritan."

And Lord de Winter retired.

Felton was indeed behind the door, and had not lost one word of this scene. Two hours passed away. Milady's supper was brought in, and she was found saying her prayers—prayers she had learned of a servant of her second husband, a most austere Puritan. Felton made a sign that she should not be disturbed, and went out quietly.

Milady knew she might be watched, so she continued her prayers to the end. She arose, came to the table, ate little, and drank only water.

An hour after, her table was cleared; this time Felton did not accompany the soldiers. He feared, then, to see her too often. She turned toward the wall to smile—for there was in this smile such triumph that it would have betrayed her.

She allowed half an hour to pass away; and with her pure, harmonious voice, began the psalm then in great favor with the Puritans:

"Thou leavest thy servants, Lord,
To see if they be strong;
But soon thou dost afford
Thy hand to lead them on."

Her voice gave to the unpolished poetry of these psalms a magic that the most exalted Puritans rarely found in the songs of their brethren. Felton opened the door quickly; his eye almost wild.

"Why do you sing thus?" said he.

"Your pardon, sir," said Milady. "I forgot that my songs are out of place in this castle."

Milady was so beautiful that Felton fancied he beheld the angel whom he had heard.

"I will be silent," said Milady, casting down her eyes with all the resignation she could impress upon her manner.

"No, no, madame," said Felton. "Only do not sing so loud, particularly at night." Feeling that he could not long maintain his severity, Felton rushed from the room.

FIFTY-ONE

Felton must be made to speak, in order that he might be spoken to—Milady knew that her greatest seduction was in her voice. With Lord de Winter her plan of conduct was easier. To remain silent and dignified, from time to time to irritate him by affected disdain, to provoke him to threats and violence to contrast with her own resignation. Felton would see all.

In the morning, Milady allowed Felton to preside over the preparations for breakfast without a word. Toward midday, Lord de Winter entered.

Milady pretended not to hear the door.

"Ah!" said Lord de Winter. "We are now playing melancholy? You would like to be at liberty on that beach! Patience! In four days' time the shore will be beneath your feet—in four days England will be relieved of you."

Milady folded her hands. "Lord," said she, "pardon this man."

"Pray!" cried the baron. "Your prayer is more generous from

your being in the power of a man who will never pardon you!" and he went out.

At the moment he went out a piercing glance darted through the opening of the door, and she perceived Felton. Then she began to pray.

"My God!" said she. "Give me strength to suffer."

The door opened gently; the beautiful supplicant pretended not to hear the noise, and continued:

"God of goodness! Wilt thou allow the frightful projects of this man to be accomplished?"

Then she pretended to hear Felton's steps and blushed, as if ashamed of being surprised on her knees.

"I do not like to disturb those who pray, madame," said Felton.

"How do you know I was praying, sir?" said Milady, in a voice broken by sobs. "I was not praying."

"Do you think, madame," replied Felton, "I assume the right of preventing a creature from prostrating herself before her Creator? The guilty are sacred at the feet of God!"

"Guilty?" said Milady, with a smile. "Say I am condemned, sir; God sometimes permits the innocent to be condemned."

"Were you innocent," replied Felton, "I would aid you with my prayers."

"I can hold out no longer," cried Milady, throwing herself at his feet. "I ask you one favor; if you grant it, I will bless you in this world and in the next."

"Speak to the master, madame," said Felton. "I am neither charged with the power of pardoning nor punishing. If you have merited this shame, you must submit to it as an offering to God."

"You think I speak of imprisonment or death. Of what consequence to me is imprisonment or death?"

"I no longer understand you, madame," said Felton.

"You are ignorant of Lord de Winter's designs upon me? He conceals them too little for you not to divine them."

"I seek to divine nothing, madame."

"Then," cried Milady, "you are not his accomplice; you do not know that he destines me to a disgrace which all the punishments of the world cannot equal?"

"You are deceived, madame," said Felton, blushing. "Lord de Winter is not capable of such a crime."

"Good," said Milady to herself. "Without thinking what it is, he calls it a crime!" Then aloud, "The friend of *that wretch* is capable of everything."

"Whom?" asked Felton.

"Are there in England two men to whom such an epithet can be applied?"

"You mean the Duke of Buckingham?" asked Felton, whose looks became excited.

"I could not have thought that there was an Englishman in all England who would have required so long an explanation to make him understand of whom I was speaking," replied Milady.

"The hand of the Lord is stretched over him," said Felton. "He will not escape the chastisement he deserves."

Felton expressed the feeling that all the English had declared toward him whom the Catholics called the debauchee, and the Puritans simply Satan.

"Do you know him, then?" asked Felton.

"At length he interrogates me!" said Milady to herself, at the height of joy. "Know him? To my eternal misfortune!" And Milady twisted her arms in a paroxysm of grief. "Sir," cried she, "that knife, which the baron deprived me of! Give it to me for a minute only! Only one minute, and you will have saved my honor!"

"To kill yourself?" cried Felton, with terror.

"I have told my secret," murmured Milady, allowing herself to sink to the ground. "I am lost!"

Felton remained standing, undecided.

"He still doubts," thought Milady. "I have not been earnest enough."

Someone was heard in the corridor; Milady recognized the step of Lord de Winter. She became silent, applying, with a gesture of infinite terror, her beautiful hand to Felton's mouth.

Felton gently repulsed Milady, and she sank into a chair.

Lord de Winter passed before the door without stopping, and the noise of his footsteps died away.

Felton remained some instants listening; then, when the sound was quite extinct, breathed like a man awaking from a dream, and rushed out of the apartment.

"Ah!" said Milady, listening to Felton's steps withdraw in a direction opposite to those of Lord de Winter. "At length you are mine!" Then her brow darkened. "If he tells the baron," said she, "I am lost—the baron knows I shall not kill myself, will place me before him with a knife in my hand, and he will discover this despair is but acted."

She stood before the glass and regarded herself; never had she appeared more beautiful.

"Oh, yes," said she, smiling, "but he won't tell him!"

In the evening Lord de Winter accompanied the supper.

"Sir," said Milady, "could you not spare me the increase of torture which your visits cause me?"

"How, dear sister!" said Lord de Winter. "Did you not come to England for the pleasure of seeing me? Besides, my visit has a motive."

Lord de Winter took a paper out of his pocket. "Here," said he, "I want to show you the passport which I have drawn up." He read: "'Order to conduct—' The name is blank," interrupted Lord de Winter. "If you have any preference, if it be not within a thousand leagues of London, attention will be paid.

"'Order to conduct to—the person named Charlotte Backson, branded by the justice of the kingdom of France, but liberated after chastisement. She is to dwell in this place without going more than three leagues from it.

"'In case of any attempt to escape, the penalty of death is to be applied. She will receive five shillings per day for lodging and food.'"

"That order does not concern me," replied Milady, coldly. "It bears another name than mine."

"Have you a name?"

"I bear that of your brother."

"My brother is only your second husband; your first is still living. Tell me his name, and I will put it in the place of Charlotte Backson. No?"

Milady remained silent. She thought that Lord de Winter had hastened her departure; that she was condemned to set off that very evening. Then she perceived that no signature was attached to the order. The joy she felt at this discovery was so great she could not conceal it.

"Yes," said Lord de Winter, "you look for the signature, and you say: 'All is not lost, that order is not signed.' Tomorrow this order will be sent to the Duke of Buckingham. The day after tomorrow it will return; four-and-twenty hours afterward it will be carried into execution."

"This abuse of power, this exile under a fictitious name, is infamous!"

"Would you like better to be hanged in your true name, Milady? You know the English laws are inexorable on the abuse of marriage."

Milady became as pale as a corpse.

"Oh, I see you prefer exile. You are not wrong after all, life is sweet. That's the reason why I take care you shall not deprive me of mine. And now, madame, *au revoir*!"

Lord de Winter saluted her ironically, and went out.

Milady breathed again. She had four days, sufficient to complete the seduction of Felton. A terrible idea rushed into her mind: Lord de Winter would send Felton to get the order signed. In that case Felton would escape her.

As she would not appear agitated, she placed herself at the table and ate. Soon she heard lighter steps.

"It is he," said she. And she began the religious chant that had excited Felton the evening before. But the door remained shut. After she had finished her song, Milady heard a profound sigh. Then steps withdrew, as if with regret.

FIFTY-TWO

CAPTIVITY: THE FOURTH DAY

The next day, Felton found Milady standing upon a chair, holding a cord of torn handkerchiefs twisted into a rope. As Felton entered, Milady leaped to the ground. He advanced slowly, and taking an end of the rope, "What is this, madame?" he asked coldly.

"Nothing," said Milady, smiling with that painful expression that she knew how to give her smile. "I had ennui, and amused myself with twisting that rope."

Felton turned his eyes toward the wall and perceived a gilt-headed screw, fixed in the wall for the purpose of hanging up clothes or weapons. He started.

"Do not question me," said the prisoner. "You know that true Christians are forbidden to lie."

"I will tell you what you were doing; you were going to complete the fatal project you cherish. Remember, madame, our God condemns suicide."

"When God sees one of his creatures persecuted unjustly,

Felton found Milady standing upon a chair,
holding a cord of torn handkerchiefs.

placed between suicide and dishonor," replied Milady, "God pardons suicide, for it becomes martyrdom."

"Explain yourself."

"That I may relate my misfortunes for you to treat them as fables? No, sir. Besides, of what importance is the death of a condemned wretch? Provided you produce a carcass, they will require no more of you; perhaps you will even have a double reward."

"You suppose that I would accept the price of your life?" cried Felton. "In a few days your life, madame, will no longer be under my care, and," added he, with a sigh, "then you can do what you will with it."

"So," cried Milady, "you ask only that you not be annoyed by my death! Cruel enough, if I am guilty; but what name will the Lord give it, if I am innocent? Do you believe that at the Last Judgment God will separate blind executioners from iniquitous judges? You are not willing that I should kill my body, but are the agent of him who would kill my soul."

"I repeat to you," replied Felton, in great emotion, "no danger threatens you; I will answer for Lord de Winter as for myself."

"Dunce," cried Milady, "who dares to answer for another man, when those most after God's own heart hesitate to answer for themselves."

"Impossible, madame," murmured Felton, who felt the justness of this argument. "A prisoner, you will not recover your liberty through me; living, you will not lose your life through me."

"Yes," cried Milady, "but I shall lose that which is much dearer to me than life. I shall lose my honor, Felton; I make you responsible for my shame."

This time Felton could not resist. To see this woman, so beautiful, overcome with grief; to resist the ascendancy of grief and beauty—it was too much.

Milady felt the flame of opposing passions burning in the veins of the young fanatic. As a skillful general, seeing the enemy ready to surrender, marches toward him with a victory cry, she rose, beautiful as an antique priestess, her throat uncovered, her hair disheveled, and went toward him, crying out in her melodious voice: "Thy God shall teach thee to repent!"

Felton stood like one petrified.

"Art thou an angel or a demon?" cried he.

"I am neither, Felton; I am a sister of thy faith."

"Yes!" said Felton. "I believe."

"You believe, and yet you deliver me up to him who defiles the world with his debaucheries—to that infamous Duke of Buckingham!"

"I deliver you up to Buckingham?"

"They have eyes," cried Milady, "but they see not; ears, but they hear not."

"Yes!" said Felton, passing his hands over his brow. "I recognize the voice which speaks to me in my dreams; I recognize the features of the angel who appears to me, crying: 'Strike, save England, save thyself!'"

A flash of terrible joy gleamed from the eyes of Milady.

Felton started as if it revealed the abysses of this woman's heart. Milady was not a woman to misunderstand this hesitation. As if the weakness of the woman overpowered the enthusiasm of the fanatic, she said: "The sword of the eternal is too heavy for my arm. Allow me to take refuge in martyrdom—my last sigh shall be a blessing for my preserver."

"Alas!" said Felton. "You must have committed great iniquities for Lord de Winter to pursue you thus."

"They have eyes," repeated Milady, with an accent of indescribable grief, "but see not; ears, but they hear not."

"Speak, then!" cried the young officer.

"Confide my shame," cried Milady, with the blush of modesty. "I could not!"

"To a brother?" said Felton.

Milady looked at him with an expression that the young man took for doubt but was nothing but observation. At this moment the steps of Lord de Winter were heard; this time he did not content himself with passing. The door opened. Felton drew back quickly, and when Lord de Winter entered, he was several paces from the prisoner.

The baron sent a scrutinizing glance from Milady to the young officer. "You have been here a long time, John," said he. "Has this woman been relating her crimes to you?"

Milady felt she was lost if she did not come to the assistance of the disconcerted Puritan.

"You fear your prisoner should escape!" said she. "Ask your worthy jailer what favor I solicited of him."

"A knife, which she would return to me a minute after she had received it," replied Felton.

"There is someone, then, concealed here whose throat this amiable lady is desirous of cutting," said de Winter, in a contemptuous tone.

"There is myself," replied Milady.

"I have given you the choice between America and the gallows at Tyburn," replied Lord de Winter. "Choose Tyburn, madame. Believe me, the cord is more certain than the knife."

Felton grew pale, remembering that at the moment he entered Milady had a rope in her hand.

"Mistrust yourself, John," said Lord de Winter. "In three days we shall be delivered from this creature."

The baron took the young officer by the arm and turned his head over his shoulder, so as not to lose sight of Milady till he was gone out.

"Well," said the prisoner, when the door was shut, "de Winter has changed his usual stupidity into prudence. Felton hesitates. Ah, he is not a man like that cursed d'Artagnan. A Puritan only adores virgins by clasping his hands. A Musketeer loves women by clasping his arms round them."

Milady feared the day would pass without her seeing Felton again. At last, the door opened. The young man advanced into the chamber, making a sign to Milady to be silent.

"The baron has related a frightful story to me," he said in a low voice. "Either you are a demon, or he is a monster. I have known you four days; I have loved him four years. Convince me."

"I am lost," said she. "Do not be lost with me."

"I came to entreat you to make no attempt upon your life till you have seen me again. If, when you have seen me again, you persist—I will give you the weapon you desire."

"I will wait," said Milady.

Felton darted out of the room and shut the door.

As for Milady, she returned to her place with a smile of contempt.

FIFTY-THREE

Milady knew she had only two days left. She should certainly return from her exile; but how long might exile last? To return after the death or disgrace of the cardinal; to return when d'Artagnan and his friends should have received from the queen the reward they had acquired by the services rendered her—these were ideas that Milady could not endure.

At ten o'clock Felton came and placed the sentinel. Two hours after, the sentinel was relieved. At the expiration of ten minutes, Felton entered Milady's apartment. "I promised to come," said Felton. "I have come."

"You promised to bring a knife, and leave it with me after our interview."

"Here is the knife," said Felton, drawing from his pocket the weapon. He offered it to Milady, who tried the point on the tip of her finger.

"Now," said she, full of melancholy, "listen. While yet young,

I was dragged into a snare. The religion I serve, the God I adore, were blasphemed, but I resisted. They wished to defile my body forever. Finally—"

A bitter smile passed over her lips.

"Finally," said Felton, "what did they do?"

"One evening my enemy mixed a powerful narcotic with my water. Scarcely had I finished my repast, when I sank into a strange torpor. I wished to run to the window and call for help, but my legs refused. I tried to pray, but my tongue was frozen. I sank upon the floor a prey to a slumber which resembled death.

"I awoke in bed in a round chamber, into which light penetrated by an opening in the ceiling. No door gave entrance to the room.

"I had vague perceptions of a horrible dream in which my strength had become exhausted; but these events seemed to belong to another life.

"As well as I could judge by the light of the sun, the day was already two-thirds gone. What had taken place during this long sleep?

"The chamber was furnished for the reception of a woman; the most finished coquette could not have formed a wish, but on casting her eyes about, found it accomplished. You may easily comprehend, Felton, that the more superb the prison, the greater was my terror.

"I sounded all the walls, in the hopes of discovering a door; but there was none.

"Night came on rapidly, and my terrors increased. I supposed it must be seven or eight o'clock in the evening, for it was quite dark.

"All at once the noise of a door, turning on its hinges, made me start. A globe of fire appeared above the opening of the ceiling, casting light into my chamber; and I perceived a man standing within a few paces of me.

"A table bearing supper stood, as if by magic, in the middle of the apartment.

"That man was he who had vowed my dishonor."

"Scoundrel!" murmured Felton.

"He came to offer his fortune in exchange for my love.

"All that the heart of a woman could contain of haughty contempt, I poured out upon this man. He advanced toward me; I seized a knife, I placed it to my breast.

"'Take one step more,' said I, 'and in addition to my dishonor, you shall have my death to reproach yourself with.'

"There was in my look that sincerity which carries conviction to the most perverse minds, for he paused.

"'Your death?' said he. 'You are too charming a mistress for me to lose you. I will pay my next visit when you are in a better humor.'

"At these words the globe of fire which lighted the room reascended. I found myself again in complete darkness. The noise of a door opening and shutting was repeated; the globe descended afresh, and I was alone.

"This moment was frightful. I was in the power of a man whom I detested—a man capable of anything."

"Who was this man?" asked Felton.

"The night passed away without any fresh attempt on the part of my persecutor. The light of day reassured me; I threw myself on the bed, concealing the knife under my pillow.

"When I awoke, a fresh meal was served.

"It was forty-eight hours since I had taken any nourishment. I ate some bread and fruit; remembering the narcotic mixed with the water I had drunk, I would not touch that which was placed on the table, but filled my glass at a fountain fixed in the wall.

"I took the precaution to empty the carafe, in order that my suspicions might not be noticed.

"Evening came. I saw the table sink through the floor; later it reappeared, bearing my supper.

"I was determined to eat only such things as could not possibly have anything soporific introduced into them. Two eggs and some fruit composed my repast; I drew another glass of water from my fountain.

"At the first swallow, it did not have the same taste as in the morning. No doubt some invisible witness had seen me draw the water.

"The same symptoms began to appear; as I had only drunk half a glass, instead of falling asleep, I sank into a state of drowsiness which left me perception, while depriving me of the strength to defend myself.

"I dragged myself toward the bed, to seek the only defense I had left—my knife—but could not reach it. I was lost."

A tremor crept through Felton's body.

"What was most frightful," continued Milady, her voice altered, "was that I retained a consciousness of the danger that threatened me.

"The lamp ascended, leaving me in darkness; then I heard the creaking of the door.

"I attempted to cry out. I raised myself up, only to fall into the arms of my persecutor."

"Tell me who this man was!" cried the young officer.

"I struggled, but my strength failed."

Felton listened. The sweat streamed down his forehead, and his hand tore his breast.

"My first impulse, on coming to myself, was to feel under my pillow for the knife I had not been able to reach. A terrible idea occurred to me."

"The idea came into your mind to avenge yourself on this man, did it not?" cried Felton.

"Yes," said Milady. "The idea was not that of a Christian, but that eternal enemy of our souls breathed it into my mind. It is of this homicidal thought that I now bear the punishment."

"Continue!" said Felton. "I am eager to see you attain your vengeance!"

"I resolved that it should take place as soon as possible. I had no doubt he would return the following night. During the day I had nothing to fear. When breakfast came, I did not hesitate to eat and drink. I concealed a glass of water.

"The day passed away. Several times I felt a smile on my lips. Felton, I dare not tell you at what idea I smiled—"

"Go on!" said Felton. "I am anxious to know the end."

"As before, my supper was brought. I sat down to table. I ate fruit. I pretended to pour water from the jug, but drank that which I had saved in my glass.

"After supper I exhibited the same marks of languor as on the preceding evening, but this time dragged myself toward my bed and lay down.

"I found my knife and grasped the handle.

"Two hours passed. I began to fear that he would not come.

"At length I saw the lamp disappear in the ceiling. The door opened and shut; a shadow approached my bed. I gathered myself up, knife in hand, and, with a cry, struck him in his breast.

"The miserable villain! His breast was covered with a coat of mail; the knife bent against it.

"'Ah!' cried he, wresting the weapon from me. 'You want to take my life, do you, my pretty Puritan? Calm yourself, sweet girl! I am not one of those tyrants who detain women by force. Tomorrow you shall be free.'

"'Beware!' said I. 'My liberty is your dishonor. I will tell everything.'

"My persecutor allowed a movement of anger to escape him. 'Then you shall not leave this place,' said he.

"'Very well,' cried I, 'then the place of my punishment will be that of my tomb. I will allow myself to die with hunger.'

"'Come,' said the wretch, 'is not peace much better than such a war as that? I will proclaim you a piece of immaculate virtue.'

"'I will denounce you.'

"'Ah!' said my enemy, jeering. 'You are very well off here. If you let yourself die of hunger, that will be your own fault.'"

"All the day, all the next night passed without my seeing him again. I neither ate nor drank. I hoped that God would pardon my suicide.

"The second night the door opened; I was lying on the floor, for my strength began to abandon me.

"'Well,' said his voice, 'are we softened? Will we not pay for our liberty with a promise of silence?'

"'I swear,' cried I, 'that no menace shall close my mouth! I will denounce you everywhere as a thief of honor!'

"'Beware!' said the voice. 'I have a means which I will employ to prevent anyone from believing a word. Promise to be silent, and riches, consideration, honor shall surround you; threaten to speak, and I will condemn you to infamy!'"

FIFTY-FOUR

After a moment employed in observing the young man who listened, Milady continued her recital.

"It was nearly three days since I had eaten or drunk. I was so weak that every time I fainted I thanked God, for I thought I was about to die.

"In the midst of one of these swoons the door opened.

"He entered the apartment followed by a man in a mask. 'Have you made your mind up?' he said.

"'I swear before God, I will take the whole world as a witness of your crime.'

"'Branded,' said he, in a voice of thunder, 'try to prove that you are neither guilty nor mad!'

"Then, addressing the man who accompanied him, 'Executioner,' said he, 'do your duty.'"

"Oh, his name!" cried Felton.

"The executioner threw me on the floor, fastened me with his bonds, and a burning fire, the iron of the executioner, was imprinted on my shoulder."

Felton uttered a groan.

"Here," said Milady, rising with the majesty of a queen. "Felton, behold the new martyrdom invented for a pure young girl."

Milady opened her robe, and red with simulated shame, showed the young man the ineffaceable impression that dishonored that beautiful shoulder.

"But," cried Felton, "that is a *fleur-de-lis* which I see there."

"Therein consisted the infamy," replied Milady. "Not the brand of England!—it would be necessary to prove what tribunal had imposed it on me—but the brand of France! By that I was branded indeed!"

This was too much for Felton. He fell on his knees before her.

"Pardon!" cried Felton. "Pardon me for having joined with your persecutors."

Milady held out her hand to him.

"So beautiful! So young!" cried Felton, covering that hand with his kisses.

Milady let one of those looks fall upon him which make a slave of a king. Felton abandoned the hand of this woman to kiss her feet.

He no longer loved her; he adored her.

When Milady appeared to have resumed her self-possession, which she had never lost, he said, "I have one thing to ask: the name of your true executioner. The other was an instrument."

"Have you not divined it?"

"What?" cried Felton. "He?"

"The truly guilty," said Milady, "the persecutor of true believers—he who, to satisfy his corrupt heart, is about to make

England shed so much blood."

"Buckingham!" cried Felton.

Milady concealed her face in her hands.

"Buckingham, the executioner of this angelic creature!" cried Felton. "And thou hast not hurled thy thunder at him, my God!"

"Men fear him and spare him."

"I," said Felton, "do not fear him, nor will I spare him."

The soul of Milady was bathed in joy.

"But how can Lord de Winter," asked Felton, "possibly be mixed up with all this?"

"Listen, Felton," resumed Milady, "by the side of base and contemptible men are often found great and generous natures. I had an affianced husband. I told him all. He girded on his sword and went straight to Buckingham Palace.

"Buckingham had left England the day before.

"'Hear me,' said my affianced husband. 'Let us be united, and then leave it to Lord de Winter to maintain his own honor and that of his wife.'"

"Lord de Winter!" cried Felton.

"Yes," said Milady, "Lord de Winter; now you can understand all. A week before Buckingham's return my affianced husband died, leaving me his sole heir, and without revealing anything to his brother. I went to France, with a determination to remain there for the rest of my life. But all my fortune is in England. Communication being closed by the war, I was in want of everything. I was obliged to come back. Buckingham heard of my return. He spoke of me to Lord de Winter, and told him that his sister-in-law was a branded woman. Lord de Winter believed all that was told him. The day after tomorrow he banishes me.

Felton, I can do nothing but die. Give me that knife!"

Milady sank into the arms of the young officer, who pressed her against his heart.

"No," said he. "You shall live to triumph over your enemies."

Milady put him from her with her hand, drawing him nearer with her look.

"Felton, I bring misfortune to all who surround me! Abandon me!"

"We will live and die together!" cried he, pressing his lips to those of the prisoner.

Several strokes resounded on the door.

"Hark," said she, "we have been overheard!"

"No," said Felton. "It is only the sentinel warning me that they are about to change the guard."

He opened the door and found himself face-to-face with a sergeant.

"You told me to open the door if I heard anyone cry out," said the soldier, "but you forgot to leave me the key. I heard you cry out; then I called the sergeant."

Milady ran to the table, and seizing the knife, exclaimed, "By what right will you prevent me from dying?"

At that moment a burst of laughter resounded through the corridor. The baron stood in the doorway.

"Here we are," said he, "at the last act of the tragedy. Be easy, no blood will flow."

Milady perceived that all was lost unless she gave Felton proof of her courage.

"You are mistaken, my lord; may that blood fall back on those who cause it to flow!"

Felton rushed toward her. He was too late; Milady had stabbed herself.

The knife had come in contact with the steel busk that defended the chests of women and glided down it, tearing the robe and penetrating slantingly between the flesh and the ribs. Milady's robe was stained with blood in a second.

Felton snatched away the knife.

"See, my lord," said he, in a deep, gloomy tone, "here is a woman who was under my guard, and who has killed herself!"

"Be at ease, Felton," said Lord de Winter. "She is not dead; demons do not die so easily." He sent off to find a physician.

FIFTY-FIVE

Felton was convinced. If an angel appeared to that young man as an accuser of Milady, he would take him for a messenger of the devil.

But Felton himself might now be watched!

Toward four o'clock in the morning the doctor arrived; the wound had closed. The doctor satisfied himself that the case was not serious.

In the morning, Felton did not come. Was Felton, suspected by the baron, about to fail her? She had only one day left.

Although she had eaten nothing in the morning, dinner was brought in at its usual time. Milady ventured to ask what had become of Felton, and was told that he had left the castle an hour before on horseback. She inquired if the baron was still at the castle. The soldier replied that he was, and that he had given orders to be informed if the prisoner wished to speak to him. Milady replied that she was too weak at present.

Felton was sent away. Felton was mistrusted.

Left alone, she arose. She traversed her chamber with the excitement of a tigress in a cage.

At six o'clock Lord de Winter came in. "You shall not kill me today," said he. "I am on my guard. You had begun to pervert my poor Felton. He will never see you again. Tomorrow you will go." With these words the baron went out. Milady had listened with a smile of disdain on her lips, but rage in her heart.

Supper was served. Distant lightning announced a storm.

The storm broke about ten o'clock. Milady felt consolation in seeing nature partake of the disorder of her heart.

All at once she heard a tap at her window, and by the help of a flash of lightning she saw the face of a man appear behind the bars.

"Felton!" cried she. "I am saved."

"Yes," said Felton, "but I must have time to file through these bars. Be ready at the first signal."

Milady shut the window and went to lie down. Amid the moaning of the storm she heard the grinding of the file upon the bars.

At the expiration of an hour, Felton tapped again.

Milady opened the window. Two bars removed formed an opening to pass through.

"Are you ready?" asked Felton.

"Yes. Must I take anything with me?"

"Money, if you have any."

"Yes, they have left me all I had."

"So much the better, for I have expended all mine in chartering a vessel."

"Here!" said Milady, placing a bag full of louis in Felton's hands.

Felton threw it to the foot of the wall.

Not a second was to be lost. She put her arms round Felton's neck, and let herself slip out the window. Felton began to descend the ladder slowly. The blast of the hurricane shook them in the air.

All at once Felton stopped. "Silence," he said, "I hear footsteps."

Both remained suspended, motionless and breathless, within twenty paces of the ground, while the patrol passed beneath them. "Now," said Felton, "we are safe."

Milady fainted. Felton continued to descend. Near the bottom of the ladder, when he found no more support for his feet, he clung with his hands; arrived at the last step, he let himself hang, and touched the ground. He stooped down, picked up the bag of money, and placed it between his teeth. Then he took Milady in his arms and set off in the direction opposite to that which the patrol had taken. He arrived on the edge of the sea and whistled.

Five minutes after, a boat appeared. The storm began to subside, but still the sea was disturbed.

"To the sloop," said Felton, "and row quickly."

The four men bent to their oars. It was almost impossible to see the shore from the boat; they would therefore be less likely to see the boat from the shore. While the boat was advancing with all the speed its four rowers could give it, Felton took some seawater and sprinkled it over Milady's face.

Milady opened her eyes.

"Where am I?" said she.

"Saved!" replied the young officer.

"Yes, the air I breathe is the air of liberty!"

The young man pressed her to his heart.

Milady looked around her. "It is there," said Felton, touching the bag of money with his foot.

They drew near to the sloop. "What vessel is that?" asked Milady.

"The one I have hired for you."

"Where will it take me?"

"Where you please, after you have put me on shore at Portsmouth."

"What are you going to do at Portsmouth?" asked Milady.

"Accomplish the orders of Lord de Winter," said Felton, with a gloomy smile. "He sent me to get Buckingham to sign the order for your transportation. He sails tomorrow for France."

"He must not sail!" cried Milady, forgetting her usual presence of mind.

"Be satisfied," replied Felton. "He will not sail."

Milady started with joy. She could read to the depths of the heart of this young man; the death of Buckingham was written there.

"Silence!" cried Felton. "We are here."

An instant after they were on the deck. "Captain," said Felton, "this is the person whom you must convey safely to France. Meanwhile, convey me to the little bay of—."

The captain replied by ordering the necessary maneuvers.

During this passage, Felton related everything to Milady—how, instead of going to London, he had chartered the little vessel; how he had scaled the wall; and how, when he had reached the bars, he fastened his ladder. Milady knew the rest.

It was agreed that Milady should wait for Felton till ten o'clock; if he did not return, she was to sail. In that case, supposing he was at liberty, he was to rejoin her in France, at the convent of the Carmelites at Bethune.

FIFTY-SIX

Felton took leave of Milady, kissing her hand. His whole body appeared in its ordinary state of calmness; only his speech had a short dry accent, which indicated something dark at work.

Both were free from the fear of pursuit; nobody ever came into Milady's apartment before nine o'clock, and it would require three hours to go from the castle to London.

Felton jumped onshore, saluted Milady, and took his course toward the city. The rapidity of his walk heated his blood; the idea that he left behind him the woman he adored as a saint exalted his mind above human feeling.

He entered Portsmouth about eight o'clock. Drums were beating in the streets; the troops about to embark were marching toward the sea.

Felton arrived at the palace streaming with perspiration. Drawing from his pocket the letter of which he was the bearer, he said, "A pressing message from Lord de Winter."

At the name of Lord de Winter, the officer let Felton pass.

Another man was entering and addressed Patrick, the duke's confidential lackey, at the same moment. Felton named Lord de Winter; the unknown would not name anybody. Each was anxious to gain admission.

Patrick, who knew Lord de Winter, gave the preference to the one who came in his name. The other was forced to wait. The valet introduced Felton into a small room where Buckingham was finishing his toilet.

"Lieutenant Felton, from Lord de Winter," said Patrick.

"From Lord de Winter!" repeated Buckingham. "Let him come in."

Felton entered. Buckingham was putting on a blue velvet doublet embroidered with pearls.

"Why didn't the baron come himself?" demanded Buckingham. "I expected him this morning."

"He desired me to tell Your Grace," replied Felton, "that he was prevented by the guard keeps at the castle. It is of his prisoner that I wish to speak to Your Grace."

"Leave us, Patrick," said Buckingham.

Patrick went out.

"My lord," said Felton, "the Baron de Winter wrote to request you to sign an order of embarkation relative to a young woman named Charlotte Backson."

"Give it to me," said the duke. He cast a glance over the paper.

"Does Your Grace know," asked Felton, "that Charlotte Backson is not the name of this young woman?"

"I know it," replied the duke, dipping the quill in the ink.

"Then Your Grace knows her real name?" asked Felton, in a sharp tone.

"I know it." The duke put the quill to paper. Felton grew pale.

"And knowing that name, my lord," replied Felton, "you sign it all the same?"

"Rather twice than once," said Buckingham.

"I cannot believe," continued Felton, in a rougher voice, "that Your Grace knows it is to Milady de Winter this relates. Will Your Grace sign that order without remorse?"

Buckingham looked at the young man haughtily.

"You are asking strange questions."

"Reply to them, my lord," said Felton. "The circumstances are more serious than you believe."

Buckingham reflected that the young man, coming from Lord de Winter, undoubtedly spoke in his name.

"Without remorse," said he. "The baron knows Milady de Winter is guilty, and it is treating her favorably to commute her punishment to transportation." The duke put his pen to the paper.

"You will not sign that order, my lord!" said Felton, making a step toward the duke.

"Are you mad?" said Buckingham.

"My lord, beware of going too far!"

"What do you say?" cried Buckingham. "I think he threatens me!"

"No, my lord, I plead. One drop of water suffices to make the full vase overflow; one fault may draw down punishment upon the head spared despite many crimes."

"Mr. Felton," said Buckingham, "you will place yourself at once under arrest."

"You have defiled this young girl. Let her go free, and I exact nothing else from you."

"You exact!" said Buckingham, looking at Felton with astonishment.

"My lord," continued Felton, "beware! All England is tired of your iniquities. God will punish you hereafter, but I will punish you here!"

"This is too much!" cried Buckingham, making toward the door.

Felton barred his passage.

"I ask humbly, my lord," said he. "Sign the order for the liberation of Milady de Winter."

"Withdraw, sir," said Buckingham, "or I will have you placed in irons."

"Beware, my lord, you are in the hands of God!"

"Help!" shouted the duke, and sprang toward his sword.

Felton held the knife with which Milady had stabbed herself; he was upon the duke.

At that moment Patrick entered the room, crying, "A letter from France, my lord."

"From France!" cried Buckingham.

Felton plunged the knife into his side.

"Ah, traitor," cried Buckingham, "you have killed me!"

"Murder!" screamed Patrick.

Felton rushed toward the staircase; upon the first step he met Lord de Winter, who seized him by the throat, crying, "I guessed too late!"

Felton made no resistance. Lord de Winter placed him in the hands of the guards, who led him, while awaiting further orders,

"Help!" shouted the duke, and sprang toward his sword.

to a little terrace commanding the sea; and then the baron hastened to the duke's chamber.

At the cry uttered by the duke and the scream of Patrick, the man whom Felton had met in the antechamber rushed into the chamber.

He found the duke reclining upon a sofa, with his hand pressed upon the wound.

"Laporte," said the duke, in a dying voice, "do you come from her?"

"Yes, monseigneur," replied the faithful cloak bearer of Anne of Austria.

"Patrick, let no one enter."

And the duke swooned.

Meanwhile, cries of despair resounded on all sides. Lord de Winter tore his hair. "Too late by a minute!" cried he.

He had been informed at seven o'clock in the morning that a rope ladder floated from one of the windows of the castle, had hastened to Milady's chamber, found it empty, remembered the verbal caution d'Artagnan had transmitted to him, trembled for the duke, galloped off like the wind, alighted in the courtyard, ascended the stairs, and on the top step encountered Felton.

The duke reopened his eyes, and hope revived.

"Gentlemen, leave me with Patrick and Laporte. What has she written to me?" said Buckingham, feebly, streaming with blood. "Read me her letter. I cannot see."

Laporte read:

My lord,

By that which I have suffered by you and for you, I conjure you to countermand those great armaments which you are preparing against France, to put an end to a war of which it is publicly said religion is the ostensible cause, and generally whispered, your love for me is the concealed cause. This war may not only bring great catastrophes upon England and France, but misfortune upon you, my lord, for which I should never console myself.

Be careful of your life, which is menaced, and you will be dear to me from the moment I am not obliged to see an enemy in you.

Your affectionate ANNE

Buckingham collected his strength to listen; when it was ended, he asked, "Have you nothing else to say, Laporte?"

"The queen charged me to tell you to watch over yourself, for she had advice that your assassination would be attempted."

"Is that all?" replied Buckingham, impatiently.

"She charged me to tell you that she still loved you."

"Ah," said Buckingham, "my death will not be to her as the death of a stranger!"

Laporte burst into tears.

"Patrick," said the duke, "bring me the small box in which the diamond studs were kept."

Patrick brought the object desired, which Laporte recognized as having belonged to the queen.

"Now the bag of white satin, on which her cipher is embroidered in pearls. Here, Laporte," said Buckingham, "these are the only tokens I ever received from her—this small box and these two letters. You will restore them to Her Majesty, and"—he looked around—"you will add—"

His eyes, darkened by death, encountered only the knife which had fallen from the hand of Felton.

"And you will add this knife," said the duke, pressing the hand of Laporte. He had just strength enough to place the bag at the bottom of the box and let the knife fall into it; then he slipped from the sofa to the floor.

Buckingham tried to smile a last time, but death checked his thought, which remained engraved on his brow like a last kiss of love.

At this moment the duke's surgeon arrived.

He approached the duke, took his hand, held it for an instant in his own, and letting it fall, "All is useless," said he, "he is dead."

As soon as Lord de Winter saw Buckingham was dead, he ran to Felton, whom the soldiers still guarded on the terrace.

"Wretch!" said he to the young man, who had regained that self-possession that never after abandoned him. "What have you done? You have served as an instrument to that accursed woman."

"I am ignorant of whom you are speaking, my lord," replied Felton quietly. "I killed the Duke of Buckingham because he twice refused to appoint me captain."

All at once his eyes became fixed upon the sea. He had recognized the sail of a sloop directed toward the coast of France.

He grew deadly pale and placed his hand upon his heart, which was breaking.

"One last favor, my lord!" said he to the baron. "What o'clock is it?"

The baron drew out his watch. "It wants ten minutes to nine," said he.

Milady had hastened her departure by an hour and a half. As soon as she heard the cannon that announced the fatal event, she had ordered the anchor weighed.

"God has so willed it!" said he, but without being able to take his eyes from that ship, on which he fancied he could distinguish the outline of her to whom he had sacrificed his life.

"Be punished, miserable man!" said Lord de Winter. "But I swear to you that your accomplice is not saved."

FIFTY-SEVEN

The king of England, learning of the death of the duke, feared that such terrible news might discourage the Rochellais; he tried to conceal it as long as possible, keeping watch that no vessel should sail until the army had gone.

But two vessels had already left the port, one bearing Milady.

During this time nothing occurred in the camp at la Rochelle; only the king, who was bored, resolved to spend the festival of St. Louis at St. Germain, and ordered an escort of twenty Musketeers.

As M. de Treville knew the great desire his friends had of returning to Paris, he fixed upon them to form part of the escort. It was then that d'Artagnan appreciated the favor the cardinal had conferred by making him enter the Musketeers—otherwise he would have been forced to remain in camp.

Aramis had written to Tours to obtain from the queen authority for Mme Bonacieux to leave the convent. Eight days afterward, Aramis received the following letter:

My dear cousin,

Here is the authorization from my sister to withdraw our little servant from the convent of Bethune, the air of which you think is bad for her. My sister sends this authorization with great pleasure, for she is very partial to the little girl, to whom she intends to be serviceable hereafter.

To this letter was added an order, conceived in these terms:

The superior of the convent of Bethune will place in the hands of the person who shall present this note to her the novice who entered the convent under my patronage.

—ANNE

The king stopped from time to time on the way to Paris. Out of the twenty Musketeers sixteen rejoiced greatly at this relaxation; but four cursed it heartily.

At length the escort passed through Paris. The king permitted M. de Treville to distribute furloughs for four days. The first furloughs granted were to our four friends. Still further, Athos obtained of M. de Treville six days instead of four, and introduced into these six days two more nights—for they set out on the twenty-fourth at five o'clock in the evening, and M. de Treville postdated the leave to the morning of the twenty-fifth.

"It appears to me that we are making trouble of a very simple thing," said d'Artagnan. "In two days, I am at Bethune. I present my letter from the queen to the superior, and bring back the treasure I go to seek. Remain where you are; do not exhaust yourselves uselessly."

To this Athos replied: "Consider, d'Artagnan, Bethune is a city where the cardinal has given rendezvous to a woman who, wherever she goes, brings misery with her. If you had only to deal with four men, d'Artagnan, I would allow you to go alone. You have to do with that woman!"

"You terrify me, Athos!" cried d'Artagnan. "What do you fear?"

"Everything!" replied Athos.

They continued as fast as their horses could carry them.

On the evening of the twenty-fifth, as d'Artagnan was dismounting at the inn of the Golden Harrow, a horseman came out of the post yard, started off at a gallop, and took the road to Paris. At the moment he passed into the street, the wind blew open his cloak and lifted his hat. D'Artagnan ran toward his horse.

"Where are you going?" cried Athos.

"It is he!" cried d'Artagnan, pale with anger. "That cursed man whom I have always met when threatened by some misfortune, he who accompanied that horrible woman when I met her first, he whom I was seeking when I offended Athos, he whom I saw the morning Madame Bonacieux was abducted! To saddle, gentlemen!"

"My dear friend," said Aramis, "he has a fresh horse, and ours are fatigued, so that we shall disable our own horses without overtaking him. Let the man go; let us save the woman."

"Monsieur!" cried a hostler, running out and looking after the stranger. "Here is a paper which dropped out of your hat!"

"Friend," said d'Artagnan, "a half pistole for that paper!"

"With great pleasure!" The hostler returned to the yard. D'Artagnan unfolded the paper.

"Nothing but one word!" said d'Artagnan.

"Yes," said Aramis, "but that word is the name of some town or village."

"'Armentières,'" read Porthos. "I don't know such a place."

"Come on!" said d'Artagnan. "Let us keep that paper carefully, perhaps I have not thrown away my half pistole. To horse, my friends!"

And the four friends flew at a gallop along the road to Bethune.

FIFTY-EIGHT

Milady arrived at Boulogne without accident. When landing at Portsmouth, she was an Englishwoman whom the French drove from la Rochelle; when landing at Boulogne, she was a Frenchwoman whom the English persecuted.

Milady had the best of passports—her beauty, and the liberality with which she distributed her pistoles. Freed from formalities by the gallant manners of an old governor of the port, she only remained long enough at Boulogne to post a letter:

To His Eminence Monseigneur le Cardinal Richelieu,
Monseigneur, His Grace the Duke of Buckingham WILL NOT SET OUT for France.
—MILADY
P.S. I report to the convent of the Carmelites at Bethune, where I will await your orders.

That evening Milady commenced her journey. Night overtook her; she stopped, and slept at an inn. At five o'clock the next morning she proceeded, and in three hours entered Bethune. She inquired for the convent of the Carmelites, and went thither immediately.

The superior met her; Milady showed her the cardinal's order. The abbess assigned her a chamber.

All the past was effaced from this woman; fixed on the future, she beheld nothing but high fortunes.

After breakfast, the abbess came to pay her a visit. Milady was charming, winning the superior by the graces of her whole personality.

Desirous of seeing how far the discretion of the good abbess would go, Milady began to tell a story about the cardinal, relating the amours of the minister with several women.

The abbess listened and smiled.

"Good," thought Milady. "She takes pleasure in my conversation. If she is a cardinalist, she has no fanaticism."

She went on to describe the persecutions exercised by the cardinal upon his enemies. The abbess only crossed herself. Milady continued, coloring her narrations more and more.

"I am ignorant of these matters," said the abbess, at length, "but one of our boarders has suffered much from the persecution of the cardinal!"

"One of your boarders?" said Milady. "I pity her."

"She is much to be pitied. But," resumed the abbess, "Monsieur le Cardinal has perhaps plausible motives for acting thus; though she has the look of an angel, we must not always judge people by appearance."

"Good!" said Milady to herself. "I am to discover something."

She tried to give her countenance an appearance of perfect candor.

"Alas," said Milady, "it is said that we must not trust to the face; but in what shall we place confidence, if not the most beautiful work of the Lord?"

"You would believe," said the abbess, "that this young person is innocent?"

"The cardinal pursues not only crimes," said she. "There are virtues which he pursues severely."

"Permit me, madame, to express my surprise," said the abbess. "You are the friend of the cardinal, and yet—"

"And yet I speak ill of him," replied Milady. "That is because I am not his friend, but his victim!"

"But this letter in which he recommends you to me?"

"Is an order for me to confine myself."

"Why have you not fled?"

"Whither should I go? This young boarder of yours, has she tried to fly?"

"No, I believe she is detained in France by some love affair."

"Ah," said Milady, "if she loves she is not altogether wretched."

The abbess looked at her.

"You are not an enemy of our holy faith?" said she, hesitatingly.

"Who—I?" cried Milady. "A Protestant? I am a fervent Catholic!"

"Then, madame," said the abbess, smiling, "this shall not be a very hard prison. You will find here, moreover, the young woman of whom I spoke. She was sent to me by someone of high rank, under the name of Kitty. I have not tried to discover her other name."

Milady smiled to herself at the idea that this might be her old chambermaid. "When can I see this young lady?" she asked.

"Why, this evening," said the abbess. "But you have been traveling four days. Go to bed; at dinnertime we will rouse you."

Milady went to bed, softly rocked by the ideas of vengeance that the name of Kitty had brought to her thoughts. She remembered that almost unlimited promise that the cardinal had given her if she succeeded in her enterprise. She had succeeded; d'Artagnan was in her power!

One thing frightened her; that was the remembrance of her husband, whom she had believed dead, and whom she had found again in Athos. But if Athos was the friend of d'Artagnan, he was the enemy of the cardinal; and she would succeed in involving him in vengeance.

All these hopes were sweet thoughts for Milady; she soon fell asleep.

She was awakened by a soft voice, opened her eyes, and saw the abbess, accompanied by a young woman whose face was unknown to her. Each examined the other with great attention; both were very handsome. The abbess introduced them and then left the two young women alone.

The novice was about to follow the example of the superior, but Milady stopped her.

"How, madame," said she. "You already wish to deprive me of your company?"

"No," replied the novice, "only you are fatigued."

"Well," said Milady, "what can those who sleep wish for—a

happy awakening?" and taking her hand, drew her toward the armchair by the bedside.

"How unfortunate I am!" said the novice. "I have been here six months without recreation. Your presence was likely to afford me delightful company; yet I expect to quit the convent at any moment."

"You are going?" asked Milady.

"I hope so," said the novice.

"I learned you had suffered persecutions from the cardinal," continued Milady. "That would have been another motive for sympathy between us."

"You have likewise been a victim of that wicked priest."

"Hush!" said Milady. "My misfortunes arise from my having said what you have said before a woman whom I thought my friend. Are you also the victim of treachery?"

"No," said the novice, "of my devotion to a woman I loved."

"And who has abandoned you?"

"I have obtained proof to the contrary, for which I thank God—for it would have cost me to think she had forgotten me. But you, madame, appear to be free," continued the novice. "If you were inclined to fly, it only rests with yourself to do so."

"Whither would you have me go, without friends?"

"Oh," cried the novice, "as to friends, you would have them wherever you went. You appear so good and are so beautiful!"

"When I said I was alone," said Milady, hoping to make the novice talk by talking of herself, "it is not for want of friends in high places. I have proof that Her Majesty herself has more than once been obliged to abandon to the anger of His

Eminence persons who had served her."

"Trust me, madame; the queen may appear to have abandoned those persons, but we must not put faith in appearances."

"Alas!" said Milady. "I believe you; the queen is so good!"

"Oh, you know her, that noble queen!" cried the novice, with enthusiasm.

"That is to say," replied Milady, "I know a number of her intimate friends. I am acquainted with Monsieur de Treville."

"Why!" cried the novice. "If you know Monsieur de Treville, you must have seen some of his Musketeers. Don't you know a gentleman named Athos?"

Milady could not help uttering a cry. "The name struck me. I have known that gentleman."

"And some of his friends, Messieurs Porthos and Aramis!"

"Indeed! I know them," cried Milady, who began to feel a chill penetrate her heart.

"If you know them, why do you not apply to them for help?"

"I am not intimate with them," stammered Milady. "I know them from having heard Monsieur d'Artagnan say a great deal about them."

"You know Monsieur d'Artagnan!" cried the novice, seizing the hands of Milady. "You know him by what title?"

"Why," replied Milady, "by the title of friend."

"You deceive me, madame," said the novice. "You have been his mistress!"

"It is you who have been his mistress!" cried Milady, in her turn. "You are Madame Bonacieux!"

The young woman drew back. "Well, yes," she said. "Are we rivals?"

"Oh, no!" cried Milady. "Never!"

"I believe you," said Mme Bonacieux, "but why did you cry out so?"

"Do you not understand?" said Milady. "I know all—your abduction, his despair, that of his friends, their useless inquiries. How could I help being astonished!"

And Milady stretched out her arms to Mme Bonacieux. These two women held each other in a close embrace. If Milady's strength had been equal to her hatred, Mme Bonacieux would never have left that embrace alive.

"Oh, you good little creature!" said Milady. "How delighted I am to have found you!"

"My punishment is drawing to a close," said Mme Bonacieux. "This evening, perhaps, I shall see him."

"This evening?" asked Milady, roused by these words. "Do you expect news from him?"

"I expect himself. Read!" said the unhappy young woman, with pride and joy, presenting a letter to Milady.

"The writing of Madame de Chevreuse!" said Milady to herself. And she greedily read the following few lines:

My dear child,
Hold yourself ready. OUR FRIEND will see you soon, to release you from that imprisonment your safety required. Prepare for your departure.

Our charming Gascon has proved himself as brave and faithful as ever. Tell him that certain parties are grateful for the warning he has given.

"Yes," said Milady, "the letter is precise. Do you know what that warning was?"

"I suspect he has warned the queen against some machinations of the cardinal."

At that moment they heard the gallop of a horse.

"Oh!" cried Mme Bonacieux, darting to the window. "Can it be he? Alas, no! It is a man I don't know, although he seems to be coming here."

The door opened, and the superior entered.

"Did you come from Boulogne?" demanded she of Milady.

"Yes," replied she, trying to recover her self-possession. "Who wants me?"

"A man who comes from the cardinal wishes to speak to a lady recently come from Boulogne."

"Oh, my God!" cried Mme Bonacieux. "Can it be bad news? As soon as he is gone, I will return."

The superior and Mme Bonacieux retired. An instant later, the door opened, and a man appeared.

Milady uttered a cry of joy; it was the Comte de Rochefort.

FIFTY-NINE

"Ah," cried Milady and Rochefort together, "it is you!"

"And you come?" asked Milady.

"From la Rochelle; and you?"

"From England."

"Buckingham?"

"Dead or desperately wounded. A fanatic has just assassinated him."

"Ah," said Rochefort, with a smile. "This will delight His Eminence!"

"I wrote to him from Boulogne. What brings you here?"

"His Eminence sent me to find you."

"I only arrived yesterday. Do you know whom I have encountered here? That young woman whom the queen took out of prison. Imagine my astonishment!"

"Does she know you?"

Milady smiled. "I am her best friend."

"Upon my honor," said Rochefort, "it takes you to perform such miracles!"

"And it is well I can, Chevalier," said Milady, "for do you know what is going on here? D'Artagnan and his friends will come for her tomorrow or the day after."

"They will go so far that we shall be obliged to send them to the Bastille."

"Why is it not done already?"

"The cardinal has a weakness for these men which I cannot comprehend."

"Tell him this, Rochefort. Our conversation was overheard; one of them took from me the safe-conduct he had given me; they warned Lord de Winter of my journey to England; they nearly foiled my mission; tell him that two only are to be feared—d'Artagnan and Athos; the third, Aramis, is the lover of Madame de Chevreuse; the fourth, Porthos, is a blustering booby."

"But they must be at the siege of la Rochelle."

"I thought so; but a letter which Madame Bonacieux has received leads me to believe that these four men are on the road hither to take her away."

"What's to be done?"

"What did the cardinal say?"

"I was to take your dispatches and return; when he knows what you have done, he will advise what to do."

"It is probable that I may not be able to remain here."

"Is this little woman to escape His Eminence?"

"Bah!" said Milady. "You forget that I am her best friend."

"I may then tell the cardinal, with respect to this little woman—"

"That he may be at ease. Return instantly. In passing through Lilliers send me your chaise, with an order to your servant to place himself at my disposal. You have, no doubt, some order from the cardinal about you? Show it to the abbess, and tell her that someone will come and fetch me. Don't forget to treat me harshly in speaking of me to the abbess. It is necessary to inspire confidence in that poor little Madame Bonacieux."

"Will you make me a report of all that has happened?"

"Why, I have related the events to you."

"You are right; only let me know where to find you. Do you want a map?"

"I know this country marvelously! I was brought up here. Let me reflect a little! That will do—at Armentières, a little town on the Lys; I shall only have to cross the river, and I shall be in a foreign country."

"You will wait for me at Armentières? Write that name on a bit of paper, lest I should forget it. There is nothing compromising in the name of a town. Now, let us see," said Rochefort, "Buckingham dead or grievously wounded; your conversation with the cardinal overheard by the four Musketeers; Lord de Winter warned of your arrival at Portsmouth; d'Artagnan and Athos to the Bastille; Aramis the lover of Madame de Chevreuse; Porthos a fool; Madame Bonacieux found again; send you the chaise as soon as possible; place my lackey at your disposal; make you out a victim of the cardinal in order that the abbess may entertain no suspicion; Armentières, on the banks of the Lys. Is that all?"

"In truth, you are a miracle of memory. Add one thing—"

"What?"

"I saw some very pretty woods which almost touch the convent garden. Say that I am permitted to walk in those woods. Perhaps I shall stand in need of a back door."

"You think of everything."

"Capital! *Adieu,* Chevalier."

"*Adieu,* Countess."

"Commend me to the cardinal."

"Commend me to Satan." Milady and Rochefort exchanged a smile and separated.

An hour afterward Rochefort set out at a gallop; five hours later he passed through Arras.

He was recognized by d'Artagnan, and that recognition, inspiring fear in the Musketeers, gave fresh activity to their journey.

SIXTY

Rochefort had scarcely departed when Mme Bonacieux reentered.

"Well," said the young woman, "what you dreaded has happened. The cardinal will send someone to take you away."

"Who told you that, my dear?" asked Milady.

"I heard it from the mouth of the messenger himself."

"Come and sit down," said Milady. "Wait till I assure myself that nobody hears us."

Milady looked in the corridor, then seated herself close to Mme Bonacieux.

"He has well played his part," said she.

"That man was not—"

"That man," said Milady, lowering her voice, "is my brother. My brother met the emissary of the cardinal. He drew his sword, and required the messenger to deliver up to him the papers of which he was the bearer. The messenger resisted; my brother killed him."

"Oh!" said Mme Bonacieux, shuddering.

"He presented himself here as the emissary of the cardinal. In an hour or two a carriage will come to take me away."

"It is your brother who sends this carriage."

"That is not all. That letter which you believe to be from Madame de Chevreuse is a snare to prevent your resistance when they come to fetch you. D'Artagnan and his friends are detained at the siege of la Rochelle."

"How do you know?"

"My brother met some emissaries of the cardinal in the uniform of Musketeers. You would have been summoned to the gate; you would have believed yourself about to meet friends; you would have been abducted."

"If this continues," said Mme Bonacieux, raising her hands to her forehead, "I shall go mad!"

"I hear a horse's steps; it is my brother setting off again. Come!"

Milady opened the window and made a sign to Mme Bonacieux to join her.

Rochefort passed at a gallop.

"*Adieu,* brother!" cried Milady.

The chevalier waved his hand to Milady.

"The good George!" said she, with a countenance full of affection.

"Dear lady," said Mme Bonacieux, "what do you advise me to do?"

"It is possible I may be deceived," said Milady. "D'Artagnan and his friends may come. There would be a very simple means—"

"Tell me!"

"To wait, concealed in the neighborhood, and assure yourself who are the men who come. I shall conceal myself a few leagues hence until my brother can rejoin me. Well, I take you with me; we wait together."

"But I am almost a prisoner."

"As they believe that I go in consequence of an order from the cardinal, no one will believe you anxious to follow me. The carriage is at the door; you mount the step to embrace me. My brother's servant makes a sign, and we set off at a gallop."

"But d'Artagnan! If he comes?"

"We will send my brother's servant back to Bethune. He shall assume a disguise and place himself in front of the convent. If Monsieur d'Artagnan and his friends arrive, he will bring them to us."

"He knows them?"

"Doubtless. Has he not seen Monsieur d'Artagnan at my house?"

"If I should happen to be any distance when the carriage comes—at dinner or supper, for instance?"

"Tell your good superior that you ask her permission to share my repast."

"Oh, delightful! We shall not be separated for an instant."

"Go down to make your request. I will take a turn in the garden."

"Oh, you are so kind, and I am so grateful!"

"Are you not the beloved of my best friend?"

"Dear d'Artagnan! How he will thank you!"

The two women parted, exchanging charming smiles.

Milady stood in need of a little silence to give all her ideas a regular plan. What was most pressing was to get Mme Bonacieux away, and if matters required, make her a hostage. Milady felt as we feel when a storm is coming on—that this issue was near, and could not fail to be terrible.

The principal thing was to keep Mme Bonacieux in her power. Once concealed with her at Armentières, it would be easy to make her believe that d'Artagnan had not come.

Revolving all this in her mind, Milady was like a good general who contemplates at the same time victory and defeat, and who is quite prepared to march forward or beat a retreat.

At the end of an hour she heard a soft voice calling her; it was Mme Bonacieux's. The good abbess had consented to her request; and they were to sup together.

On reaching the courtyard, they heard a carriage stop at the gate.

Milady listened. "It is the carriage my brother sends for us," she said.

The bell of the convent gate was sounded; Milady was not mistaken.

"Go to your chamber," said she to Mme Bonacieux. "You have perhaps some jewels you would like to take. We will snatch some supper; we must keep our strength up. In a quarter of an hour you will be safe."

Milady ran up to her apartment, found Rochefort's lackey, and gave him his instructions.

He was to wait at the gate. If by chance the Musketeers should appear, the carriage was to set off as fast as possible and wait for Milady at the other side of the wood.

If the Musketeers did not appear, Mme Bonacieux was to get into the carriage as if to bid her *adieu,* and she was to take her away.

Mme Bonacieux came in and to remove all suspicion, Milady repeated to the lackey the latter part of her instructions.

"You see," said Milady, when the lackey had gone out, "everything is ready. The abbess suspects nothing. Drink a finger of wine, and let us be gone."

Milady poured her a small glass of wine. Mme Bonacieux just touched the glass with her lips.

"Come!" said Milady, lifting hers to her mouth. "Do as I do."

Her hand remained suspended; she heard the rattling of a distant gallop. She grew pale and ran to the window, while Mme Bonacieux, rising all in a tremble, supported herself upon her chair to avoid falling. Nothing was to be seen. Only the galloping drew nearer.

"Oh, my God!" said Mme Bonacieux. "What is that noise?"

"Either our friends or our enemies," said Milady, with her terrible coolness.

The noise became louder; the horses could not be more than a hundred and fifty paces distant. If they were not yet to be seen, it was because the road made an elbow. The noise became so distinct that the horses might be counted by the rattle of their hoofs. Milady gazed with all her attention; it was just light enough to see who was coming.

All at once she saw the glitter of laced hats and the waving of feathers; she counted two, then four horsemen. One preceded the rest by double the length of his horse. She recognized d'Artagnan.

"It is the uniform of the cardinal's Guards," she said. "Fly! Make haste!"

Mme Bonacieux sank upon her knees. Milady tried to raise her, but could not. They heard the rolling of the carriage, which at the approach of the Musketeers set off at a gallop.

"For the last time, will you come?" cried Milady.

"My strength fails me. Flee alone!"

"And leave you here? Never!" cried Milady.

All at once she paused; she ran to the table and emptied into Mme Bonacieux's glass the contents of a ring. It was a grain of a reddish color, which dissolved immediately.

Then, taking the glass with a firm hand, she said, "Drink. This wine will give you strength!" And she put the glass to the lips of the young woman.

"This is not the way that I wished to avenge myself," said Milady, replacing the glass upon the table with an infernal smile, "but we do what we can!" And she rushed out.

Mme Bonacieux saw her go without being able to follow her. She was like people who dream: they are pursued and in vain try to walk.

A great noise was heard at the gate. Every instant Mme Bonacieux expected to see Milady, but she did not return.

At length the noise of boots resounded on the stairs. There was a great murmur of voices. All at once she uttered a cry of joy; she had recognized the voice of d'Artagnan.

"D'Artagnan!" cried she. "This way!"

The door of the cell opened; several men rushed in. D'Artagnan fell on his knees before his mistress. Athos replaced his pistol in his belt; Porthos and Aramis, who held their drawn swords in their hands, returned them to their scabbards.

"Oh, my beloved d'Artagnan! You have come at last! Oh, it was in vain she told me you would not come! How happy I am!"

Athos, who had seated himself, started up.

"*She!* What she?" asked d'Artagnan.

"My companion. She who, mistaking you for the cardinal's Guards, has just fled away."

"Of what companion are you speaking, dear Constance?" cried d'Artagnan. "Can you not remember her name? Help! Her hands are icy cold. She is ill!"

While Porthos was calling for help, Aramis ran to the table to get a glass of water, but stopped at seeing the horrible alteration in the countenance of Athos, who, standing before the table, his hair rising from his head, was looking at one of the glasses.

"Oh!" said Athos. "God would not permit such a crime!"

"Water!" cried d'Artagnan.

"Poor woman!" murmured Athos, in a broken voice.

Mme Bonacieux opened her eyes under the kisses of d'Artagnan. "She revives!" cried the young man.

"Madame!" said Athos. "In the name of heaven, whose empty glass is this?"

"Mine, monsieur," said the young woman, in a dying voice.

"But who poured the wine that was in this glass?"

"Oh, I remember!" said Mme Bonacieux. "The Comtesse de Winter."

The four friends uttered the same cry. At that moment the countenance of Mme Bonacieux became livid; a fearful agony pervaded her frame, and she sank into the arms of Porthos and Aramis.

"She revives!" cried the young man.

"D'Artagnan!" cried Mme Bonacieux. "Where art thou? Do not leave me!"

D'Artagnan hastened to her. Her face was distorted with agony; a convulsive shuddering shook her body; the sweat rolled from her brow.

"Call for help!"

"Useless!" said Athos. "For the poison which *she* pours there is no antidote."

"Yes, yes!" murmured Mme Bonacieux. "Help!"

Then she took the head of the young man between her hands, looked at him as if her whole soul passed into that look, and pressed her lips to his.

"Constance!" cried d'Artagnan.

A sigh escaped from Mme Bonacieux, and dwelt for an instant on the lips of d'Artagnan. That sigh was the soul, so chaste and loving, which reascended to heaven.

D'Artagnan pressed a corpse in his arms. The young man fell by the side of his mistress as pale and as icy as herself.

At that moment a man appeared in the doorway. He saw Mme Bonacieux dead, and d'Artagnan in a swoon.

"I was not deceived," said he. "Here is Monsieur d'Artagnan; and you are his friends, Messieurs Athos, Porthos, and Aramis."

They looked at the stranger with astonishment. It seemed to all three that they knew him.

"Gentlemen," resumed the newcomer, "I am in search of a woman who," added he, with a terrible smile, "must have passed this way, for I see a corpse."

The three friends remained mute—for although the voice

reminded them of someone they had seen, they could not remember under what circumstances.

"Gentlemen," continued the stranger, "since you do not recognize a man who probably owes his life to you twice, I must name myself. I am Lord de Winter, brother-in-law of *that woman.*"

Athos rose, and offering him his hand, "Be welcome, my lord," said he. "You are one of us."

"I set out five hours after her from Portsmouth," said Lord de Winter. "I arrived three hours after her at Boulogne. Finally, I lost all trace of her. I was going about at random when I saw you gallop past. I called, but you did not answer; I followed, but my horse was too fatigued to go at the same pace with yours. And yet it appears you have arrived too late."

"You see!" said Athos, pointing to Mme Bonacieux dead, and to d'Artagnan, whom Porthos and Aramis were trying to recall to life.

"Are they both dead?" asked Lord de Winter.

"No," replied Athos, "Monsieur d'Artagnan has fainted."

At that moment d'Artagnan opened his eyes. He threw himself on the corpse of his mistress.

Athos rose, embraced him tenderly, and said to him, "Friend, be a man! Women weep for the dead; men avenge them!" Athos made a sign to Porthos and Aramis to go and fetch the superior.

"Madame," said Athos, passing his arm under that of d'Artagnan, "we abandon to your care the body of that unfortunate woman. She was an angel on earth before being an angel in heaven."

D'Artagnan sobbed aloud.

"Weep," said Athos, "heart full of love! Would I could weep like you!"

And he drew away his friend, as affectionate as a father.

All five took their way to the town of Bethune and stopped before the first inn they came to.

"Now, gentlemen," said Athos, when he had ascertained there were five chambers free in the hotel, "let everyone retire to his own apartment. I take charge of everything."

"It appears, however," said Lord de Winter, "if there are any measures to take against the countess, it concerns me; she is my sister-in-law."

"And me," said Athos. "She is my wife!"

D'Artagnan smiled—for he understood that Athos was sure of his vengeance when he revealed such a secret. Porthos and Aramis grew pale.

"Retire to your chambers," said Athos. "D'Artagnan, give me the paper which fell from that man's hat, upon which is written the name of the village of—"

"Ah," said d'Artagnan, "I comprehend!"

"You see, then," said Athos, "there is a god in heaven still!"

SIXTY-ONE

Athos procured a map of the province, perceived four different roads from Bethune to Armentières, and summoned the four lackeys of the Musketeers.

They must set out the next morning at daybreak, and go to Armentières, each by a different route. If they discovered Milady's retreat, three were to remain on guard; the fourth was to return and serve as a guide to the four friends.

Athos then girded on his sword and left the hotel. At length he met a belated passenger, went up to him, and spoke a few words. The man he addressed recoiled with terror, and only answered by pointing.

Athos plunged into the street the man had indicated with his finger and went toward a small house. No light appeared through the chinks of the shutters; no noise gave reason to believe that it was inhabited.

Three times Athos knocked. The door at length was opened, and a man appeared. Athos explained the cause of his visit and the service he required. The man refused. Then Athos took from his pocket a small paper on which two lines were written, accompanied by a signature and a seal, and presented them. The tall man read these lines and bowed to denote that he was ready to obey. Athos returned the same way he came.

At daybreak the superior of the convent sent to inform the Musketeers that the burial would take place at midday. At the door of the chapel d'Artagnan looked for Athos; but Athos had disappeared.

Faithful to his mission of vengeance, Athos had requested to be conducted to the garden and went out into the forest.

His suspicions were confirmed; the road by which the carriage had disappeared encircled the forest. Athos followed the road for some time, his eyes fixed upon the ground. At the end of three-quarters of a league, the ground was trampled by horses. Between the forest and this accursed spot was the same track of small feet as in the garden; the carriage had stopped here. Milady had come out of the wood and entered the carriage.

Satisfied with this discovery, Athos returned to the hotel and found a lackey impatiently waiting for him.

At the village of Festubert, the lackey had learned that the evening before, a lady had been obliged to stop. Later, the woman had continued her journey.

The valet took the crossroad, and by seven o'clock in the morning he was at Armentières.

Athos had just received this information when his friends returned.

At eight o'clock in the evening Athos ordered the horses to be saddled, and Lord de Winter and his friends notified that they must prepare for the expedition.

In an instant all five were ready. Each examined his arms, and put them in order. Athos came down last and found d'Artagnan already on horseback.

"Patience!" cried Athos. "One of our party is still wanting," and he set off at a gallop.

He returned, accompanied by a tall man wrapped in a large red cloak. Lord de Winter and the three Musketeers looked at one another. All were ignorant as to whom this man could be.

The little cavalcade took the route the carriage had taken. It was a melancholy sight—these six men, traveling in silence, sad as despair.

SIXTY-TWO

It was a stormy night. Occasionally, by the light of a flash of lightning, the road stretched before them; the flash extinct, all remained in darkness.

Several times Lord de Winter, Porthos, or Aramis tried to talk with the man in the red cloak; but to every interrogation he bowed without response. A man sheltered beneath a tree advanced into the middle of the road. This lackey acted as guide.

Another flash illuminated all around them. By its bluish splendor, they distinguished a little isolated house on the banks of the river. One window was lighted.

"Here we are!" said Athos. He sprang from his horse and went up to the window.

By the light of a lamp he saw a woman seated near a dying fire. She leaned her head upon her hands. It was she whom he sought. Milady raised her head, saw close to the panes the pale face of Athos, and screamed.

Athos pushed the window open and leaped into the room.

Milady rushed to the door. More pale and menacing than Athos, d'Artagnan stood on the threshold. Milady recoiled, uttering a cry. D'Artagnan drew a pistol from his belt; but Athos raised his hand.

"Put back that weapon, d'Artagnan!" said he. "Come in, gentlemen."

D'Artagnan obeyed. Behind d'Artagnan entered Porthos, Aramis, Lord de Winter, and the man in the red cloak.

Milady had sunk into a chair. Perceiving her brother-in-law, she uttered a terrible cry.

"Charlotte Backson, who first was called Comtesse de la Fère, and afterwards Milady de Winter, Baroness of Sheffield," said Athos. "We wish to judge you according to your crime."

D'Artagnan advanced.

"Before God and before men," said he, "I accuse this woman of having poisoned Constance Bonacieux, who died yesterday evening."

He turned toward Porthos and Aramis.

"We bear witness," said the two Musketeers.

D'Artagnan continued: "I accuse this woman of having attempted to poison me. A man named Brisemont died in my place."

"We bear witness," said Porthos and Aramis.

"I accuse this woman of having urged me to murder the Baron de Wardes. As no one else can attest the truth of this accusation, I attest it myself." And d'Artagnan passed to the other side of the room.

"Your turn, my lord," said Athos.

The baron came forward.

"Before God and before men," said he, "I accuse this woman of having caused the assassination of the Duke of Buckingham."

"The Duke of Buckingham assassinated!" cried all present.

"Yes," said the baron, "assassinated. On receiving the letter you wrote to me, I had this woman arrested, and gave her in charge to a loyal servant. She corrupted this man; she made him kill the duke. At this moment, Felton is paying with his head!"

A shudder crept through the judges.

"That is not all," resumed Lord de Winter. "My brother died of a strange disorder which left livid traces all over the body. My sister, how did your husband die? Assassin of Buckingham, assassin of Felton, assassin of my brother, I demand justice."

Lord de Winter ranged himself by the side of d'Artagnan, leaving the place free for another accuser.

Milady let her head sink between her hands.

"My turn," said Athos, himself trembling. "I married that woman when she was a young girl; I gave her my wealth, I gave her my name. One day I discovered that she was branded with a *fleur-de-lis*."

"I defy you to find any tribunal which pronounced that sentence against me," said Milady, raising herself.

"Silence!" said a hollow voice. And the man in the red cloak came forward.

Milady examined with increasing terror that pale face. Then she suddenly cried, "No, no!" rising and retreating to the very wall.

"Who are you?" cried the witnesses.

"Ask that woman," said the man in the red cloak.

"The executioner of Lille!" cried Milady, a prey to insensate terror.

Everyone drew back. The unknown resumed. "Yes, I am the executioner of Lille. That woman was once a nun in the convent of the Benedictines. A young priest, with a trustful heart, performed the duties of the church of that convent. She undertook his seduction, and succeeded.

"She prevailed upon him to reach another part of France, where they might live at ease because unknown; money was necessary. The priest stole the sacred vases and sold them; but they were arrested.

"She seduced the son of the jailer and escaped. The young priest was condemned to ten years of imprisonment, and to be branded. I was executioner of the city of Lille. I was obliged to brand the guilty one: my brother!

"I swore that this woman should share his punishment. I caught her and imprinted the same disgraceful mark upon her.

"My brother succeeded in making his escape. They fled together into Berry, and there he obtained a little curacy. This woman passed for his sister.

"The lord of the estate on which the chapel was situated saw this pretend sister, and became enamored of her. Then she became the Comtesse de la Fère—"

All eyes were turned toward Athos, whose real name that was, and who made a sign that all was true.

"Determined to get rid of an existence from which she had stolen everything," resumed the executioner, "my poor brother returned to Lille and hanged himself. That is the crime of which I accuse her; that is the cause for which she was branded."

"Monsieur d'Artagnan," said Athos, "what is the penalty you demand against this woman?"

"Death," replied d'Artagnan.

"Lord de Winter," continued Athos, "what is the penalty you demand against this woman?"

"Death," replied Lord de Winter.

"Messieurs Porthos and Aramis," repeated Athos, "what is the sentence you pronounce upon this woman?"

"Death," replied the Musketeers.

Milady uttered a frightful shriek.

"Charlotte Backson, Comtesse de la Fère, Milady de Winter," said Athos, "you shall die."

At these words, Milady's strength failed her. She did not attempt the least resistance.

SIXTY-THREE

The moon, reddened by the last traces of the storm, arose behind the little town of Armentières. Not a breath of wind now disturbed the atmosphere.

Two lackeys dragged Milady. The executioner walked behind them, and Lord de Winter, d'Artagnan, Athos, Porthos, and Aramis behind the executioner. On the bank of the river, the executioner approached Milady and bound her hands and feet.

She cried, "You are cowards—ten men combined to murder one woman. He who touches a hair of my head is himself an assassin."

"The executioner may kill without being an assassin," said the man in the red cloak, rapping upon his immense sword. "This is the last judge; that is all."

As he bound her, Milady uttered savage cries.

"If I have committed the crimes you accuse me of," shrieked Milady, "take me before a tribunal. You are not judges!"

"I offered you Tyburn," said Lord de Winter. "Why did you not accept it?"

"Because I am not willing to die!" cried Milady, struggling. "I am too young to die!"

"The woman you poisoned at Bethune was younger, and yet she is dead," said d'Artagnan.

"I will enter a cloister," said Milady.

"You were in a cloister," said the executioner, "and you left it to ruin my brother."

Milady uttered a cry of terror. The executioner carried her toward the boat.

"My God!" cried she. "Are you going to drown me?"

These cries were so heartrending that d'Artagnan, who had been eager in pursuit of Milady, sat down, covering his ears with his hands. His heart failed him. "I cannot consent that this woman should die thus!" said he.

Milady caught at a shadow of hope. "D'Artagnan!" cried she. "Remember that I loved you!"

The young man rose.

But Athos rose likewise. "If you take one step farther, d'Artagnan," said he, "we shall cross swords." D'Artagnan sank on his knees. "Come," continued Athos. "Executioner, do your duty."

"Willingly, monseigneur," said the executioner.

Athos made a step toward Milady.

"I pardon you," said he. "I pardon you for my lost honor, my defiled love, and the despair into which you cast me. Die in peace!"

Lord de Winter advanced in his turn.

"I pardon you," said he, "for the poisoning of my brother, and the assassination of His Grace, Lord Buckingham. I pardon you for the death of poor Felton. Die in peace!"

"And I," said M. d'Artagnan. "Pardon me, madame, for having by a trick unworthy of a gentleman provoked your anger; and I pardon you the murder of my poor love. I pardon you, and I weep for you. Die in peace!"

"I am lost!" murmured Milady. She arose, and cast around her one of those piercing looks. "Where am I to die?" said she.

"On the other bank," replied the executioner.

He placed her in the boat, and Athos handed him a sum of silver.

"Here," said he, "is the price of the execution, that it may be plain we act as judges."

"That is correct," said the executioner. "And now let this woman see that I am not fulfilling my trade, but my debt." And he threw the money into the river.

The boat moved off, bearing the guilty woman and the executioner. The friends saw it gain the opposite bank; the figures were black shadows on the red-tinted horizon.

Milady had contrived to untie the cord that fastened her feet. She jumped lightly ashore and took to flight. But the soil was moist; she slipped and fell.

They saw the executioner raise his arms slowly; a moonbeam fell upon the blade of the large sword. It fell with sudden force; they heard the hissing of the scimitar and the cry of the victim, then a truncated mass sank beneath the blow.

Three days afterward the four Musketeers were in Paris; they had not exceeded their leave of absence.

SIXTY-FOUR

Although warned that the man she loved was in danger, the queen, when his death was announced, would not believe the fact. The next day she was obliged to believe; Laporte arrived, bearer of the duke's dying gift.

The king displayed his joy, but soon again became dull and indisposed. He felt that in returning to camp he should reenter slavery; nevertheless, he did return.

The return to la Rochelle, therefore, was profoundly dull. Our four friends, in particular, astonished their comrades; they traveled together, side by side, heads lowered. As soon as the escort arrived in a city, the four friends retired to a secluded cabaret, where they conversed in low voices, looking around to see that no one overheard.

One day, when the four friends had stopped at a cabaret on the high road, a man coming from la Rochelle pulled up at the door to drink a glass of wine.

"Holloa, Monsieur d'Artagnan!" said he. "Is not that you?"

D'Artagnan raised his head. It was his stranger of Meung. D'Artagnan drew his sword.

The stranger jumped from his horse, and advanced to meet him.

"Ah, monsieur!" said the young man. "This time you shall not escape me!"

"I was seeking you; in the name of the king, I arrest you. You must surrender your sword, monsieur."

"Who are you?" demanded d'Artagnan.

"I am the Chevalier de Rochefort," answered the other, "equerry of Monsieur le Cardinal Richelieu. I have orders to conduct you to His Eminence."

"We are returning to His Eminence, Monsieur Chevalier," said Athos. "Accept the word of Monsieur d'Artagnan that he will go straight to la Rochelle."

"I must place him in the hands of Guards who will take him into camp."

"We will be his guards, upon our word as gentlemen; but," added Athos, knitting his brow, "Monsieur d'Artagnan shall not leave us."

The Chevalier de Rochefort saw that Porthos and Aramis had placed themselves between him and the gate; he understood that he was at the mercy of these four men.

"Gentlemen," said he, "if Monsieur d'Artagnan will surrender his sword to me and join his word to yours, I shall be satisfied with your promise."

"You have my word, monsieur, and here is my sword."

"This suits me the better," said Rochefort, "as I wish to continue my journey."

"If it is for the purpose of rejoining Milady," said Athos, coolly, "it is useless; you will not find her."

"What has become of her?" asked Rochefort, eagerly.

"Return to camp and you shall know."

On the morrow they arrived. The cardinal and the king felicitated each other upon the fortunate chance that had freed France from the enemy who set all Europe against her. On returning to his quarters, the cardinal found d'Artagnan, without his sword. This was d'Artagnan's second interview with Richelieu, and he felt it would be his last.

"Monsieur," said the cardinal, "you have been arrested by my orders. Do you know why?"

"No, monseigneur, for the only thing for which I could be arrested is still unknown to Your Eminence."

"What does that mean?" he said.

"If monseigneur will tell me what crimes are imputed to me, I will tell him what I have really done."

"You are charged with having corresponded with the enemies of the kingdom; with having surprised state secrets; with having tried to thwart the plans of your general."

"Who charges me with this, monseigneur?" said d'Artagnan, who had no doubt the accusation came from Milady. "A woman branded by the justice of the country; a woman who espoused one man in France and another in England; a woman who poisoned her second husband and who attempted to assassinate me!"

"What do you say, monsieur?" cried the cardinal, astonished. "Of what woman are you speaking?"

"Of Milady de Winter," replied d'Artagnan, "of whose crimes

Your Eminence is doubtless ignorant."

"Monsieur," said the cardinal, "if Milady de Winter has committed the crimes you lay to her charge, she shall be punished."

"She has been punished, monseigneur. She is dead."

"Dead!" repeated the cardinal.

"Three times she attempted to kill me, and I pardoned her; but she murdered the woman I loved. My friends and I took her, tried her, and condemned her."

D'Artagnan then related the poisoning of Mme Bonacieux, the trial in the isolated house, and the execution on the banks of the Lys.

A shudder crept through the body of the cardinal. "So," he said, "you have constituted yourselves judges, without remembering that they who punish without license are assassins?"

"Monseigneur, I willingly submit to any punishment Your Eminence may inflict."

"I know you are a man of a stout heart, monsieur," said the cardinal, with a voice almost affectionate. "I can therefore tell you you shall be tried, and even condemned."

"Another might reply to Your Eminence that he had his pardon in his pocket. I content myself with saying: I am ready."

"Signed by whom—the king?" The cardinal pronounced these words with an expression of contempt.

"No, by Your Eminence. Monseigneur will doubtless recognize his own handwriting."

And d'Artagnan presented to the cardinal the paper that Athos had forced from Milady, and had given to d'Artagnan.

His Eminence took the paper, and read:

It is for the good of the state that the bearer of this has done what has been done.
—RICHELIEU

The cardinal sank into a reverie, but did not return the paper to d'Artagnan.

"He is meditating by what punishment he shall cause me to die," said the Gascon to himself.

Richelieu rolled the paper in his hands. At length he fixed his look upon that open countenance, read upon that face all the sufferings its possessor had endured in the course of a month, and reflected what resources his courage and shrewdness might offer to a good master. On the other side, Milady had more than once terrified him. He felt a secret joy at being relieved of this dangerous accomplice.

Richelieu slowly tore the paper that d'Artagnan had relinquished, then approached the table, wrote a few lines upon a parchment, and affixed his seal.

"That is my condemnation," thought d'Artagnan. "He will spare me the tediousness of a trial."

"Here, monsieur," said the cardinal to the young man. "The name is wanting in this commission; you can write it yourself."

D'Artagnan took the paper; it was a lieutenant's commission in the Musketeers. "Monseigneur," said he, "this favor I do not merit. I have three friends worthier—"

"You are a brave youth, d'Artagnan," interrupted the cardinal. "Do with this commission what you will."

"I shall never forget this," replied d'Artagnan. "Your Eminence may be certain of that."

The cardinal turned and called, "Rochefort!" The chevalier entered immediately.

"Rochefort," said the cardinal, "you see Monsieur d'Artagnan. I receive him among the number of my friends."

Rochefort and d'Artagnan coolly greeted each other; the cardinal observed them with his vigilant eye. They left the chamber at the same time.

That evening d'Artagnan repaired to the quarters of Athos, whom he found in a fair way to empty a bottle of wine. D'Artagnan related what had taken place, and drawing the commission from his pocket, said, "Here, my dear Athos, this belongs to you."

Athos smiled. "Friend," said he, "for Athos this is too much; for the Comte de la Fère it is too little. Keep the commission."

D'Artagnan left Athos's chamber and went to that of Porthos. He found him admiring himself before a glass.

"Is that you, dear friend?" exclaimed Porthos. "How do you think these garments fit me?"

"Wonderfully," said d'Artagnan, "but I offer you a dress which will become you still better."

D'Artagnan related to Porthos the substance of his interview with the cardinal, and took the commission from his pocket. "My friend, become my chief."

Porthos cast his eyes over the commission and returned it to d'Artagnan.

"Yes," said he, "that would flatter me, but I should not have time to enjoy the distinction. The husband of my duchess died; I shall marry the widow. Keep the lieutenancy, my dear."

The young man then entered the apartment of Aramis,

finding him with a prayer book. He described his interview with the cardinal, and said, for the third time drawing his commission from his pocket, "Accept this commission. You have merited it more than any of us by your wisdom."

"Alas, dear friend!" said Aramis. "Our adventures have disgusted me with military life. After the siege I shall enter the house of the Lazarists. Keep the commission, d'Artagnan; you will be a brave and adventurous captain."

D'Artagnan went back to Athos, whom he found still at table contemplating the charms of his last glass. Athos took a quill, wrote the name of d'Artagnan in the commission, and returned it to him.

"I shall have no more friends," said the young man. "Nothing but bitter recollections." And tears rolled down his cheeks.

"You are young," replied Athos, "and your bitter recollections have time to change themselves into sweet remembrances."

“Keep the commission, d’Artagnan; you will be a brave and adventurous captain.”

GLOSSARY

almoner ✦ A chaplain or church official who distributes charity to the poor.

Anne of Austria ✦ The queen of France, following her marriage to King Louis XIII. Although she was born in Spain, her mother was from Austria.

auberge ✦ An inn or tavern, usually a place to stop for food or drink in *The Three Musketeers*.

Bastille ✦ More formally known as the *Bastille de Saint-Antoine*, first built as a fortress to protect the east end of Paris, later turned into a prison. In the eighteenth century, the storming of the Bastille by French citizens to gain access to gunpowder and weapons stored there marked the beginning of the French revolution.

cabinet ✦ A small, private room.

carte blanche ✦ The power to make decisions and act freely, without the approval of a higher authority.

chaise ✦ A light two or four-wheeled carriage.

chevalier ✦ A knight, though it is often used in *The Three Musketeers* as a term of flattery.

commissary ✦ A deputy, someone delegated to perform a duty.

courtier ✦ An attendant to the king, queen, or other figure in the royal court; also a person with no official role who is frequently in attendance at the court or in the presence of royalty.

crown ✦ An English coin introduced in 1526.

curé ✦ A Catholic priest.

fleur-de-lis ✦ A symbol associated with the French monarchy, with a shape said to be based on the lily or iris. It was an old French custom to brand criminals with this shape.

For-l'Évêque ✦ A prison in Paris open from 1674–1780.

habitués ✦ Those who frequent a particular location or are ardent supporters.

harquebus ✦ A portable, long-barreled gun used from the fifteenth through seventeenth centuries.

league ✦ A unit of length seldom referred to in modern times, varying anywhere from 2.4–4.6 miles in different countries at different times, based upon the distance a person or a horse can walk in an hour.

Lieutenant Criminel ✦ An officer of the French judicial court who decided criminal cases.

livre ✦ The currency of France until 1795, but the livre coin did not actually exist at the time of *The Three Musketeers.* Approximately ten livres equaled the value of one pistole.

louis d'or ✦ Although Dumas mentions this coin in the novel, it was not actually used in France until 1641. In *The Three Musketeers*, its value is equivalent to the pistole.

Louvre ✦ The Palais du Louvre was the formal royal palace for the French monarch in Paris until Louis XVI moved the seat of power to Versailles in 1672. In 1791 the Louvre opened as a museum, which remains its function to this day.

M. ✦ Abbreviation for Monsieur.

mercer ✦ A textile merchant.

Mme ✦ Abbreviation for Madame.

Palais du Cardinal ✦ Residence of Cardinal de Richelieu, later the Palais Royal.

pistole ✦ An old unit of French currency worth approximately ten livres, typically used when referring to very large sums of money.

poniard ✦ A lightweight dagger.

Tyburn ✦ A village in England notorious for its gallows. It was the primary execution location for London criminals.

wicket ✦ A small gate or door.